A veteran of the U.S. Navy, **Paul Carr** spent his months at sea reading classic mystery and detective novels. He studied economics at Mercer University and worked in financial and computer-related positions before authoring six crime novels, including four Sam Mackenzie thrillers and two Detective Michael Dalton Florida Keys mysteries. He lives with his wife, Elaine, on a lake in Georgia, where he is busy on his next novel.

THE BLACK PALMETTO

PAUL CARR

W🌐RLDWIDE

TORONTO • NEW YORK • LONDON
AMSTERDAM • PARIS • SYDNEY • HAMBURG
STOCKHOLM • ATHENS • TOKYO • MILAN
MADRID • WARSAW • BUDAPEST • AUCKLAND

W☀RLDWIDE™

Recycling programs
for this product may
not exist in your area.

ISBN-13: 978-1-335-99394-6

The Black Palmetto

First published in 2014 by Paul Carr.
This edition published in 2021.

Copyright © 2014 by Paul Carr

This edition published by arrangement with Harlequin Books S.A.

For questions and comments about the quality of this book,
please contact us at CustomerService@Harlequin.com.

Harlequin Enterprises ULC
22 Adelaide St. West, 40th Floor
Toronto, Ontario M5H 4E3, Canada
www.ReaderService.com

Printed in U.S.A.

THE BLACK PALMETTO

ONE

THE SUN MELTED into the horizon like a rogue reactor headed for the other side of the world. Sam Mackenzie's eyes ached as he rode the last mile staring into its glare.

"That's the place up ahead," Sam said.

Simone sighed. "Good. Maybe we can put a bullet in Sean Spanner and get back to civilization."

She was joking. Probably.

Sam had shown Spanner's photograph at a gas station in Marathon, and the cashier said he'd filled up and paid with a hundred-dollar bill. When their guy asked about a place to stay on Iguana Key, the gas man told him about the Blue Iguana, twenty miles south on US-1. The cashier also told them the make and model of the car that Spanner had driven.

Sam turned into the motel entrance and took in the old beach lodging, a stucco two-story, thirty or forty years old. About a dozen cars sat in the lot. The lighted sign out front hissed and buzzed. It had an iguana figure perched on top, rimmed in bright blue neon.

"This place gives me the creeps," Simone said.

Sam parked, and they entered the office. A window air conditioner to their right dripped water on the tile floor. The temp seemed only a couple of degrees below that outside. Perspiration beaded on Sam's neck.

The desk clerk sat on a stool behind the counter. He had shoulder-length hair, wore a short-sleeve uniform shirt, and seemed somewhere between young and middle-age. A nametag on his pocket read Chris. Grinning, he displayed yellow teeth and a lot of gum.

"Your lucky day, folks. I got one room left."

His breath wafted across the counter. Garlic and weed.

"We're looking for a guy." Sam showed him the picture used on Spanner's I.D. card at the government lab in Homestead.

Chris glanced at the photo. "Never seen him." He seemed to notice Simone for the first time, eyes lingering on her shapely, nearly six-foot figure. His jaw sagged in a leer. Bad move.

Despite having the looks of a movie star, she could hurt him a hundred different ways. A source had told Sam she'd been recruited out of Yale by the CIA, and had gotten booted after ten years for leaving dead bodies all over Eastern Europe. Sam had once asked her about it, and she'd said, "Hey, I killed them before they could kill me." Sounded right to Sam, and he never mentioned it again. Though no longer with the CIA, contractors working for the agency called on her often. She and Sam, a former SEAL, had worked together on a previous case, so she'd brought him on as a partner to help her find Spanner.

Laying a twenty on the counter, Sam snapped his fingers to get the guy's attention. "Take another look. He's supposed to be staying here."

Chris eyed the bill and chuckled. "Sorry, against policy to rat out the guests."

Sam shook his head and added another twenty.

"You cops?" Chris asked.

"No," Sam said, "we're not cops."

The long-haired man scooped up the money. "He checked in two nights ago and paid for a week. I haven't seen him since."

"Which room?" Simone asked.

He shrugged and smiled. "Can't remember."

She pulled her 9mm and pointed it at Chris. His eyes popped wide. No more leers.

Sam touched her arm. "I think he'll remember."

Her eyes narrowed. "He better."

The clerk backed away from the counter and eyed the phone, maybe wondering who he could call.

"I want to apologize for my friend, Chris. She's a little impatient. Now, I'll give you another twenty if you tell us what we want to know, but if you don't, I'll just take a walk and you two can hash it out."

Chris eyed the gun. "Okay, I accept your apology. Number thirteen, last unit on the end."

"Has anyone been in the room?" Simone asked.

"No, the maid said he had the privacy sign on the door."

"You have any idea where he went?"

He gave her a shrug. "You might check Chopin's. It's on the highway going into town. The guy asked about a place to get a beer and I told him about it."

"When was that?" Sam asked.

"I told you, two nights ago."

Sam stepped behind the counter and took the key from a pigeonhole on the wall.

"Hold on. You can't take that."

"Just borrowing it for a few minutes," Sam said.

When he came back around, Simone said, "Check it out. I'll stay here with Chris and make sure he doesn't do anything stupid." He got a pair of latex gloves from his car and stretched them on.

The parking space in front of the unit lay vacant. A Do Not Disturb sign hung on the doorknob. Sam pulled his 9mm, unlocked the door and swung it into the room.

"Spanner, you in there?"

No answer. He entered, the gun out front. The place was hot. It'd been tossed, the mattresses of both beds askew, covers on the floor. Drawers stood open and empty. A duffel bag sat atop the dresser, unzipped. It contained socks, underwear, and a toilet kit. He scanned the bathroom and found nothing but a couple of towels on the rack and a bar of soap on the sink. A wrapped bar lay on the edge of the tub as if Spanner had never used the shower.

Sticking the gun in his holster, Sam went back to the bedroom and dumped the contents of the toilet kit onto the dresser. Just the regular stuff: toothbrush and toothpaste, a razor, shaving cream, deodorant. Leaving the items there, he pulled pairs of socks apart and found nothing but stray strands of thread. No clothes hung on the rack outside the bathroom. If Spanner brought clothes, they were probably still in his car.

The cover for the air conditioner stood loose on the floor, leaning against the low wall unit. Sam moved the cover aside and spotted something on the floor. A small piece of paper, like a band used for wrapping a stack of cash. The metal enclosure had a space in the bottom where twenty or more stacks of cash could have been stashed. Sam put the band into his pocket, moved the cover back where he'd found it, and strode out of the room.

Back in the office, the mood still seemed pretty chilly between Chris and Simone.

Sam motioned for her to follow him, and they went outside.

"Somebody tore the room apart searching for the money. I think Spanner had it in the air conditioner. The cover was off, and this was on the floor under it." He showed her the band.

"No sign of the flash card?"

Sam shook his head. "Maybe Spanner had it in his pocket. Let's get a room in case we don't find Spanner tonight."

She raised an eyebrow. "You want to stay here?"

"Probably won't be another place between here and Key West. We could go back north if you want."

She peered up the highway as if she might be able to see all the way to Marathon, and sighed. "No, let's just get a room here and get this done."

Chris didn't seem too happy they were staying, but brightened when Sam gave him the extra money he'd promised.

Jiggling the key in the lock, Sam thought he had the wrong room, but it finally snapped open. Heat rushed his face when he swung the door open. He stepped inside and reached for the air conditioner knob. It came off in his hand, and he stuck it back on and twisted. The tired old unit groaned with displeasure as the compressor spun up.

"Some place, huh?" Simone said.

"Yeah, a real palace. Which bed do you want?"

She dropped her overnight bag on the one nearest the bathroom. "This one's okay."

Although they'd been intimate after their previous

job together, Simone had told Sam she'd met a guy named Karl, spelled with a "K," that she was pretty serious about. She'd said she wanted to maintain a strictly professional relationship for this job. That had deflated Sam, but after a time, he decided it might be best anyway. If not best, at least safest.

Sam nodded. "Let's go check out that place the desk guy mentioned, and maybe get something to eat."

"Okay with me. I'm starving."

They rode out of the lot at dusk and turned onto a road headed inland toward Downtown Iguana Key. A mile or so later he spotted Chopin's, set back from the highway among a stand of puny palm trees, the parking lot paved with what appeared to be pieces of old roofing shingles. A sign advertised food and drinks. About thirty cars sat out front.

Inside, the air was frigid, which probably accounted in part for the full house. A man met them and asked if they planned to dine. He stood about chest-level to Sam, which made him about five feet tall, and weighed at least three hundred pounds. His massive arms were covered with green tattoos that resembled rattlesnake watermelons. Gray hair topped his head, gathered in a ponytail. He steered them to a table near the bar, took their drink orders, and returned a couple of minutes later with a beer and a martini.

"You Chopin?"

The short man stared for a second and glanced at Simone as if considering whether or not to answer, then nodded. "Yep."

"Nice name."

His eyes narrowed. "That supposed to be some kind of wisecrack?"

"No, I like it."

The stern expression melted away, and Chopin seemed to relax.

"Sorry, I get some ribbing around here. At least you know how to pronounce it. My mama wanted me to be a concert pianist. You in town on business?"

"Vacation," Sam said.

"Yeah, right," the wide man said with a grin. "What can I get you for dinner?"

They scanned the menu for a few moments and decided on shrimp baskets.

"Okay, that'll only take a few minutes."

Before he could leave, Sam pulled out the photograph.

"You see this guy in here a couple of nights ago?"

Chopin stiffened. "You cops?"

"No, we're just looking for him."

The man picked up the picture and studied it.

"What'd he do?"

"He took something that didn't belong to him. I was hired to get it back."

Chopin shook his head. "Nah, never seen him before." He laid the picture on the table and walked away.

"You think he knows something?" Simone asked.

"Yes. Might not be as easy to get it out of him as it was the motel guy, though."

A woman sat at the next table over. Though with another man, she stared at Sam until he gave her a smile, and she turned away. A modern Cleopatra, she had black hair and bangs, her dark eyes like magnets. Then Sam noticed the man staring, too.

Simone touched his arm and whispered, "You know that chick?"

"No, I don't."

"Could've fooled me."

"What do you care? You said you're crazy about some guy named Karl."

Simone's eyes tightened. "Look all you want."

TWO

A YOUNG MAN wearing an apron, who probably doubled as a cook, brought their food to the table. Chopin had disappeared somewhere behind the bar.

Simone remained quiet as they ate, seemingly in a bad mood. She'd gotten angry about what Sam had said, but he didn't care much for mixed signals. Maybe she had a thing with Karl, and maybe she didn't.

When they finished, Sam paid the bill and left a tip. Simone headed outside, and the man who had stared earlier got up and caught Sam at the door.

"I saw you flashing that picture," the man said, his voice low. He glanced back into the restaurant, beyond the bar area, and frowned. "I might know something about him, but I can't talk right now. You staying at the Blue Iguana?"

"Yeah."

"Okay, meet me behind the place, next to the beach, in an hour."

"I'll be there."

The man went back to his table and Sam strode out the door.

"You mad at me?" Sam asked Simone when he got into the car.

She sighed and peered out the window. "No, I'm just tired. I need to get back and catch some Zs."

"You sure?"

"Yes, I'm sure."

"'Cause we can talk about this thing you have with Karl if you want."

Simone turned and smiled. "There's nothing to talk about. I shouldn't have said anything about the girl back there. We just need to get this job done and get out of this place, okay?"

"Sure, let's get it done." He told her about the man speaking to him at the door.

"Maybe he knows where we can find Spanner."

"I hope so."

"Let's get going. It's like an oven in here."

THEY DECIDED SAM would go to the meeting alone, since the guy had waited until Simone walked out the door before saying anything. At 9:35 p.m. Sam went out through the sliding door leading to the beach. They'd taken the room next to the one Spanner had rented.

He stood next to the wall, waiting until his eyes adjusted to the moonlight. The grassy grounds behind the motel extended about fifty feet to a narrow beach and a lapping surf. A full moon shone from the east, reflecting off the white sand and transforming the Caribbean into an endless expanse of tarnished pewter.

Something made a noise in the palmetto scrub bordering the motel on the side. It sounded like someone moving in the brush, crunching dead fronds. A shiver raced across Sam's neck as he pulled his gun. He hugged the motel wall and eased to the corner, closer to the brush, his pulse thumping in his ears. A light from the front of the motel cast a dim glow over the area on the side. The noise grew louder then changed to a scrubbing sound as it cleared the palmettos and slid onto the grass into view. It resembled a dragon, about five feet long with spines down its back and claws that could probably hurt you. Something like a beard hung underneath its chin. An iguana. Probably harmless, but he didn't want to give it the impression of being cornered. He stepped backward and the creature snapped its head in his direction. It jerked around and thrashed back into the palmettos.

The gun back in his holster, Sam peered across the grounds between the motel and the beach. No sign of anyone. He checked his watch. 9:50 p.m. Maybe the guy had changed his mind. After another ten minutes, he gave up and stepped around the motel to scan the parking lot. Six cars had been there when they'd returned from Chopin's, and no new cars had arrived.

Back in the room, he told Simone about the no-show and the iguana.

Headed into the bathroom, she said through the open door, "There's a brochure on the dresser that tells about the iguanas on the island. Apparently the place has lots of them. Probably why there aren't any other motels along this stretch of beach. It said they're pretty harmless, as long as you leave them alone. If you get too close, they can bite, and pop you with their tails."

"Yeah, well, I'm going to steer clear."

A minute later she came out carrying her clothes, dressed in a short nightgown. Sam remembered she liked to sleep that way.

Pulling small bottles from her bag, she poured gin and tonic into two glasses filled with ice atop the small table in the corner.

"No sign of your guy, huh?"

Sam sighed. "No, and that's too bad. He probably knows something that would help us."

"Probably just some wacko."

"Yeah, maybe."

She sat down on the bed, pulled her legs up, and leaned back against a couple of pillows. "Aren't you going to have a drink?"

He shook his head. "I think I'll go back to Chopin's and see if I can find him. Maybe he just had too much to drink and forgot about the time."

As he said it, he remembered the way the guy had scanned the place before speaking. A feeling of dread gnawed at his stomach.

Simone's smile leaked away. "Okay, suit yourself. I'm turning in after I watch the news, so be quiet when you get back."

He looked at her lounging there in her short nightie, and wished he had accepted the drink offer. It could have turned out that Karl with a "K" didn't mean as much to her as she'd let on. Too late now. The moment had passed. She pulled the sheet over her legs and turned the TV on with the remote.

"Yeah, I'll do that," he said and strode out the door, closing it behind him.

A few minutes later he turned into the driveway leading to Chopin's and parked. Floodlights illuminated the parking lot. On his way to the door he noticed a throng of people standing by a car toward the far corner of the lot. A couple of men wore police uniforms.

"That's the guy," a man said, pointing in Sam's direction.

One of the officers turned, seemed to zero in on him, and hurried over.

Uh oh. The dread returned, this time full blast. Something had happened to the man. Too late to run. He still had the gun in his holster, the butt sticking out. Maybe his shirttail covered it up.

"You got some ID?" the officer asked. The name-tag above his shirt pocket identified him as Lt. Lonnie Cates. Muscle bound, like a steroid freak, he stood a few inches shorter than Sam, had oily, slicked back hair, and a pencil-thin mustache that had taken some time in front of the mirror.

Sam pulled out his driver's license and handed it to Cates.

The lieutenant studied it for a few moments. "You're from Miami?"

"That's right. What's the problem?"

Cates narrowed his eyes, stuck the license into his shirt pocket, and took Sam by the arm.

"Come on. I'll show you what the problem is."

Cates' fingers dug into his arm. They reached the throng and the people parted. The man who wanted to meet him earlier lay on the ground between two cars. He looked dead. Another man knelt over him.

"Chief Boozler," Cates said to the kneeling man, "this is the guy. He could be a professional hit man."

The chief turned his head to stare at Cates, rolled his eyes and stood. Unlike the officer, he wore civilian clothes, stood over six feet, and carried a few extra pounds about the middle.

"Don't you think it's kinda soon to be drawing conclusions, Lonnie?" Boozler asked.

Cates' eyes darted to the people standing by. "Sure, Chief. Too early for that."

Boozler took the license and turned it so he could

read it in the light of the floods. After a few seconds, he handed it back to Cates and glared at Sam.

"This is Jake Bell," the chief said, pointing to the man on the ground. "Somebody stabbed him. A witness saw you talking to him earlier this evening. Mind telling me what you were talking about?"

Sam didn't see any reason to lie, at least for the most part.

"I came here looking for a man." He removed the photo from his shirt pocket and handed it to the chief. "His name is Sean Spanner. I showed the picture to the bar owner inside, and Mr. Bell here saw it. After we ate, he came up to me and said he knew something about Spanner. He said to meet him at the Blue Iguana in an hour, but he didn't show up. I came back here to see if I could find him."

Boozler nodded. "Why are you after this Spanner guy?"

"He stole some money, and I came here to get it back." Sam didn't see any need to go into the stolen flash drive. The simpler the better at this point.

"You a private detective?"

"No, not a detective. Just a friend of the man who lost the money. Doing him a favor."

"Who is this man?"

"Sorry, I'm not at liberty to say."

The chief clicked his tongue, turned his head for a moment, and fixed Sam with a stare.

"Son, this man was just murdered, and his father has more money than anybody between Key West and Miami. I think you better come up with a name."

Sam shook his head. "Sorry. He had nothing to do with this man's death, and neither did I."

Boozler drew a deep breath, let it out, and turned toward Cates. Probably about to tell the officer to put the cuffs on him.

"You're wasting your time asking me about this," Sam said. "My guess is that someone did something to Spanner for the money I mentioned, and killed Jake Bell because he knew about it."

The chief narrowed his eyes. "That assumes what you're telling me is the truth. Since you won't come clean about who you're working for, I'm not inclined to believe anything else you say."

"Listen, Chief, my girlfriend is back at the motel. She's was with me from the time I left this place until a few minutes ago when I came back to see why Jake didn't show up. You can call her if you want." He pulled out his cell phone and held it up.

Boozler seemed to consider that for a moment and nodded. "Okay, ring her up."

When Simone answered, Sam said, "Honey, the man who was supposed to meet me was killed outside the bar where we were earlier. I know, that's terrible. Yes, the Chief of Police is standing here, and he wants to ask you some questions."

Simone picked up right away on the conversation. She knew what to say. Sam handed the phone to Boozler, who introduced himself and began with the questions. A couple of minutes later, he thanked her and handed the phone back.

Sam dropped it into his pocket. "So, okay if I go?"

Cates, who had been listening a few feet away, said, "You're not going anywhere until you answer the chief's questions."

Boozler glared at him, shook his head then turned

back. "Yeah, you can go, but you can't leave town. I need that photo you showed me and any information you have about the guy."

He handed over the photo. Simone had a duplicate, so he didn't care about parting with this one. The chief wrote down Spanner's name and car model, along with Sam's phone number, in a pocket-sized pad.

"Okay, give him his license, Lonnie."

Lieutenant Lonnie Cates stared at Sam for a couple of beats, his thin lips pursed. He adjusted his gun belt before taking the license from his pocket and handing it to Sam.

Sam turned to head back to his car. When he did, he saw the woman who'd been sitting with Jake Bell earlier inside the restaurant. She stared for a moment then someone stepped into his line of vision. By the time the person passed by, she'd disappeared, so Sam went toward his car.

The woman caught up with him. "Hey, I know you didn't kill Jake. I saw you leave with your girlfriend."

"Yeah? Why didn't you say something about it to the chief?"

She smiled. "I thought you were doing pretty well." Her large eyes shone blue in the glow of the floodlights, her lips like ripe strawberries. Something fluttered inside Sam's chest.

THREE

THE WOMAN HELD out her hand. "I'm Lora Diamond. I work for the local newspaper."

Newspapers usually blabbed too much about things they shouldn't.

He shook her hand. "Sam Mackenzie. You a reporter?"

She nodded. "You want to get a cup of coffee and talk about what happened here tonight? There's an all-night diner over on US-1."

He didn't need to become part of a news story, even for a beautiful reporter, but maybe Jake Bell told her something.

"As long as you don't mention my name anywhere."

Lora raised an eyebrow. "Why do you have a problem with that?"

"I don't want to be in the papers, that's all."

She gave him a sardonic smile. "I could just go with what I already have. Stranger in town. Spoke with the victim a little while before he was killed. That would get everybody's attention."

"Yeah, you could do that. Probably wouldn't be in your best interest, though."

She backed up a step and glanced in the direction of the police. "Why, what would you do?"

Sam smiled. "I wouldn't do anything, but the man I'm working for might shut down your newspaper."

"Who is this guy you work for?"

"Sorry that's all I can say about it."

"Ah, I get it," she said, grinning, "this is some kind of government thing."

"No comment."

"Okay, you win. No names. I'll even let you clear the story. How about it?"

Maybe she'd keep her word. He hoped so, because he did want to talk to her. "I guess that sounds okay."

THEY LEFT IN separate cars, and Sam followed her to the diner, which sat across the road from the beach. Only one person seemed to work the night shift. The waitress served the counter and the booths, and maybe even cooked in the back.

After ordering coffee, Lora took out her notebook and laid it on the table. "So, what can you tell me that isn't classified?"

Sam smiled. "Why don't you tell me what you know about Sean Spanner?"

"I don't know anything about him. Jake seemed anxious to tell you something about the guy, but when I asked him what it was, he wouldn't say."

"Did you leave before he did?"

"We went out to the parking lot at the same time, a minute or so after you left. He said he had to talk to you about something at the motel, but wouldn't tell me what it was. I waited before pulling out, so he wouldn't see me, and then I drove to the Blue Iguana, hoping to eavesdrop on your conversation. When Jake didn't show, I went back to Chopin's in case he showed up there again. I got there just a few minutes ahead of you, and the police were already there, standing over his dead body."

"You don't seem too shook up about it."

"What? Oh, Jake and I weren't dating if that's what you think. I met him at Chopin's to get some information for a story about a big development his father is building in Marathon."

"Did you get it?"

"Some of it, but when you came in and flashed that photo, he got quiet and didn't say much after that."

She tried to get him to tell more about why he was searching for Spanner, and Sam told her about the cash.

"And that's it? He stole some money and you're trying to get it back? That doesn't sound much like government work to me."

She grinned when she said it, and he thought she might be loosening up.

"I never said anything about the government. You did."

"Yeah, but you led me to believe I was right."

"Sorry about that, but I really can't say any more about it."

Lora pushed back from the table and crossed her arms. "I guess that about does it, then."

Sam didn't want her to leave, telling himself that she might know something else of value. "What keeps a newspaper reporter busy in a town like this?"

After taking a sip of coffee, she said, "There's more going on here than you'd think. We had a murder here a couple of months ago. I wrote four stories on it."

"What happened?"

"A man's body was found over on the highway, stabbed in the chest. Nobody could identify him."

"You seem pretty matter-of-fact about it," Sam said, "like that sort of thing doesn't bother you."

She frowned. "Oh, it bothered me at first. It was the biggest thing to happen here in a long time. No one could remember anyone ever being murdered on Iguana Key. They never found the killer."

They were quiet for a moment. Sam checked his watch. 10:35 p.m. "You have any ideas about who could have killed Jake?"

She gave him a stare. "Not a clue. Maybe it had something to do with what he planned to tell you."

Maybe it did. "I'd like to see the stories you wrote about the other murder."

"You think the same person killed Jake?"

Maybe it had nothing to do with Spanner, but two murders so close together in this backwater town seemed suspicious.

"Could be."

She checked her watch. "It's too late tonight, but I could get the issues for you tomorrow if you drop by the newspaper office."

Sam smiled. "Don't you keep copies at home?"

Raising an eyebrow, she said, "Yeah, but I don't know you. You think I'm going to take you to my house?"

"It was worth a try."

A smile teased at the corner of her mouth. She stared for a moment. "Okay, why not. You seem pretty harmless. But you have to tell me something else about this guy you're searching for."

"Sounds like a good trade."

SAM FOLLOWED HER about a mile down US-1. They turned right and rode another half-mile to a subdivi-

sion. In the dark it looked like a development from the
1940's and 50's. Cabana-style homes built with painted
cinder blocks. Mature palms dotted the front lawns. No
garages or carports.

Lora turned into a driveway, pulled the car behind
the house, and stopped. A light inside a screened porch
cast a glow on her car and the back yard. They got out,
and she went through the screened porch and in the
back door. Sam followed her inside past an entrance
hall to the kitchen.

"Have a seat and I'll get the stories. How about a
drink?"

"Sure, if you have a beer."

Nodding, she opened the refrigerator and took out
two bottles.

"Glass?"

"No, bottle's fine."

She handed one to him, opened her own, and disappeared down the hall.

Sam twisted off the cap, drank down a third of the
bottle and sat. The kitchen had no plaques with homey
slogans on the wall, no magnets or photos on the refrigerator, no napkins or salt and pepper shakers on
the table. The stovetop and sink had a layer of dust on
their surfaces. It all appeared as if she'd just moved
in. A coffee pot sat on the counter in the corner. It had
some leftover brew in the decanter, so she'd used that.

"Here they are," she said, stepping back into the
kitchen. She sat across from him at the table and laid
several news clippings in front of him.

Scanning through them, he learned little more than
what she'd told him in the diner. The man had been
stabbed with a knife and left in a ditch on a road a hun-

dred yards or so from the Overseas Highway. Lieutenant Lonnie Cates was quoted as saying the man probably had been homeless, unkempt and wearing dirty clothes, and he might have gotten into a squabble with another homeless person. The victim had what looked like jail-house tattoos on his arms and legs. Nothing in the stories told him anything about who the killer might be.

"The police didn't have any theory about the killer's identity?"

"If they did, they wouldn't tell me about it. I got the impression they didn't know anything, and didn't want to go to the expense of an investigation for a home-less man."

He sighed, finished his beer, and studied her face. She was even more beautiful now in this light, her hair black as ink, eyes a deep blue, flawless skin.

Her eyebrow inched up. Probably watching the gears turn inside his head.

"Time for you to go. I have to send in my report on Jake's murder and get up early tomorrow."

Sam smiled and stood. "Yeah, I guess it is time to go."

"Before you leave, you promised to tell me some-thing else about Sean Spanner."

Hmmm. He'd hoped she would forget about that.

"Let's see. The police took the photo I had, but I can give you a description." He described the man and she wrote it down in her pad.

"Okay, that's good, but I assumed you'd give me something else about why he's here."

"That's a good question. I don't know why he's here. I just know he left Miami a couple days ago, and I can only assume he came here to see somebody about hiding him."

Something rattled outside the door.

"You hear that?" Sam asked.

"What?"

"There was a noise on the porch."

Her eyes narrowed. "Hey, is this a ploy to get me to ask you to stay."

"No, I heard something."

He went through the dimly-lit entrance hall and tried to peer through the glass of the back door. The porch lay in darkness. He flipped the light switch, but it didn't work.

Stepping back to the kitchen, he said, "You have a flashlight?"

Lora reached into a cabinet and pulled one out. Returning to the entry hall with his gun drawn, he opened the door and eased out to the darkness.

He splashed the light on the screen door. It hung ajar. Turning to see what had happened to the porch light, he sensed movement to his right. Someone slapped the flashlight from his hand, and Sam spun and kicked with his right foot. His shoe brushed cloth, but nothing else. A split second later the silhouette of a man burst out the screen door. Sam ran out behind him and up the drive to the street. He couldn't see anything in the dark, and heard only the crunch of his own footfalls on the gravel. A car started somewhere down the block, and when he got to the street it was gone. Back in the house, he told Lora what had happened, his pulse still thumping in his ears.

"You're just trying to scare me. I never heard anything."

"No, I'm not. Somebody was out there."

"Okay, I'll call the police." Frowning, she picked up her phone from the table, dialed 911, and told the operator she thought she had a prowler. She closed the phone and said, "They're coming out, so you can go now."

The time for friendly conversation had passed. Now she just wanted him gone.

"Okay, but I still want to clear the story before you print it."

"That's fine. I'll send in a quick write-up about Jake's murder for the morning edition, and save the bigger story for the next day. You can drop by the paper tomorrow afternoon and check it out."

FOUR

BEFORE SAM COULD use the key, Simone swung the door open. She stood there in the short nightie, the gun hanging down by her side. A pretty sexy pose, but she probably hadn't intended it that way. She seemed oblivious to her attraction of men. He entered and closed the door behind him. The room felt frigid.

"Where've you been? I thought they must've arrested you."

He didn't want to get into another discussion about Lora Diamond.

"I spoke with a reporter after the police let me go."

"Why would you do that?"

Laying his gun on the dresser and emptying his pockets, he said, "Another murder happened a couple of months ago, and this reporter covered the stories on it."

When he turned around, she'd gotten into bed and sat propped up on pillows with the cover pulled up under her arms.

"You think it could be the same guy?"

He sat on the other bed and told her about the similarities of the killings. "A place this size probably doesn't have many homicidal maniacs."

She stared for a couple of beats. "Well, I'm glad they didn't arrest you. I'd hate to have to put down some policemen getting you out of there."

The words might have been intended as humor,

but he knew her pretty well. She just might do what she'd said.

Sam grinned. "Yeah, me too."

Simone yawned, turned on her side, facing him, and moved the pillow underneath her head.

"Turn off the light when you go to bed," she said, her eyes closed, her words already dreamy.

After brushing his teeth and undressing, he sat on the bed and watched her sleep, her body rising ever so slightly with shallow breaths, her lips smiling as if in a nice dream, like an innocent child. Smiling himself, he turned off the light, pitying the poor soul who might think that and try to take advantage of her.

THE HEARSE WANDERED across the center line. Alton Cox dozed at the wheel, head back, mouth open. Harpo Crum peered out the windshield and saw the grill of a semi in their path. His pulse fired in his ears as he grabbed the wheel.

"Watch out, man!"

The semi's horn blasted as it squeezed by, the driver throwing them the finger.

Alton awoke and coughed, his eyes darting. They'd stopped at a bar along the highway for a few drinks since the body didn't have to be in Lauderdale until morning. As always, Alton had way too many. He'd spilled whiskey on the guy next to him, and the man got in his face about it. One thing led to another and Alton ended up on the floor, the man kicking him in the face with the pointed toes of his cowboy boots. Harpo finally persuaded the cowboy to stop, and dragged Alton out of the bar.

Harpo drove the first couple of hours after that,

Alton sleeping it off in the passenger seat. He awoke when Harpo pulled off the highway to get some malt liquor, and went to the restroom to rinse the blood off his face. When he returned, he insisted on driving. Harpo had been glad to oblige, but now he thought that might have been a mistake. He didn't want to become road kill pasted onto the grill of a semi. Taking a long pull on the bottle of malt liquor, he felt his nerves begin to smooth out.

"What about my bottle?" Alton asked. He still looked drunk.

"Want me to drive?"

"No, man, just give me my bottle."

"Sure, buddy, hold on." Harpo pulled a quart of Colt 45 from the bag at his feet, twisted off the cap, and handed it to him. "You see that car following us? He's been back there since we left the bar. Even stopped at the store when we got the malt."

"Don't worry about it. You just got the heebie jeebies cause of that stiff we got back there. I know a bar up ahead that stays open all night. We'll stop for a couple of shots and maybe you can chill out."

Harpo shook his head and sighed. Alton should have learned his lesson when the tips of the cowboy's boots were stuck up his nose.

The hearse felt hot and laden with moisture, windows wide open, the odor of the sea and the moldy casket floating in the air. Within a couple of minutes they rolled onto a bridge that seemed a mile long.

Harpo sighed and fiddled with the little crystal radio he'd bought for a dollar at a flea market. The guy said it was over fifty years old, and Harpo had brought it along because the hearse's radio had gotten stolen a few months before. Inserting the tiny speaker plug into his ear, he adjusted the antenna and found only one station. A man with a Southern accent preached about sins of the flesh. Another program would probably come on eventually, so he settled back to listen to the preacher for a while. He dropped the radio into his shirt pocket and took a long drink of the malt. The expanding image of the trailing car caught his attention in the mirror outside his window.

Harpo twisted around in his seat until he could eyeball the car. It sped up and cut into the passing lane. "Watch out, man, the car is coming around us."

"He's the one better watch out," Alton said.

The sedan sped by, pulled into their path, and braked until its rear bumper banged the front end of the hearse. The driver stuck his arm out the window and motioned for them to pull to the side.

"What's wrong with that guy?" Alton said, pumping the brakes.

"He wants us to pull over."

Alton rolled his eyes. "I know that, Sherlock."

Jamming the brakes again, he slowed to a stop behind the car.

"See what he wants, and make it quick. Give me the high sign if he tries anything."

Harpo grinned. "Yeah, I'll do that. Maybe you can take care of him like you did that cowboy."

The stranger got out of the car and stood there, waiting. He appeared to be holding something behind his back.

Harpo turned up the bottle of malt liquor, draining it, and got out. Wiping his lips with the back of his hand, he walked on shaky legs in front of the hearse. "What's the problem, dude?"

The man approached, humming a song that sounded like an old television show. Alton hit the high beams, lighting up the guy's face, and Harpo recognized him.

"Hey, you're that—"

It happened in the blink of an eye. Something exploded, knocking him back. Harpo stumbled against the hood of the hearse, and the guy turned and walked around toward the driver's door. Harpo felt funny, his chest burning, and he realized he'd been shot. He coughed. Fluid came up from his throat.

The man jerked the driver's door open. Alton cursed, but the gun exploded again, and he fell over in the seat. The shooter grabbed his shirt front and pulled him back up behind the wheel. He peered out at Harpo, his eyes shining in the dash lights, begging for help, his mouth stretched wide in a silent scream. Harpo wanted to do something, but then his head went into a spin and he passed out.

When Harpo awoke he was back in his seat next to Alton, the motor idling. They just sat there on the vast concrete expanse of the bridge, life leaking away, as if waiting for the Pearly Gates to open. He wondered if he would be on the list to get in. The radio preacher, still channeling through the earpiece, talked about redemption and how sinners should pray for forgiveness. Harpo wondered if he could be forgiven for the things he'd done.

The car in front of them had disappeared. Lights glared in the mirrors, and he tried to turn and see out of the back window. His chest felt as if it had a flare burning inside it. After a few moments of struggling, he managed to see the sedan behind them. The man reached inside it and came out with an object of some kind. In the dim light it resembled a can of beans. He stepped to the front of his car and held the object in the illumination of the headlight, as if reading the list of ingredients. Then he strode to the hearse, twisted something on the top of the can, and tossed it behind Alton next to the casket. In the next instant, he reached in the window, cut the wheel to the left, and punched the old Caddy into drive.

The vehicle lurched forward, headed to the other side of the bridge toward the rail. Although Alton seemed to be breathing, his eyes were closed, his face a jaundiced death mask. Harpo didn't know what might happen now, but he knew it'd be bad, and he willed his hand to move to the door handle. He also took the radio preacher's advice and prayed. As he felt the snap of the latch, everything turned a blinding white, and he wondered if this might be the crossing-over light he'd heard about. But then he felt the heat and a sense of flying, and the light went out.

FIVE

CHIEF BOOZLER ARRIVED for work at 9:30 a.m. He hadn't gotten to bed until after five. Lonnie Cates met him at the door.

"The mayor came by to see you, Chief. He wants you to stop in. And there's something I need to tell you when you have a chance."

Chief Boozler knew the mayor would come around as soon as he heard about the murder. "Lonnie, will you get me a cup of coffee and bring it to me in his office? I might as well get this over with."

The chief winked at him as he walked by and Lonnie broke into a big grin. Boozler sauntered into the mayor's outer office and told the secretary he needed to see her boss.

"Go on in. He's expecting you."

Sighing, Boozler entered and sat down, rubbing his sleepy eyes, acknowledging the mayor only after he got completely situated.

"Morning, Rich. I understand you were busy last night. Have time to tell me about it?"

"That's why I'm here. I guess you know it was Jake Bell who got murdered. His father was beside himself when I called him, but he seemed more angry than hurt. Course, people express their grief in different ways. Morton ranted and raved over the phone about how we'd better fry the animal that did it or he'll do it himself."

Lonnie Cates came through the open door and handed the cup of coffee to the chief. Boozler thanked him and took a sip.

Donald Meyer's eyes narrowed. Probably jealous. Word was his secretary would never bring him coffee.

"It sounds like you have a good suspect. I heard about the guy from Miami."

Boozler tried not to smile. "You must have been talking to Lonnie."

Meyer nodded.

"You know," the chief said, "there's no shortage of people around here who might kill Jake Bell."

"Yes, well, that might be true, but we need to make sure Morton knows we're doing our jobs. Maybe you should arrest the man from Miami until you find more evidence."

Bell had bought the mayor's office with campaign funds, and satisfying him was Meyer's number one priority. "Sorry, but it doesn't work that way." Boozler took a sip of coffee and glanced at his watch. The mayor's time was up.

Back in his office, Boozler turned on the computer and brought up his e-mail. He hated electronic systems and didn't use them often. There were a couple of messages from fraternal police organizations, probably wanting money from him, one from the Iguana Key Chamber of Commerce, one from the mayor, and one from a parole officer with the Florida Department of Corrections. The last message probably deserved his attention most because Boozler had already ignored it for a few days. The parole officer was searching for a man named Fletcher Spikes, who had been paroled a couple of months before and had disappeared. A report in the Tallahassee office mentioned a dead John Doe in Iguana Key. Doe had a tattoo on his arm, and the parole officer asked in the e-mail if any photos of it had been made.

Fletcher Spikes.

Lonnie entered his office. "I did some searches on Mackenzie, the dude from Miami. He looks pretty suspicious."

Boozler leaned back and scratched his head, still thinking about the e-mail. "Yeah? How so?"

"I didn't find anything. No arrests, no credit rating, nothing. Not even a driver's license. It's like he doesn't exist."

"Maybe you made a mistake. We saw his Florida license."

Lonnie shook his head. "Could've been fake. I think we should bring him in."

SAM SAT AT the table in the interrogation room and stared at Police Chief Boozler. A cruiser had shown up at the diner at 9:45 a.m. while he and Simone ate breakfast. They probably didn't have anything to link him to the murder of Jake Bell, but there was no telling what else they might dig up if they talked to the right people.

"What are you doing in Iguana Key, son?"

"I told you last night why I'm here. I'm searching for Sean Spanner. Surely you don't think I had anything to do with that murder."

"Have you ever been here before this trip?"

"No, never, except driving through to Key West."

"You sure about that?"

Sam wondered where this was going. He thought he could see something sinister crawling in the chief's eyes, but wasn't sure what it might be. He shifted in the chair. "Yes, I'm sure. I think I'd remember."

The chief nodded, took a sip from his coffee cup. "Sure you weren't here a couple of months ago?"

Sam recalled the murder Lora had mentioned.

Without waiting for an answer, the chief got up, stepped out of the office for a few seconds and returned. "We had another dead body turn up a couple of months ago. Stabbed, like Jake Bell."

An officer entered the door and handed Boozler a file folder. He opened it on the table and studied its contents for a few moments.

"Can you verify your whereabouts on April 6th?"

Sam tried to remember. "I think I was refinishing my boat deck during that time. The dock master helped me. Give him a call and he'll tell you."

He wrote down the man's name and telephone number for the chief, who didn't seem very convinced.

"Will he know where you were twenty-four hours a day?"

"Probably not, but he saw me during the day that whole week."

The chief shrugged. "Okay, I'll call him."

Sam hoped he was right about the dates, and if wrong, maybe his friend would catch the drift and give the right answer anyway.

Boozler made a copy of his driver's license and let him go after a few more minutes.

"We're not finished with you, so stay in town. I'm going to check out this license. My Lieutenant said it didn't show up when he researched it. You better hope that was some kind of mistake."

Check all you want. That's one thing I have that is legitimate.

Sam left the room and called Simone to pick him up. She said she was in the parking lot, so he went outside and spotted the car, the engine running, the windows closed to keep in the cool air. When he reached to open the door, Lora Diamond pulled in beside them and lowered her window.

"I heard they rousted you again. You have a few minutes to talk about it?"

"I think I'm all talked out."

The sun bore down on his neck, tingling his skin with ultraviolet wattage.

"You sure? I'll spring for a beer at Chopin's."

After a moment's hesitation, he said, "Hold on."

He got inside the car with Simone and said, "You up for talking with the reporter?"

Her lips tightened into a smirk. "She's the reporter you mentioned last night?"

"Yeah, she's the reporter."

"Sure, why not. Let's hear what Cleo has to say."

Sam lowered the window and told Lora they'd meet her there.

Simone backed out and drove away. "So, you weren't going to tell me about her, huh?"

He grinned. "I didn't see any reason to go into it."

"That's the only reason? 'Cause, you know, I'm cool."

Glancing at her, he wondered if she really was cool, or just talking.

SIX

SAM SPOTTED LORA at a table in the corner. She stood and introduced herself to Simone, extending her hand.

"Let's get this over with," Simone said, ignoring the outstretched hand.

Smiling, seeming a little embarrassed, Lora glanced at Sam and sat back down. A waiter arrived at the table and they ordered. Sam and Lora made small talk until the drinks arrived, while Simone sat pushed back from the table, her legs crossed, one foot moving up and down to a slow cadence.

"You seem to have gotten yourself into some trouble after you left my place," Lora said. "I thought you might need my help."

"What kind of help?" He took a long drink of the cold beer.

Chopin stood behind the bar a few feet behind Lora's chair, wiping it with a towel, pretending not to listen to their conversation. The round man with the tattoos finally looked in their direction, and Sam gave him a nod. He cut his eyes away.

"I thought you might need a lawyer," Lora said.

Sam gave her a quick smile. "What I need is information on Sean Spanner. You think you could help me with that?"

"I told you last night, I don't know anything about this Spanner man."

"Jake must've said something about him," Sam said. "Think hard."

Lora shook her head. "But he didn't. Wait..." She peered down at the table for a couple of moments.

Simone's foot stopped moving, and she uncrossed her legs and eased up to the table. "What did he say?"

"He said something like, 'the questions about the Marathon job make sense, now.'"

"What questions?"

"He wouldn't tell me. He just clammed up after that, with a serious expression on his face, as if he might be obsessing about something. Then he told me to wait at the table when he went to talk to you. I was pretty miffed by then, so I left and followed you two to the motel."

Sam nodded. "What kind of job is it they're doing in Marathon?"

The reporter shrugged. "A new shopping center."

"Does it involve any concrete?"

Lora raised an eyebrow. "Concrete? I guess it might. The Bell Company pours a lot of concrete. Why?"

Leaning back in his chair, Sam drank from his beer bottle and glanced at Simone. Her eyes widened.

"Nothing," Sam said. "Just wondering what a construction job would have to do with Sean Spanner."

He drained his beer. "We need to get going."

"So that's it? That's all you're going to tell me?"

Simone stood and headed for the door.

"Sorry, that's all there is to tell." He got up from his chair. "I still want to see the story before you run it in the paper. I'll drop by your office this afternoon about five."

Lora stood and said, "Okay. In case you change your

mind about the lawyer, Charles Ford is good, and I can talk to him for you. You might need him more than you think."

Why did she keep bringing up the lawyer? "It sounds like you might know something I don't."

"Well, I heard the police did some research and couldn't find any records on you, like you're off the grid. That's the kind of thing that gets their attention."

"Who told you that?"

"Sorry, I have to protect my sources. What do you have to say about it?"

"The chief just brought me in for some more questions. He dragged out a file on the two-month-old murder you mentioned last night. Then he let me go. That's all there was to it."

He turned and strode out the door.

When they got into the car Simone said, "You think somebody killed Spanner and put him under some poured concrete?"

"If he's dead, the killer might have planned on doing that, but I think he would've changed his mind when he saw me talking to Jake Bell."

"Yeah, that makes sense. And you just mentioned it to keep the reporter busy for a while."

He nodded as he started the car. "The guy couldn't have known whether or not Bell mentioned that to me when he asked about a meeting."

"He was probably in the restaurant," Simone said, "and saw you flash the photograph."

Sam pulled out of the parking lot, drove down to the next block, and turned into a gas station. He got out and filled the car in the midday sun. A bead of perspiration ran down the side of his face. While the pump ticked away the gallons, he watched Lora Diamond's car exit Chopin's lot and turn toward the Overseas Highway.

When he got back in the car Simone said, "She's headed to Marathon. Let's go back and talk to Tattoo Boy."

Smiling, Sam said, "We do think alike."

CHIEF BOOZLER WAS about to go across the street for lunch when Officer Dudley Crew came into his office with a sheet of paper.

"I found the record of Mackenzie's Florida driver's license. The lieutenant must have missed it. I also got this from a contact with the Department of Defense." He handed the report to the chief.

The chief studied the profile, which said only that the man had been a Navy SEAL ten years or so before. There was nothing else. No duty locations, no assignments, nothing but blank space.

"SEALs are special forces, right?" the chief asked.

"Correct, sir. It stands for 'Sea, Air, and Land.' They're big into underwater demolition."

"You mean explosives?"

"Yes, sir."

"So the absence of information about this guy probably means what he did was classified."

"That would be my interpretation. Or illegal."

Boozler laid the report down and smiled. Dudley knew his computers.

"That all you needed?" the officer asked.

"Yeah, but I want you to do something on another case. How about checking the files for that John Doe murder and see if there are any photographs of the victim."

Crew left and returned within a few minutes.

"The evidence list contained an entry for ten photographs taken of the victim, but they were missing from the box."

"What could have happened to them?"

Crew shrugged. "Somebody probably took them out and forgot to put them back."

When Crew had gone, the chief pulled up the e-mail from the parole officer to give him the news in a reply. Within minutes, he got another e-mail from the guy asking to have the body exhumed. He said he'd seen the tattoos on his parolee, so he'd drive down and examine the ones on the body of the John Doe to see if they matched.

Just what Boozler needed, some state guy coming in asking questions. He forwarded the e-mail to Lonnie, asking him to get an exhumation order from the local judge.

On his way out, he stopped by his secretary's desk and asked her to set up an appointment with the prosecutor, Dale Edison, at one o'clock. He might as well go over everything with him, too, and make sure they were on the same page about the Jake Bell case. Then he strode out the door, thinking about SEAL operatives and all the ways they probably had to kill a man. He also thought about the grief his office would catch from Morton Bell if they didn't soon come up with a credible solution to his son's murder.

BOOZLER ENTERED EDISON's outer office. The prosecutor's secretary had stepped away, so he proceeded around her desk to knock on Edison's closed door. It opened when he reached out, and Edison stood there with a leather-bound bible in his hand. The chief wondered what that was about, pretty sure the guy wasn't a religious person.

The prosecutor jerked when he saw the chief and just stood there for an awkward moment. He wore a dark gray suit that matched the color of his tinted glasses.

"Can I help you, Rich?"

"We're supposed to have a meeting at one."

"Huh. I guess I didn't get the message. Come on in." He laid the book down on the corner of his desk, and a tiny cloud of fine white powder puffed from its pages. It could have been a number of things, but the first that came to mind was cocaine. Edison had always seemed a little familiar, like someone who had crossed paths with Boozler in the past. He had never thought much about it, but when he saw the powder a little alarm sounded off in Boozler's head.

Edison's face flushed red when he saw Boozler looking at the book. He sat down and said, "This meeting about the Bell murder?"

The chief averted his eyes to his notes. "Yes, I thought I'd go over what we have so far and make sure we're all on the same page."

With the awkward moment seemingly past, he laid out the facts about the case. He also told Sam Mackenzie's story and what they'd learned since the night before. "I'd bet a week's salary he killed lots of men as a SEAL. He could have killed the guy we found two months ago on the highway, too. I checked out his alibi during that time. The guy he told me to call said he'd been with him all that week working on Mackenzie's boat, but he couldn't vouch for his time after four or so each day. That would've been plenty of time for him to drive down US-1, kill a man, and get back to Miami in time for a few hours' sleep before morning. I'd like to arrest him, but the only evidence we have is that he spoke with Jake Bell about an hour before the murder."

Edison took off his glasses, rubbed his eyes, and sighed. He stood and walked to his window. The bright afternoon sun traced his six-foot silhouette. "Morton called this morning. He's heard about Mackenzie and doesn't know why we haven't brought him in. But I'm with you. We don't have enough on him for an arrest."

When he returned to his chair, Boozler studied his eyes. Despite the brightness at the window, his pupils seemed as large as blueberries.

"Got anybody else that might be connected at all?" Edison asked. "Morton will be gunning for us if we don't do something soon."

Boozler shook his head. "Nobody else, but I've got Lonnie and a couple of other officers working on it. We should turn up something soon."

Edison chuckled. "Lonnie, huh?"

"Lonnie's okay. He just runs off at the mouth a little too much."

The prosecutor smirked. "We agree on that last part."

Boozler stood and left the man sitting there with his arms crossed on his chest. The cocaine-in-the-bible angle might be something he would investigate further on his own. Maybe drop by after hours and get a peek inside the book. Probably had a cutout for a mirror and a snorting straw. *Never know when you might need a prosecutor in your back pocket.* And he would need to think more about where he might have seen Edison before he'd come to work in Iguana Key. It bothered him when something nagged at him he couldn't put his finger on.

He stopped by Lonnie's desk and asked if he'd gotten the exhumation order signed by the judge. The lieutenant picked up an envelope and tapped its edge on his desktop. "Right here, Chief. You want me to deliver it to the funeral home?"

"We'll both go in case Howard Tim gives you a hard time. That guy from Tallahassee is coming down this evening. It'll be better if we have that body out of the ground so he can examine it and be on his way."

SEVEN

WHEN SAM AND SIMONE entered the door of Chopin's, the fat man stood behind the bar straightening liquor bottles on the wall. He wore a T-shirt with *Juilliard* stenciled across its back. They took seats on barstools and Chopin turned around.

"Didn't you two just leave?"

"Yeah," Simone said. "But we wanted to talk to you without the local mouthpiece listening."

The corners of his pudgy mouth turned up in a smile. "Sugar, you can talk to me anytime you want. Get you a drink?"

"Yeah," Simone said, "give us a beer."

The bartender filled two frosted mugs and set them on coasters in front of them. He fixed a stare on Sam, his palms flat on the bar.

"Way I hear it, you been keeping the fuzz hopping around here."

Sam smiled. "You attend Juilliard?" He remembered the man saying something about being a pianist the night before.

Chopin looked down at the front of his shirt, which bore the same decoration as the back. He grinned. "Yeah. Master of Music. I used to play concerts at the Lincoln Center, but I got tired of that gig and moved south to open this bar."

"Just like that, from Juilliard to bartender."

Chopin shrugged. "Pretty much. Hard to live up to a name like mine in the music business."

"You recognized the guy in the photo we showed you last night," Simone said. "Why didn't you tell us about him?"

Smiling, he said to Sam, "I don't blab to pigs."

Sam raised an eyebrow. "I told you, we're not with the law."

"I know what you said, but you got the look. I can spot you guys a mile away."

Simone gave Sam a sidelong glance. He winked, and she took a sip of her beer, set it down on the bar, and slid it to one side.

She grabbed Chopin by the front of his shirt with both hands and jerked, scrubbing his corpulence against the bar, bringing his face to within inches of her own.

"Would cops smash your nose on this bar?" she asked.

The round man just stared at her beautiful face and grinned.

Reaching his arm between them, Sam said, "Hold on. I think he'll tell us."

She released him and he staggered back against the liquor racks behind him, rattling the bottles, still grinning.

Clearly not the effect she'd hoped for. "Okay, piano boy, tell us what you know about Sean Spanner, or I can get a lot rougher."

Chopin said to Sam, "She do this for free, or do I have to pay?"

Sam shook his head. "Better not provoke her."

He must have seen something sinister in her eyes, because the grin leaked away.

"All right, he was here. He didn't talk to anybody, including me. He just sat at the bar drinking beer. Every now and then he called somebody on his cell phone, but I don't think he ever got anybody to answer."

Sam took a drink of the beer and set it down. "How long did he stay?"

"I don't know, maybe an hour. I kind of lost track, we were so busy."

"You're sure he didn't talk to anybody else?"

"I didn't notice it if he did. I can ask the waitress on duty that night. She served him a couple of beers while I was busy."

He stepped through a door going to the rear of the building and came back in less than a minute, a blonde woman dressed in jeans trailing behind him.

"Tell them about the guy," Chopin said.

The woman eyed them then turned to her boss. Her expression said, *You sure about this?*

"They're not cops," he said.

She turned to Sam. "Not much to say. I asked him if he was just visiting town, and he said he was. Said he lived in Miami. He didn't seem to want to talk, so I left him alone."

"He didn't say anything about who he was visiting?" Sam asked.

The blonde's eyes narrowed. "No, I told you everything he said. He rob a bank or something?"

"Not a bank, but he stole something, and we need to get it back."

Chopin told her she could go back to work, and when she'd gone Sam asked if he knew about the murder that had happened two months before.

"Sure, everybody around here knew about it."

"You have any theories about who did it?"

He raised an eyebrow, scanned around the bar, and leaned in closer. "Some guys were in here from Miami a few weeks ago, and after a few drinks I could tell they were connected. You know, mob—"

"Yeah, I get the picture."

"Anyway, I mentioned that body out on the highway to them and told them the word was it was a mob hit. They said no way. Said if it was their kind of business they would know about it. They acted like it insulted them that I would even mention it. I gave them a couple of drinks on the house and they went away happy, but I could tell they were hiding something."

The guy seemed like somebody who could be connected himself.

"So you pegged it as a mob hit?"

"Yeah. Those guys wouldn't admit something like that to me."

"If you're wrong, and it happened to be somebody in town, who would you put your money on?"

Chopin seemed to study on the question then frowned. "I didn't know the guy who got whacked, and I never heard anybody else say they knew him, so I don't have any idea."

THE BEAUTIFUL RIVER FUNERAL HOME sat on a man-made canal fed from the Gulf of Mexico, patiently awaiting the next dearly departed. An imposing structure, it was overshadowed only by its massive billboard that rose a hundred feet in the air.

The lieutenant parked the cruiser behind the facility, and he and the chief went in through the employee entrance. They passed the open door of the bookkeeper's office and Boozler tapped on the jamb.

She turned around. "Can I help you?"

"We have an exhumation order. Can you get Howard out here?"

She motioned for them to follow her down the hall and swung open the door to a large room. Two embalming tables stood close to the far wall. Howard Tim leaned over one of them, fiddling with a machine of some kind.

"Lieutenant Cates and Chief Boozler are here to see you," she said through the doorway. "You want them in the lobby?"

The undertaker came over. "This isn't a hotel. The front room is called Heavens Hall."

The bookkeeper wrinkled her nose, as if smelling a foul odor. "Well, Heavens Hall, whatever." She turned and went back toward her office.

When Tim saw them standing there, he said, "Officer Cates, Chief. Nice of you to stop by."

He led them down the hall to the front room, where there were several chairs and a sofa.

"It's Lieutenant," Cates said when they stopped.

"Beg your pardon?"

"It's Lieutenant Cates, not Officer."

"Oh, sorry." He turned to the chief as if to dismiss Lonnie. "What can I do for you?"

The chief held up the court document. "I've got an exhumation order for that John Doe you buried back in April. A parole officer from Tallahassee is coming here today to check it for identification."

The undertaker took off his glasses, polished the

thick lenses with a handkerchief, and put them back on. "Can you say that again?"

"The medical examiner reported a tattoo on the Doe's upper arm, and the parole guy thinks he might be his missing parolee. The judge says we can dig him up. We need it done post-haste."

The undertaker ran his fingers through his hair and sighed. "I can't believe this."

"What's the problem?"

Howard Tim frowned. "I received a call from a Lauderdale funeral home asking me to dig up John Doe and bring him up there. The body's gone."

Boozler felt his pulse thumping at his temple, his face heating up. "When did this happen?"

Howard Tim frowned. "I got the call yesterday afternoon. We disinterred the deceased about 8:00 p.m., and the hearse left here at 10:00 p.m."

"You must be out of your mind, Howard. Nobody ever identified that body."

"Well, what am I supposed to do? The man who called said the Fort Lauderdale Police Department had identified the man as a local citizen. He said the family was having a belated funeral, and the deceased had to be there by this morning. I told him you would have to approve it, but he assured me he'd already talked to you and everything was arranged."

"Nobody talked to me." The chief sighed, took his notebook from his pocket, and sat down in an imitation leather chair.

"Did the body get delivered to Lauderdale?"

"Well there must have been a snag somewhere. I called the funeral home up there twice this morning. My men never arrived with the body. They didn't return here, either, and neither of them have a cell phone, so I don't know what happened. I suppose I shouldn't have given them any money up front. They probably got drunk and forgot where they were going."

The undertaker stared for a moment and opened his mouth, but closed it again.

"What is it?" Boozler asked.

"Well, there was something else. The funeral home manager didn't seem to know what I was talking about."

After staring at him for what seemed like a full minute, the chief said, "Do you think it could have been somebody in town who called you?"

Howard shook his head. "I told you, it was somebody in Lauderdale."

"How do you know? Did you see the caller ID?"

"Well, no, it was late, and I didn't think about it, but I can go find it right now. The call should still be there."

Boozler rolled his eyes. "Lonnie, go with him."

They went to the phone in Howard Tim's office and found the number. It had a local area code, which extended from Miami to Key West. Fort Lauderdale had a different code.

"Okay, Howard, as you can see, the call didn't originate in Lauderdale, so it could have been somebody calling from here in town. Think back. Did it sound like anybody you know?"

The undertaker's eyes seemed even larger than usual, like golf balls behind those thick lenses. He wiped his forehead with the sleeve of his suit coat, and blinked a couple of times.

"Well, it did sound like somebody I've heard, but I thought it was just my imagination."

"Who?"

The tall man pulled off his glasses and rubbed his eyes. They were like tiny dots after seeing them behind the magnifiers.

"Gee, I'm sorry, Rich, I just don't know. If I'd thought more about it then—or if I heard him again—I might be able to say who it was." He replaced the specs. "Wait, my bookkeeper answered the phone. Maybe she recognized the voice."

Howard motioned for them to follow him, and they went to her office.

When the undertaker asked her, she seemed to concentrate for a moment. "I remember the guy calling. He had a nice voice. Now that you mention it, he did sound familiar."

They gave her a minute, but she couldn't come up with a name.

"Well, think about it," Lonnie said, "and call us if it comes to you."

Back in the lobby, Boozler said, "I suppose this person promised to pay you for this illegal service you performed."

"Well, uh, yes, he did, but I didn't think it was illegal."

"You've pulled some good ones, but this one might just land you in jail. I'll let you know if the prosecutor wants us to bring charges."

Howard Tim opened his mouth to speak, but coughed and tried again. "You know," he stammered, "I don't get enough from the city to bury a John Doe or an indigent. I do that as a public service. And this man said he would send me a check for two thousand dollars if I got the deceased there by morning."

"You get enough for those burials, or you wouldn't

do them." Boozler took a deep breath and let it out. "I suggest you get on the phone and find that body."

They hurried out of the funeral home, and the chief's face still felt hot when they got back to the station. Boozler went into his office and slammed the door.

About an hour later, Lonnie knocked then let himself in.

"What is it?" Boozler asked. He'd taken a drink a few minutes earlier and hoped the lieutenant couldn't smell it.

Lonnie frowned. "Got some bad news. I found out the call originated from a burner phone that can't be traced."

Boozler shook his head. "We can't seem to catch any luck today." He got up from his desk. "I'm leaving for a while. There's something I need to take care of."

EIGHT

SAM AND SIMONE drove away from Chopin's, headed toward downtown Iguana Key.

"Do you believe her?" Sam asked.

"The waitress?"

He nodded and adjusted the rearview mirror.

"No, I think she's holding something back."

"Me, too. I wonder if they talked more than she said, and maybe she met him after work."

"Yeah, Spanner's a good-looking dude. I could go for him."

Sam grinned. "You mean if not for Karl?"

Simone gave him a stare. "Yeah, except for that."

"I'm thinking maybe you just made up Karl to keep us focused on this mission."

She smiled and raised an eyebrow. "No, that's your ego talking. Karl is real."

"Whatever you say."

"No, really."

"Okay, fine. Back to the waitress. Let's get a sandwich and go back and wait for her to take a break. I smelled cigarettes when she came in to talk to us, so she'll probably head out for a smoke every hour or two."

They stopped at a drive-thru and got burgers and fries. Doubling back, they pulled into the parking lot next door to Chopin's so they could watch the back of his place. An hour passed, the air conditioner lugging to keep the car cool, before the woman came out. She got a cigarette from a Toyota, walked to the shade of the building, and lit up. With the smoke in her hand, she stood there, taking the occasional puff and staring into space. A minute or so later she took out her phone and punched some buttons.

Sam backed out and drove to within a few yards of where she stood.

"Go get her," Sam said. "She might feel more threatened by me."

"You got that right." Simone got out and strode over.

When the barmaid saw her, she closed the phone and dropped her cigarette to the ground. After stubbing it with the toe of her shoe, she turned to go back inside. Simone caught up and stepped in front of her. Whatever she said got lost in the car noise. The girl shook her head and started around toward the door, but Simone blocked her again and took her by the arm. She tried to pull away, but couldn't manage it, and after a few moments of dirty looks and what might be harsh words, she seemed to sigh and headed to the car with her captor.

"I told you," she said from the back seat, "I didn't talk to the guy."

"We think you did," Sam said. "And if you care anything about him at all, you should tell us what happened, because he could be in a lot of danger."

"What do you mean?"

"You know about Jake Bell dying in front of the place last night."

"Yeah, sure. You mean whoever killed Jake might kill Sean, too?"

There it was. First name basis.

"You got it."

Silence.

"Chopin wouldn't like it if he knew I took off early that night to meet the guy. I said I didn't feel well and asked if I could leave."

"Don't worry," Simone said. "He'll never know about it. Just tell us."

After hesitating again, she said, "Okay, if he's in some kind of danger, I want to help. Just don't mention it to my boss. I left about 9:00 p.m. that night and he was waiting in the parking lot. We went to my place for a while and had some drinks. He kept trying to call whoever it was he wanted to talk to, and the guy finally answered."

"What did he say?"

"I don't know. I went in the other room to give him some privacy."

"How do you know it was a man?" Sam asked.

"When the guy answered, Sean said, 'Hey, dude, this is your old buddy.' That's when I left the room, and when I came back in, he was off the phone. He said he had to leave, and he'd come back in a couple of hours. But he didn't. I waited until after midnight before going to bed. I decided he probably just wanted to get out of there and came up with the call as an excuse."

A glow shone on the woman's face in the sunlight that Sam hadn't noticed inside Chopin's. Her big baby blues and full lips, framed by the Nordic hair, were all quite appealing. Spanner hadn't left because he didn't want to be with her.

"Think back," Simone said. "Surely you heard something else, even a word or two might be important."

The barmaid shook her head. "No, nothing else." But then she cast her eyes down to her side, as if in concentration. "Well, there was something. I didn't know what it meant, and I don't see how it could be important."

Like pulling teeth.

"Tell us," Sam said. "You never know."

"Well, as I was leaving the room, I heard him say, 'Yeah, from the Palmetto.'"

"Palmetto?"

"That's what he said."

"Could be the town of Palmetto," Simone said, "up on the west coast of Florida."

"Yeah, it sounded like he was talking about a place." After a protracted silence, she said, "Can I go? Chopin's gonna rake me over for staying out so long."

"Okay," Sam said, "but one more thing. Were you calling him when we just drove up?"

"Yeah, I was worried."

Simone reached over the seat. "Let's see the phone." She took it, punched some buttons, and wrote down the number.

Returning it, Simone said, "I entered my number. Call us if you remember anything else. We'll let you know if we find him."

The door opened and she started out, but stopped. "I just hope he isn't in any kind of trouble, even if he did stand me up."

As she hurried toward Chopin's back door, Sam turned the car around and drove away.

"We don't know much about Spanner, do we?" he asked.

"Not really. All they told me is that he's been working at the research center in Miami for about a month, and all of a sudden he left, taking the flash card and the money with him."

"They would've done a background check on him."

"They did, but he came up squeaky clean. He didn't work in a high security area, so they didn't spend a lot of time and money on it."

"But what he took came from a high security area, right?"

"Yes, top secret. I don't think they know how he got in there."

"What do they do at the facility?"

Shrugging, she said, "It's a defense contractor site. Some kind of research, maybe weapons development work."

"Is it big?"

"I'd say. It covers a couple of square miles out in the boonies near Homestead."

Sam shook his head. "They have to know something else we can use. Call your contact and mention the reference to Palmetto."

Simone shrugged. "I can give it a try." She opened her phone and punched in a number.

"I KNEW HE wouldn't tell me anything else," Simone said upon hanging up. "He made that pretty clear in the briefing."

"Nothing on Palmetto?"

"No, he said he didn't know anything about it."

"Huh. You think he's lying?"

"I wouldn't be surprised. He seemed pretty snappy about me asking."

That didn't sound good.

Sam took out his phone and called John Templeton Smith III. J.T. had served as an intelligence officer in the Navy and became one of their top computer experts.

Now, about a dozen years later, he used his knowledge in various criminal activities. He'd tried honest work a few times, but it didn't work out. Too boring and not enough pay. The FBI kept him on their radar all the time, but he somehow managed to stay at least one step ahead of them.

"Sammy, what's going on?"

"J.T., I'm on a guy's trail, and I wondered if you could help me out." He told him about Spanner and Palmetto and gave him the guy's phone number.

"You think that's his real name?"

"Probably not, but it's all we have."

"Who're you working with down there?"

Sam glanced at his partner and grinned. "Simone."

She raised an eyebrow.

J.T. whistled. "Is she as hot as ever?"

"Yep, smoking."

Simone hit him on the arm, but smiled, her face flush.

"Okay, I'll check this out, but something is nagging me about the Palmetto thing."

"What?"

"Well, if I remember correctly, a few years ago there was a rumor going around about something called Black Palmetto. It was supposed to be an elite assassination unit. Not exactly government-sanctioned, so nobody ever owned up to it. But if a kill couldn't be explained away by the other groups, the rumors credited the Black Palmetto with it. It might have been just legend, though. Your guy probably couldn't have anything to do with that."

After Sam closed the phone, Simone said, "Do you think it's wise to bring J.T. in on this?"

"Sure, why not?"

"Isn't he a little light in the integrity department?"

"Some people might think so, but he's never hung me out to dry." He said it with a pang of guilt. While J.T. had always been pretty loyal, he could get greedy when a lot of money figured into the equation, and Sam always kept that in mind.

Simone rolled her eyes. "Okay, but if this job turns upside-down because of him, it's on you."

"Hey, chill out. It'll be fine. You know anything about Black Palmetto?"

She frowned. "Was that his explanation for the Palmetto reference?"

"No, but he mentioned it. You didn't answer my question."

"Yes, I know about it. It got disbanded a year or so ago, after a couple of the operatives went off the reservation and killed their handlers."

"You're kidding."

"No, we had to go in and clean up the mess. We erased everything we could find."

"What happened to the assassins?"

She gave him a stare. "Sorry, that's classified."

That probably meant they had died. He was about to ask why she hadn't told him all this earlier, but his phone chirped.

Glancing at the display, he said, "It's Lora, the reporter."

Simone smirked.

"Hello."

"The story's ready, and I'll be here until four if you want to take a peek." She gave him directions to the place.

"Okay, I'll be there in about ten minutes." He closed the phone.

Sam told Simone he wanted to go by there and check out what she had written. "Shouldn't take long, though."

"Do you think that's really necessary?"

"Yeah. I don't want any attention I can avoid."

A smile grew on her face. "You really think I'm smoking?"

"Did I say that?"

"Yes, you said it."

He grinned. "Then I guess I do."

She reached across and ruffled his hair.

THEY LOCATED THE newspaper office, went inside, and found Lora Diamond's cubicle. She turned in her chair and handed Sam a paper copy of the story. After reading it, he gave it to Simone. She scanned it for about ten seconds and handed it back.

He laid it on her desk. "Looks good." She had kept his involvement to a minimum.

Lora leaned back in her chair and smiled, her eyes locking on his a couple of beats too long.

"I always protect my sources. Let me know if there's anything I can do to help you find your guy."

Though he didn't have much use for reporters, this one seemed to be growing on him. Simone elbowed him in the side. "Let's go."

He turned to her and she rolled her eyes, as if to say, *Can't you see she's playing you?*

"Okay," Sam said, "I guess that does it, for now."

Lora's eyes widened, as if she just remembered something. "Oh, yeah. I went to the construction site up in Marathon, but didn't see anything out of the ordinary. It looks like they might be about half-finished with the shopping center. Nobody was working, probably because of Jake's death."

"We'll drop by there," Sam said, "but not today."

"I'll give you the address when you're ready to go. Oh, yeah, I set up an appointment for you with the attorney. I know what you said about not needing one, but this isn't Miami. You might be in a precarious position. He said he'd see you at 4:30 p.m."

Sam glanced at the clock on the wall of her cubicle: 4:25 p.m. Sam didn't want to meet with the guy, but he didn't want to be rousted by the police, either.

"You've got time. His office is right across the street."

CHARLES FORD SEEMED FRAIL, had thinning hair, and stood only about five-two. He had a facial tic under his right eye, and wore an empty expression that seemed almost catatonic. Lora had filled Sam in before going over so he wouldn't be surprised. "Don't stare," she'd said. "He hates that."

After introductions, Sam and Simone took a seat in front of Ford's desk. The lawyer wore a beige suit that appeared to be made of linen. He smiled at Simone. The tic rippled down the side of his face.

"Okay, tell me what happened," Ford said.

Sam decided to play along. When he finished the story, Ford nodded. "That jibes with what Lora said. It's a good thing you came in."

"They didn't seem too interested in arresting me for it."

Between tics, Ford's face morphed into something

that resembled a smile, like an expression on a cat with a mouse under its paw.

"Wait until Morton Bell enters the picture," Ford said.

"What do you mean?"

"His only son was murdered. After he pitches a fit, they'll be glad to lock you up."

"I don't think they can do that," Sam said.

The attorney did the cat smile again. "They can do anything they want. You're a stranger in town. You made an appointment to meet Jake. An hour later they found him dead. That will be simple logic for Morton Bell."

"You paint a pretty dismal picture of the local law."

Shrugging, the lawyer said, "Left to their own devices, they'll never find this killer, but they will need someone to blame."

NINE

CHIEF BOOZLER RETURNED to headquarters shortly before 5:00 p.m. and passed Lonnie's desk on his way to his own office.

"I found out about the hearse, Chief."

"What hearse is that, Lonnie?"

"You know, the one the gravediggers used to move the body. The state boys said a vehicle crashed through the rail of a bridge up above Key Largo, over Blackwater Sound. It might be the reason those two clowns never made it to Lauderdale with that body. And that isn't all. A bomb of some kind was used. Maybe military. They found pieces of metal and human tissue. But most of it probably fell into the water."

The chief stared for a moment. "Okay, good work, Lonnie. Get me the details on that bomb. There aren't many places to get a military bomb around The Keys."

"I can't imagine why anyone would want to blow up a hearse."

"What if someone wanted to destroy the body? You know that call to Howard Tim was a phony."

"But why would somebody want to destroy a corpse?" Lonnie asked, smiling.

The chief rolled his eyes.

"Use your head. Remember the guy who's coming from Tallahassee to examine the tattoo? Maybe somebody didn't want him to see it."

"You really think so? Oh, oh yeah. I get the picture now."

About time.

"Get Dudley to help you, Lonnie. No need in you shouldering all the responsibility on this."

"That's okay. I can handle it. Dudley's got other things to do."

"Yeah, well, get him anyway. That's an order." He stepped away, headed for his office, leaving Lonnie to pout at his desk.

Before entering the door, he asked his secretary if the parole officer had called.

"No calls. I've been at my desk since you left earlier."

Scratching his head, he said, "Huh, he's supposed to be here by five."

Shrugging, the secretary grabbed her purse and stood to leave. "Unless you have something else, Chief, I'm calling it a day."

"No, that's okay. I won't be here much longer, my-self."

Back behind his desk he turned his concentration to a budget proposal the city manager had left there the day before.

Morton Bell thundered in through his door. "What's wrong with you, Rich? Your brain going soft like these other idiots around here?"

A hammer pounded behind the chief's eyes.

"What's the problem, Mort?"

"Why'd you let that murderer go? Jake is stone-cold dead, and that killer is running free to do whatever he pleases. I want you to arrest him, right now!"

"Sorry Mort, I can't do that. I don't think he killed your son."

"Well, nobody around here would've done it, and he spoke with Jake no more than an hour before…" His mouth twisted out of shape and tears ran down his cheeks. He mopped them with the backs of his hands.

"I know you're upset, and you have a right to be. But the prosecutor decided we don't have enough evidence to convict. We'd be wasting our time, while the real killer is still out there."

"Okay, fine. If you won't lock him up for me, let's see if you'll do it for the mayor."

The older man stormed out and down the hall. Boozler didn't like the sound of that. He got along just fine with the mayor, but he also knew the man was defenseless when it came to Morton Bell.

Bell had spread enough money around Iguana Key to get the mayor elected, and he had become the best puppet imaginable. Though Bell didn't call on him often, when he did, he expected attention.

Within ten minutes Morton came marching back past his door, a sneer on his face, and stomped out of the building. Then, just about the time Boozler expected the mayor, Charles Ford came in. He hadn't even heard the door open again. Ford entered the office without saying a word and sat down.

"Well, if it isn't Mr. Personality," the chief said. "What do you want?"

Ford stared for several beats. "Has the mayor been in yet?"

"What are you talking about?"

"You know precisely what I'm talking about. I just saw Morty leaving."

The chief thought about it before responding. "No, he hasn't. What does—"

"Splendid, it will save you some measure of face to not have to reverse a moronic decision."

"You're representing Mackenzie?"

"As a matter of fact, I am. So just turn Meyer down and be firm. It will be considerably less painful for you both in the long run."

"Why would I do that for you?"

Ford leaned back in his chair and crossed his legs. A couple of beats passed. The corners of his mouth seemed to turn up, as if in a smile, Boozler wasn't sure.

"Perhaps the voters would like to know how a public servant could afford a Range Rover."

The blood pulsed past Boozler's ears like noisy windshield wipers. His head felt as if it might pop. This creep had coerced him into releasing a suspect for the John Doe murder two months ago, and now he might get away with it again. Did he know where the money came from, or was he just bluffing?

Boozler took a deep breath and sighed. "What about Morton?"

"What about him? He can take a hike."

"You are a ruthless bloodsucker."

Ford nodded. "I'm glad we understand each other."

"What if Mackenzie is guilty? Wouldn't that make you feel bad?"

The little man's right eye twitched. "Nice try. I suspect any number of jealous husbands would like to have Jake's genitals bronzed and displayed on their mantels."

"That's dangerous talk. If Morton heard you make a statement like that, there's no telling what he might do. And no jury around here would convict him, either."

Ford chuckled. "The day I'm afraid of a rich redneck

like Morton Bell is the day I'll tear down my shingle. I'm leaving now, and I suggest you do the same."

Though Boozler made no comment as the lawyer left the room, he had to agree. It would be easiest if he couldn't be found. He stood and kicked the wall on his way out, bursting a hole in the thin wood panel.

THE LITTLE SHACK sat about fifty feet from the bend in the waterway. Harpo Crumm lay on the floor atop a blanket, inching his way back from death's door. He dreamed of people with flowing robes, and angels, everything bright and sunny, in living color.

He found himself quoting Bible verses he'd never read, and witnessed strange visions. The woman who owned the shack said it was because of the fever and pain. But part of it was because of the voices in his head. Voices that told about things that happened somewhere around the beginning of time. But they also told the news and weather, advertised a new club on South Beach, and urged him to vote for some guy he'd never heard of running for Dade County Commission.

After rolling out the door of the exploding hearse, Harpo had floated to the bank of the Sound with his arms wrapped tightly around a piece of a dead tree. The little boy had found him, and he and his mother had pulled Harpo out of the water and dragged him into the shack. He didn't know why he remained with the living, instead of shoveling coal down below, but here he was, and he thought it might be a sign.

Salt water had washed away most of the blood, but he had an ugly gash on his chest where the bullet had ricocheted off the little radio in his shirt pocket. He also had an inflamed knot on one side of his forehead with a piece of metal sticking out of it. The woman said it looked a lot like the tip of the antenna on the portable radio she had in her kitchen, only smaller. She wanted to take him to a hospital to get it out. Alas, she didn't have transportation or a phone.

Few people knew Harpo Crumm had been a hospital corpsman with the military in an earlier life. He had almost forgotten it himself. But he remembered just long enough to tell the woman he needed antibiotics if she could find some. She left on foot and came back several hours later carrying a pint jar full of capsules the size of jumbo jellybeans. The label prescribed the medicine for someone named Heifer. The pills weren't a flavor of antibiotic Harpo recognized, but they would have to do. He took double the prescribed dose, and for the next twenty-four hours his head simmered and buzzed, while the tunes and visions just kept on playing.

TEN

Boozler drove around for a few minutes, thinking about Morton Bell. The old guy would get what he wanted, one way or another, but he wouldn't get it tonight. They had always been adversaries, primarily because of their first meeting. As a teen, Rich had come down from Miami to a June bash held at the Bell estate. Mitzi, Morton's only daughter, had invited him. Though he'd seen her at the beach a few times, they'd never actually been on a date. With hair the color of honey, blue eyes that would cause a compass to go haywire, and a body that drew ogles from every boy on the beach, he assumed she was out of his league.

About an hour into the party, Mitzi pulled him aside and asked if he wanted to walk on the beach. He'd said yes, of course. They each left the crowd, going in different directions, and he met in her backyard. After stepping into the sand, away from the lights and noise inside, she took him by surprise with a kiss. The kiss, and what followed, led him to believe she had more experience than he had thought. Certainly more than he had.

Five minutes later, they lay half clothed in the sand. Then old Morty stepped through the dunes with a flashlight and started yelling. He grabbed Boozler by the ankle and dragged him through the sand and shells for what seemed like a hundred yards, cursing the entire time. For days after that, Boozler suffered from scratches and scrapes on various parts of his body.

Mitzi went off to boarding school the following week, and the next time Boozler saw her was at Christmas, when she came home for the holidays. He had thought of little else for those months, and the minute he heard she was home, he drove down the Overseas Highway and rode by her house. It appeared her parents were away, and he wanted to surprise her. But when she opened the door, he was the one who got the surprise. She seemed different, not as pretty as he'd remembered, and she frowned when she saw him. The reason became clear when a grown man peeked around the corner.

"What is it, Mits?" the guy asked.

"Oh, just some kid."

Rich was crushed. He thought he might never get over it, but like other things, that feeling soon passed.

In the years since, he and Morton had spoken few words to each other.

Boozler checked his watch. 7:00 p.m., just enough time. He turned down a county road lined with scrub and live oaks and came to a frame house on a shaded lot. Ellen, a striking woman of forty, met him at the door. She had been seeing him for a year or so, and since she had already been married and divorced a couple of times, she didn't want to try again. That suited him just fine, since he already had a wife.

"Get in here, you big lug. I've been wondering when you'd be back. It's been a week now."

Twenty minutes later, Boozler lay back and rested his head on the soft pillow, listening to his own pulse in his ears, savoring the sweet exhaustion. His eyelids

felt as if connected to lead weights, and his conscious-
ness slipped away.

"Did you get it done or not?" the man asked.

*They had just sat down at the private table in the
corner of the restaurant and ordered drinks. Boozler
didn't like the man's tone, but being a rookie cop, he
knew he had to watch what he said.*

"Yeah, I did it."

*"You wear gloves?" Concern pinched at the corners
of the man's eyes.*

"Of course. I know what I'm doing."

*The man took a deep breath and let it out, now re-
laxed. "Yes, I suppose you do."*

*Drinks arrived, and Boozler took a long pull from
the glass in front of him. "Now, let's talk about what
you're going to do for me," Boozler said.*

*The man's eyes changed as he peered at something
over Boozler's shoulder. When he turned in his seat, another face glared down at him. A young man, no more
than twenty-years-old, but his eyes seemed much older.*

*"Here's what we're going to do for you," the new
person said. Then he pulled a gun from his pocket and
rammed it into Boozler's ear.*

Boozler sprang upright in Ellen's bed, his face drip-
ping with sweat.

"What's wrong Rich?" Sleep slurred her speech.
"You have a bad dream?"

Boozler stared at her for several beats, then jumped
off the bed and put on his clothes.

"Rich?"

"I've got to go," he said, maybe more to himself
than to Ellen.

"But what's wrong?"

He ran out of the house without speaking again, started the car, and pressed the accelerator to the floor. The tires screeched as the cruiser left the driveway and entered the blacktop.

AFTER SEARCHING THE roads of Iguana Key for more than an hour, searching for Sean Spanner's car, Sam and Simone had given up and driven to a seafood grill on the beach of Sugarloaf Key. She ordered a shrimp salad with mineral water, and he chose a grilled snapper sandwich and a beer. They both had coffee after the meal. As the waiter brought the check, the phone chirped in Sam's pocket. He took it out and looked at the display. J.T.

"The Black Palmetto stuff I mentioned earlier might have something to do with your guy after all," J.T. said.

"What did you find?"

"Spanner's a fake. The information on his job application at the research center belongs to a real person in Scranton, P.A. who went missing about the time your guy came on the scene."

"How do you know that?"

"I called all the Spanner numbers in Scranton until I found a brother. He said Sean hasn't been seen since leaving his job a few months ago. The police haven't been able to find a trail."

"You think our Spanner killed him?"

"Yeah, maybe. It's the kind of thing an assassin might do if he needed a solid identity."

"Which means he got himself hired at the research facility so he could steal something. Anything else?"

"Not much. I did get in touch with a dude who knew one of the operatives back when the Palmetto was piling up the kills. He said the operation fell apart when two of the operatives went nuts and killed everybody in charge. It was at a place somewhere close to Homestead."

Huh. Maybe the same place as the research facility. Simone hadn't mentioned that.

"My source also said somebody in Congress had a hand in organizing the group, but he didn't know who."

"That might be important. See if you can find out who it is."

"Yeah, I planned to do that." J.T. paused for a moment. "Sounds like you could use me down there. I can research this stuff from anywhere, and leaving here might get me off the Fed's scope for a few days. You know how it is."

Sam had mentioned the money Spanner had taken, and J.T. probably thought it would be up for grabs. The money wouldn't matter one way or another if they didn't find it, and they hadn't made much headway. Zeroing in on the cash might lead them to Spanner. Maybe they needed some greed stirred into the pot. If it turned out that the Palmetto group had something to do with this, he might need some extra firepower, and J.T. could handle a gun as well as anyone he knew. Simone wouldn't like it, though. He glanced at her and she shook her head. Could she hear J.T.'s voice from across the table?

She reached and tapped him on the wrist. "Don't do it."

Guess she could, or could read his mind.

Averting his eyes, Sam said, "Yeah, come on down." He told J.T. where they were staying, closed the phone, and relayed the conversation.

Simone listened, her arms crossed, eyes narrowed.

When he finished, she said, "I warned you about him. If this blows up in our face, you're going to be sorry."

Maybe she was angry, or maybe she just didn't want to talk about the Black Palmetto.

"This Palmetto business keeps coming up. Why didn't you tell me about their site being in Homestead?"

Shrugging, she said, "What does that have to do with what's going on here?"

"It might have a lot to do with it. If that facility had records lying around that named names in an illegal assassination activity, maybe Spanner took them and tried to use them to blackmail somebody in Iguana Key."

Shaking her head, Simone said, "There weren't any records lying around. I told you, we got rid of everything."

"Maybe you missed something."

"No, we got everything. Computers, servers, books, papers. We torched them inside a government van, then crushed it and dropped the burned metal block in a hole where no one will ever discover it."

Sam stared for a moment. "Is the research facility where the Black Palmetto was?"

She sighed. "It's in the same building."

The Palmetto angle sounded more and more plausible.

"What if somebody had another set of books locked away off site, for protection in case something like this happened?"

At first she smirked, but then seemed to remember something. Sam could see the gears turning in her head.

"You know, we grilled the people who worked there and turned up a few things they'd taken home, but there was this one guy who had left a month or so earlier. A psychiatrist. We never talked to him. But if he did have something, I don't know how it could have gotten back into the research facility for Spanner to steal."

SAM FELT SURE he had locked the motel door when they'd left, but it now hung ajar. He put his finger to his lips and then pointed at it. With their guns at the ready, he reached inside, flipped the light switch, and kicked the door open. A body lay on the floor next to the far wall. Stepping inside, he scanned the rest of the room, and then eased past the body to the bathroom. His pulse pounded in his ears as he leaned around the corner of the jamb. Nobody there.

"It's clear," he said, returning to the bedroom where Simone knelt over the body.

"You have some gloves?" she asked.

"Yeah, I'll get them."

Stepping outside, he scanned the parking lot for any signs of life. A calico cat lay in a clump of palmetto, chewing on a dead chipmunk. The cat stopped, peered up at him and bared its teeth, as if to say, *This is mine, man. You get your own.*

He got the gloves and stretched on two of them. Back inside, he closed the door and handed a pair to Simone.

It appeared that the man had died quickly. All the blood seemed to be contained on the front of his shirt. A shotgun lay close to his fingers, and a designer ball cap sat askew atop his head. Sam picked up the gun and smelled the end of the barrel. It hadn't been fired recently.

"His name is Morton Bell," Simone said, examining the dead man's driver's license. "Maybe he's Jake

Bell's father. He smells like booze. Probably got drunk and came here to kill you."

"Yeah. Somebody else must've had the same idea and was waiting here. He opened the door, came into the dark room, and the killer mistook him for me."

Standing up, Simone said, "You're a popular guy."

"Yeah, right. I wonder how they got in."

"Somebody could have called that clown at the desk and offered him some money to leave it open. He would have done it."

"We can't call the cops," Sam said.

Simone's eyes widened. "No, they'd haul you off, for sure."

She made two drinks from what remained of the gin and tonic and handed him one.

Sam took a swallow and set the glass down. "I'll check outside for his vehicle. Any keys in his pocket?"

"Maybe. Hold on." She pulled a set of keys from his right-hand pocket. One had a Mercedes emblem on it.

After scanning over the few vehicles in the lot, Sam spotted the car on the street. Seeing no security cameras in the area, he stepped over to the Mercedes, got inside, and drove it to their motel room door. A large plastic drop cloth lay on the other bucket seat. More evidence that Bell had come there to kill him.

He tore open the drop cloth package, spread the plastic over the passenger seat, and popped the right-side door. Back inside, he took the cap off Bell's head and put it on his own.

"You like the dead man's cap?" Simone asked.

"Somebody might see me driving his car, and maybe they'll think it's him."

Glancing at the plump body, Simone said, "Fat chance of that."

They carried Bell's body out to the car, wrapped the plastic around him, and positioned him so he would ride low in the passenger seat. Sam buckled him in. The trunk would have been a better place for transport, but it would complicate Sam's plans for later. Simone brought out the shotgun, and he propped it against the center console, its barrel tip on the floor at Bell's feet.

It was deathly quiet as Sam eased the Mercedes out of the parking lot. Simone followed in his car. Driving toward town, he passed Chopin's, which was now closed, its parking lot empty. He was tempted to pull in and leave the car there, but Chopin probably didn't need that kind of grief, either.

As he neared town, he saw the headlights of an approaching vehicle. It got closer and he was reasonably certain it was a police cruiser. His pulse pounded in his ears. If he got caught driving Bell's car with his dead body in it, it would mean a death sentence. Glancing at the corpse, he wondered if any of Bell's dead face might be visible in the headlights of the police car. With his eyes fixed on the road, he reached and found the seatbelt buckle, and popped it. The body fell over, and the plastic-covered head came to rest on the console between the seats. He snugged the cap down as close to his ears as possible, and slid down in the seat to seem more the dead man's height, which he guessed at about five-six.

A right turn came up and he decided to take it. The cruiser slowed, reached the intersection a few moments after he did, and stopped, as if waiting to turn in behind him. As Sam spun the wheel, he felt the glare of the headlights in his eyes, and turned and reached for the radio, as if trying to locate a station, hoping the person in the police car wouldn't see much of his face. Once on the side street, he peered in the rear view mirror and watched the cruiser sit there, motionless. Then it accelerated on down the road and out of sight.

Hopefully, Simone noticed the cruiser and hung back. Sam lifted the cap and wiped his perspiring face with his shirtsleeve. He made a couple more turns to get back on the highway and began scanning for a place to ditch the car.

As he entered downtown, he passed a building about the size and shape of a trolley car. The sign out front, almost as big as the structure itself, proclaimed that Madame Zena could read your palm and tell your fortune. A Dumpster sat off to the side, between Madame Zena's and a jewelry store. Spotting no security cameras on either building, Sam turned in next to the Dumpster, cut the engine, and got out.

Leaving the door open, he got back into the seat on his knees, and dragged the body over the console to the driver's side and into a sitting position behind the wheel. He removed the plastic, found the drop-cloth bag he'd taken it from, and stuffed the bloody shroud inside. After closing the door, he strode away, carrying the wadded plastic, watching for any sign that someone might have seen anything he'd done. All quiet. Simone hadn't showed, so he phoned and told her where to pick him up. As he eased past Madame Zena's, the door opened, and he dropped down at the corner of the building.

A seductive voice of indeterminate age called out. "Who's there? Is that you, Morton?"

Sam hadn't expected anyone to be sleeping in such a tiny place, and he certainly hadn't expected anyone who knew Morton Bell. He wondered if that might be an omen.

He crept around the building, then through the shadows for a hundred yards or so until he saw Simone coming down the street. Though reasonably sure Madame Zena hadn't seen him, he did wonder about the extent of her powers, and if she had already viewed the undoing of Morton Bell in her crystal ball.

ELEVEN

SAM ASKED SIMONE to pull to the side of the road next to a wooded area. Finding a place to ditch the wad of plastic took only a few minutes. A large pine lay on the ground, probably blown over by high winds that left the root system hanging above a four-foot-wide hole in the ground. He stuck the plastic into a crevice in the dirt wall at the bottom of the hole and jammed in a sandstone rock to conceal and hold it in place. It wouldn't be discovered for years, if then.

Back in the car, Simone said, "What about the cap?"

He had forgotten about that. It probably contained his and the dead man's DNA. Taking it off, he said, "I'll get rid of it later, along with our gloves. I don't think we should stay in the motel tonight."

"Yeah, me either. Let's get our stuff and head up the road, maybe to Marathon."

Remembering their earlier conversation about Homestead, he said, "You mentioned a psychiatrist that had been associated with the Black Palmetto, who wasn't there at the end. Why would they employ a psychiatrist?"

Giving him a sidelong glance, she said, "Because the Palmetto wasn't your normal black ops unit. I was told that those guys were crazy. It's one of the reasons they all crashed and burned."

"Crazy? You mean insane?"

"Yes. Each of the assassins had killed someone or attempted it before being recruited into the program. Somebody high up, probably the congressman J.T. mentioned, had the bright idea that sociopaths would be more effective as hit men than traditional candidates, the rationale being that it's easier to teach a killer how to use weapons than it is to turn a sharpshooter into a killer."

Sam raised an eyebrow. "That's an interesting idea, but I can't imagine anybody actually thinking it would work."

"Well, they did, but it didn't last long before self-destructing."

"What happened to the psychiatrist?"

"I heard he turned sour over the whole concept, after a couple of bad incidents, and the leadership sent him packing."

"You remember his name?"

She squinted her eyes in the glow of the dash lights. "It was Emerson something. Like Whitehurst. No, Whitehall. That's it, Emerson Whitehall. He lived in Miami."

"Shouldn't be too hard to find somebody with a name like that."

HARPO DIDN'T KNOW how long he'd been out this time, but he finally felt like standing and pacing around the little shack. His chest wound had been nothing less than a miracle. Maybe a little sore, but no swelling or pain.

The name of the woman who had saved him was Twyla. She came into the room, saw him on his feet, and told him he should lie down, get his rest. Twyla fussed a lot over Harpo, but he thought she might be the

most beautiful woman he had ever seen; flawless skin
the color of creamed coffee, and almond shaped eyes.
That first day when he awoke in the yard, he knew she
had been sent from heaven to guard over him, the aura
around her face so bright it burned his eyes.

"Don't worry. I just need to walk around a little, get
my legs back."

"But that knot on your head. I'm afraid you'll have
a stroke or something."

"I'll be fine." He patted her hand and felt an uncom-
mon warmth course into his fingertips and up his arm.
"You just sit on the porch and have some lemonade. I'll
be back in a little while."

She didn't argue, but concern pinched at the corners of her eyes.

As he descended the porch steps, his head felt as
if it might go into a spin. After resting a moment, the
dizziness faded. Just a little walk, that's all he needed.

The day before, after the fever had left him, he realized that part of the radio had gotten stuck in his head
during the explosion. It'd been put there for a reason,
and he didn't plan to take it out. The words had led him
to pray for his own meager salvation, and for Twyla and
the boy. And here he stood, a miracle. Snipping off the
tip of the antenna had left just a little knot on his head.
Reception had never been better.

As he made his way up the path through the undergrowth and neared the highway, he heard traffic noises,
along with the inspirational words of Dr. Eddie Worth,
his favorite of all the voices. He stepped into a clear-
ing next to the road, and his head began to buzz, sweat
pouring over him like a hot spring. The world around

him started to spin again, but Dr. Worth kept on preaching, loud and clear, and Harpo knew he'd be okay.

As he sat down next to the road, the spinning subsided. A viper of about six feet, with great venom pockets on the sides of its head, slithered over the asphalt toward him, but he remained steady and unafraid. He closed his eyes and prayed. When he finished, the snake had almost reached his leg. Its eyes were blood red, its fleshy tongue flicking forked tips like ice picks. It would strike, of that Harpo had no doubt. Then a semi appeared, seemingly out of nowhere, the tires so close Harpo could see between the rubber tread. The truck's horn blasted, and its giant tire struck the serpent's head with a popping sound, leaving a paper-thin patch about the size of a tri-fold wallet attached to a still-wriggling body.

Harpo stood and wiped perspiration from his forehead with the back of his hand. After a moment of deliberation and a smile, he turned and headed back to the house. It had become crystal clear why he had been spared. He knew what he had to do.

Chief Boozler had just entered his office and turned on the light when Lonnie appeared at his doorway.

"We got a 911 a few minutes ago. The embalmer at the funeral home found Howard Tim and his bookkeeper dead when he got to work this morning."

"What?" He felt his face flush, his head throb from too much Jack Daniels the night before. "Do you know how they were killed?"

"I don't know about the woman, but Tim was stabbed in the chest. According to the operator, the caller was pretty hysterical, screaming into the phone."

Boozler had gotten a late start after a fitful night of sleep and had rushed out of the house without washing his face or combing his hair. He ran his fingers through his oily mane. "You get the ball rolling?"

The lieutenant nodded. "I sent a cruiser to secure the crime scene. The techs and the medical examiner are on their way." He paused and seemed to give the chief a quick once-over. "You want me to get you some coffee?"

The embalmer who had reported the murders sat on the ground by the back door in the morning sun. An officer stood close by. He stepped over to the cruiser when the chief and Lonnie got out.

"You get his statement?" Boozler asked.

"Yeah, there wasn't much to it." The officer pulled out his notebook. "He reported for work at his normal time and found the bookkeeper with her head down on her desk. He thought she was sleeping. Then he went to the embalming room to get started and found the owner on the floor. He said there was a lot of blood, and he ran out here and called 911."

Boozler peered at the man by the door. He seemed very still, staring down at the ground. "Is he okay?"

"I think so. He said he took a Valium."

As they headed inside, the embalmer said, "Hey, Chief, I got four-day's pay coming. When do you think I'll get it?"

The chief ignored him and walked on.

Two crime scene technicians worked around the bookkeeper's desk, dusting for prints and vacuuming the carpet. Lonnie and the chief eased down the hall to the embalming room where the medical examiner pulled a bloody instrument of some kind from Howard Tim's chest and dropped it into a plastic evidence bag.

"What's that?" Lonnie asked.

"A trocar. They use it for embalming. The tip is sharp, for inserting into a blood vessel. Interesting murder weapon, don't you think?" Without waiting for an answer, he continued. "I think the secretary's neck is broken." He stood and sighed. "I just finished with Jake Bell. My practice is going to suffer if this keeps up."

"We need to establish a time of death as soon as possible," Boozler said, peering down at the body.

The M.E. stowed his instruments in his medical bag. "I'll do my best to get it to you in a couple of hours." He paused. "I'm guessing these murders are probably related to Jake's."

Boozler turned to the doctor. "What makes you say that?"

"I know they appear different: a knife on Jake, the trocar on Tim, and the girl with a broken neck." The M.E. pursed his lips and stared at the floor, as if in thought.

The chief raised an eyebrow. "So what makes you think they're related?"

"This all seems impersonal, like the killer is just doing a job."

Boozler kneaded his brow, his face flush. "Doing a job? What are you talking about Doc?"

The M.E. frowned and shook his head. "Nothing. Forget it. I'll get you the time of death by noon."

The chief thought he might let it go, but Lonnie jumped in. "Wait a minute. Tell us what you think."

Boozler shot him a glance.

"To tell the truth," the doctor said, "I don't know

what I think. We hadn't had a murder in Iguana Key for almost ten years, and now we've had four. The laws of probability would—"

"Yeah, yeah, probability," Boozler said. "People don't die from probability, Doc."

"You're absolutely right, Chief, so I'll come right out and say it. It seems as if all these people were killed by a professional. Why? I don't know. That's your job."

He closed his bag and strode out the door. The chief just sighed and shook his head.

Outside, Boozler put on his sunglasses and ambled toward the car. "Did you find out anything else about that hearse bombing?"

"Yes, sir, they said it was an incendiary device, most likely military, definitely not homemade."

The chief didn't comment, just opened the car door and got in.

When they arrived back at headquarters, Boozler said, "Lonnie, have a couple of officers bring Mackenzie in."

"You gonna arrest him?"

"I don't know yet, but he worked with explosives in the Navy, and he could've set off that bomb. Maybe he killed Tim and the girl to keep them from identifying his voice."

"But Mackenzie isn't even from around here. I don't think Mr. Tim would know his voice."

"Just get him in here, Lonnie."

Boozler started to leave, and Lonnie said, "Wait, I was just thinking about something. Dudley and I overheard a guy in the diner a month or so ago talking about being out at Ted Carter's place. He said he was there to do some repairs and saw some explosives in his barn.

Ted ran him off when he realized he'd seen them. Why don't we go out there and check it out?"

Sighing, Boozler said, "Okay, we can do that, but have the officers pick up Mackenzie. I want him here when I get back."

He went into his office, closed the door, and opened the bottom drawer where he kept a bottle of J.D. He took a long pull from it and put it away. Leaning back in his chair, he closed his eyes, let the alcohol seep into his brain, smooth out the rough edges. Things just kept getting worse and worse. He had to do something. Maybe one more drink would help for now.

Lonnie said he would bring the cruiser around. It took about twenty minutes to get to the Carter place. They rode down the long, winding driveway that had gone to seed. Lonnie hit the brakes, and the cruiser slid to a halt in front of the farmhouse. A shroud of fine dust settled around them.

Ted Carter had served in the military in the Middle East, and said little about his experiences when he returned home to Iguana Key. He became a recluse, and probably would have moved away had it not been for his father dying and leaving him a broken down farm. Though he didn't know anything about farming, the rent was free. The only drawback: his mother lived there, too, and they didn't get along very well.

As the two lawmen got out, the chief unsnapped his holster. Lonnie did the same. They ascended the steps to the front porch, and Lonnie opened the rusty screen door and knocked. He stepped back to let the spring snap it shut.

Ted's mother appeared in the doorway, dressed in

blue denim overalls. Though she weighed at least three hundred pounds, she had a surprisingly pretty face.

"Hello, Rich, Lonnie."

Her breath drifted through the rusty screen door. It smelled like bacon.

"Maude," Chief Boozler said, "we wondered if we could talk to Ted."

The woman gazed past them, an uneasy expression on her face. "I guess so. He's out in the barn."

"We heard he has a stockpile of explosives. Do you know anything about that?"

"Sorry, you'll have to ask him. He doesn't tell me anything about his business."

The chief gave her a mock salute. "Okay, we'll check with him, then."

As they turned away, she said, "I guess you know he doesn't care for visitors."

"I heard something about that. It happens to some of the vets returning from the war. How long has he been back?"

She squinted her eyes. "About a year. It was right before Ralph left."

Boozler put on his best sad smile. She had married Ralph after Ted's father died, but one day he went for a pack of Marlboro and never came back. Rumors spread that Ted had done away with the man for his insurance money, but no one who mattered ever took them seriously.

A silence stretched into several uncomfortable beats.

Without another word, they stepped into the yard and headed for the barn. The door stood open, and they eased inside. The veteran sat at a table in the corner, cleaning the barrel of a rifle, a can of beer near his right hand. He looked as if he hadn't shaved for a week.

"Ted, how's it going?" the chief asked.

He laid down the weapon and turned to face them. "I got nothing to say to you two clowns."

Lonnie glanced at the chief, his hand moving to his holster.

Boozler shook his head, and the lieutenant dropped his hand back to his side. "This shouldn't take long. We just have a few questions—"

"I'm not answering any questions!"

He obviously had already consumed a few beers.

"You can't talk to the chief like that, Ted," Lonnie said. "We can take you in if—"

"Lonnie," Boozler said, "it's okay." He turned to Ted. "We need to know about your explosives. A vehicle was blown up on a bridge over Blackwater Sound by a military-grade bomb."

"I didn't have anything to do with that."

Chief Boozler moved closer. "So you heard about it?"

"News travels fast." Ted grinned and stood up. "Now, you need to get out of here and leave me alone."

"Sorry, but we have to see those explosives," Lonnie said.

"You got a warrant?"

"We can get one in an hour if that's what you want, but we won't be going anywhere until it arrives, to make sure you don't do anything stupid."

Ted's eyes narrowed, and he reached to push Lonnie out of his way. Lonnie hit him in the chest with the palm of his hand, and tripped him from behind with his foot. Ted's back slammed against the floor, and his breath *whooshed* from his lungs. Dropping to one knee, Lonnie pinned him at the throat with his right hand.

"You better just answer the questions before I get rough with you, Ted."

Ted caught his breath, turned his head and spat. "You'll be sorry you did that."

"Yeah? Big talk for a drunk."

The chief touched Lonnie on the shoulder. "That's enough."

"Get off of me," Ted said. "I'll show you the stuff, but then you're going to leave."

Lonnie got up and pulled him to his feet.

"You better get him under control," Ted said to the chief, brushing pieces of hay from his shirtfront.

"Just show us, and we'll get out of your hair."

He led them outside and around the building to a shed that probably hadn't been painted in twenty years. The door had an old hasp on it with rusted screws. A padlock secured it. Ted grabbed the hasp and pulled it off the door, screws and all, leaving rusty holes in the old pinewood. He pulled the door open, its hinges squeaking, and reached inside for a kerosene lamp. After lighting it with a match from his pocket, he adjusted the flame and entered the shed. The floor was concrete, and a hinged metal door measuring about four-feet-square lay in the middle. It resembled a shallow, upside-down, roasting pan.

Ted set the lamp down, lifted the door open, and lay it back on the concrete. The top of a ladder was visible inside the opening. He retrieved the lamp, got onto the ladder and descended into the pit. When he reached the bottom, Chief Boozler motioned for Lonnie to go next and then followed. At the bottom was a concrete-walled room with two cots at one end and a large metal footlocker at the other.

"What's that odor, Ted?" Lonnie asked, sniffing.

"Probably some bad canned goods we put down here a long time ago." Ted went to the locker, lifted the top and leaned it back on the wall, and stepped aside. "This is everything. Knock yourself out."

The chief took the lamp from him and held it over the top of the open locker. Several olive-drab colored objects lay in the bottom.

"What are these things?" the chief asked, picking one up.

"Like you said, explosives."

"Where'd you get them?"

"That's none of your business."

It really didn't matter where he had gotten the bombs. "Okay, what kind of damage would they do?"

"One of those would destroy that house up there."

The chief stared at him for a moment. "Having this stuff is probably a Federal offense, Ted, but I'm not interested in that. You have an alibi for Saturday night?"

"What are you talking about? I haven't done anything."

"Saturday night, Ted."

"I was here all night, okay? Ask my mother. She'll tell you."

"Don't worry, we will."

Chief Boozler put the bomb back and stepped away. "I think we've seen enough."

"Wait," Lonnie said as he moved closer and peered inside the locker. "There's something in the corner." After stretching on latex gloves from his pocket, he reached in and pulled out a rolled-up towel. It was damp with a red substance that resembled blood. He unrolled it, and a knife about eight inches long lay inside.

A rancid odor wafted up to Boozler's nose. The knife had smears of the same red substance on the handle and blade. The chief felt his stomach clench. His temples throbbed to an erratic beat. Dread buzzed inside his head.

The veteran ran his hands through his greasy hair and took a deep breath, looking sick in the jaundiced light of the kerosene lamp.

"I don't know anything about that. Anybody could've gotten in here and left it. You saw that rusty lock up there, how it came loose in my hand."

He reached into the locker and ran his hands over the explosives. "I had eight of these in here. I know that for sure because I moved them down here from the barn a while back and I counted them. Now there's only seven. Somebody stole one of them and left that knife in there. Somebody trying to frame me."

TWELVE

FINDING THE PSYCHIATRIST proved to be more difficult than Sam had thought. An Internet search on Simone's phone came up empty. They spent the night in Key Largo, rose early, and called J.T. He had arrived at Miami International late the night before and checked into an airport hotel. Still half asleep when Sam called, he mumbled he'd get back to them when he found the address. An hour passed, and the phone chirped as they reached the outskirts of Miami. Though J.T. hadn't found the man, he had made some progress and was awaiting a call from a source with a mobile phone company.

At 10:00 a.m. they stopped at a restaurant in Coconut Grove for coffee and a sandwich. J.T. finally called back after their second cup and said he'd located Whitehall in North Miami, through a mailing address for his phone bill.

The residence turned out to be an old hotel named Kingly Court. It didn't seem like a place where a psychiatrist might live; cinder block construction, weeds in the lawn, peeling paint on the sign.

They parked and went inside a dingy lobby. A counter ran across one side with nobody behind it. Upon ascending a wooden staircase with a threadbare carpet runner, they located room 210 and Sam knocked on the door. No one responded, so he knocked again.

Casting a sidelong glance at Simone, Sam said, "J.T. seemed pretty certain this is where he lives."

She rolled her eyes. No faith.

The floor squeaked somewhere on the other side of the door. Emerson Whitehall probably stood there peering at them through the peephole.

"Who is it?" A deep, muffled voice.

They had discussed on the drive up what they would say.

"FBI," Sam said. "We need to speak with Dr. Emerson Whitehall."

The door eased open a few inches. A bearded and bespectacled face peered around it. The man appeared to be in a bathrobe and smelled like stale beer.

"Let's see some ID."

Sam pulled out a badge emblazoned with the FBI seal, his photo, and a fake name. He'd had it made by a counterfeiter in Miami for occasions such as this.

Emerson Whitehall studied it for what seemed like a long time then glanced at Simone.

"What about her?"

She sighed and pulled out a similar ID, though without the seal, flashed it and put it away.

He stared for a few heartbeats, a frown on his face, and Sam expected him to ask her to take it back out for a closer examination. Then the man took a deep breath and let it out with a sigh.

"Okay. Just checking. Can't be too careful after what happened."

They went inside and sat on a sagging sofa in the tiny living room. Whitehall took a chair across from them that had been reupholstered in shiny vinyl. A table next to him held a lamp with cobwebs stringing from the shade like moss on oak trees. It also held three beer cans with their tabs popped open. A box sat on a table in the corner of the room, overflowing with framed documents. Sam guessed they might be professional certifications and diplomas. A tabletop TV sat next to the box, muted, a rerun of an old detective show playing.

"Get you something to drink?" the doctor asked.

Both of them shook their heads, and Sam said, "Have something if you want to, though."

"Oh, don't worry, I will." He picked up one of the beer cans and held it up as if in a toast, then took a large swallow and set it down. "So, what does the FBI want from me?"

"We have a problem," Sam said. "One of the guys from the Black Palmetto program stole some information from a research center in Homestead and disappeared in the Lower Keys."

He smiled. "I don't work there anymore."

"Yes, we know."

"What kind of information?"

Sam leaned back on the sofa and looked fleetingly at Simone. She gave him the simplest of nods.

"We don't know for sure, but whatever it is, we believe he used it to blackmail another member of the program, and now has disappeared. We need to get the information back."

The psychiatrist took another long slug of the beer, emptying the can, and set it down on the table. He wiped his mouth with the back of his hand.

"What does this have to do with me?"

"We know you left there under adverse circumstances."

"'Adverse circumstances.' I suppose that's one way

of looking at it. They fired me because I wouldn't march to their idiotic agenda."

Sam shook his head and gave him a sad smile, as if to say, *I know exactly what you mean.* "We know they trained mental patients to be assassins. I assume that's what you didn't agree with."

"That's correct. And I heard recently that the entire operation imploded on them. I must say, that bit of news gave me a certain amount of satisfaction."

"How did you hear about it?"

With a wave of dismissal, he said, "I still have my sources."

Sam supposed it didn't matter who told him.

Whitehall got up and got another beer from a refrigerator in a tiny kitchen off the living room.

"You sure you won't have one?" he said as he popped the top. Not waiting for an answer, he ambled back to his chair and drank deeply from the fresh can.

"Now, where were we?"

Simone spoke up. "The guy we're after worked at the research center located in the same building where the Black Palmetto operated. We have it on good authority that the operation was completely erased after the program…imploded, to use your words, so we're at a loss as to how the man could've stolen anything pertaining to it."

"Erased? What does that mean?"

"We were told that all papers and equipment were destroyed. So we're pretty sure he didn't get the information from there…" She let the words trail off.

The psychiatrist's eyes widened. "You think he got it from me?"

"That had occurred to us," she said.

He shook his head. "No way."

"You left under a cloud," Sam said, "and, given the business those guys were in, a person like you probably would have taken something with you for your own protection."

Whitehall narrowed his eyes and took another slug of beer. "If I had done that—and I'm not saying I did—I would have been smart enough to safeguard it. Nobody would have gotten their hands on it."

Simone raised an eyebrow. "Given your disdain for the operation, maybe you told our guy where to find the information."

"I wouldn't do that, either."

"Okay, let's say we believe you. If he didn't get the information from you, where did he get it?"

The doctor scratched the whiskers on his chin. "You said everything in the place got destroyed?"

"Yes, everything."

"What about the safe?"

Simone widened her eyes at Sam then turned back to Whitehall. "What safe?"

"I had a wall safe built into the closet in my office. You wouldn't know it existed just to glimpse inside, but a button on the edge of the inside door trim opened a concealed panel in the back wall. The safe sat behind the panel."

"What was inside?"

"An up-to-date account of everything we did. At least it was up-to-date when I left."

That probably explained why the people at the center were mum on the stolen information. They probably didn't know anything about the safe until a new occupant came in one day and found it standing open.

A security video likely caught Spanner, or whatever his real name was, leaving the office. Had he closed the safe behind him, maybe no one would have ever been the wiser.

"Nobody else knew about the safe?" Simone asked.

He shook his head. "No. Well, only one other person."

"Who?"

"The man who installed it. His name was Arthur Benetti. Artie had been a carpenter before killing a man and getting sent to prison. I treated him there for several months before the Homestead program got him out."

Simone pulled the photo of Sean Spanner from a pocket in her jeans, stepped over to Whitehall, and held it up for him to see.

"Is this Arthur Benetti?"

The doctor took it, studied it for a couple of beats, and handed it back. "Yes, that's Artie."

Returning to the sofa, Simone gave Sam a smile. *Now we're getting somewhere.* This was a good turn of events, but something bothered him.

"Why would you entrust a convicted killer with installing a secret safe for you?" Sam asked.

Whitehall seemed to consider that for a moment. "I don't know for sure. He did have a bad temper that could lead to violence, and he exhibited no remorse for killing a man who made a pass at his girlfriend. But something about him made me think he wouldn't betray my confidence. And to my knowledge, he never did, at least not while I remained there at the facility."

The psychiatrist obviously knew more about human motivation than Sam did, so he let it go. Spanner/Benetti probably had no reason to rob the safe until the program ended and he saw a way to make some money from it, or maybe get even with some people.

"Did you keep cash in the safe?" Simone asked.

He seemed to consider that before answering. "Yes, due to the nature of the program, we dealt in a relatively large amount of cash. None of it belonged to me, so I left the money in the safe when I checked out of there." Grinning, he added, "I thought they'd have to come to me to find it, but then I never heard from them."

"But you heard from someone in Homestead recently, right?" Simone asked.

He grinned. "Yes, I told them about the money and a small computer card with classified information on it. But that all I told them."

So, that's how the lab people knew what had been taken.

"How much money did you leave behind?"

"If I remember correctly, a little over half a million. I kept a ledger with it to account for expenditures and the balance."

They now had a name, Arthur Benetti, and a theory concerning how he might have stolen the information and the cash from the facility. But they still didn't know any more about the person in Iguana Key whom he'd visited.

"Okay," Sam said, "back to the part about you keeping some information about the program for your own protection."

"I didn't say I did that."

"Well, let's pretend you did. Black Palmetto bit the dust months ago, and there's nobody left there to threaten you. So if you had some information, it would be safe to share it with us."

The psychiatrist grinned. "Good try. If I did have any such information, the last thing I would do is share it with someone in law enforcement. The man who hired me is still around, and you might just be trying to build a case for prosecuting an innocent psychiatrist who unknowingly got tangled up with an illegal government operation."

The FBI gambit had worked to get them inside, but now it had morphed into a roadblock. If they came clean about it, Whitehall might tell them more, but he might also toss them out and clam up for good.

"Is the offer for a beer still good?" Sam asked.

"Yes, indeed." He smiled, drained his can, and got up to get more. "How about the young lady?"

Simone declined.

When he returned, and they'd both had a long drink, Sam said, "What did they do to you when you left?"

"What do you mean?" Then he scanned the room around him. "Oh, you're referring to my living conditions."

Sam nodded, took another drink.

"The founder had connections in high places, and he convinced the AMA to pull my medical license because of some trumped-up charges. Now I teach night classes at the junior college. That gig barely pays for this place."

"The founder? Who was that?"

Whitehall's eyes appeared out-of-focus, the alcohol having its way.

"Senator Blaine. I assumed you knew that."

"Sure. Just getting the story from you."

"Have you tried to get your license reinstated?" Simone asked.

"Of course, but nothing has worked. Whoever black-balled me made sure it would stick."

"Maybe we could help."

He stared for a moment before saying, "Why would you do that?"

"Simple. You help us and we'll help you."

THEY LEFT A few minutes later. Before closing the door, the psychiatrist said, "By the way, I didn't buy the FBI routine for a minute."

They had given him J.T.'s e-mail address. He promised to send them a list of names of the men recruited for the Black Palmetto. He also said he would give them more information only after they showed good faith in restoring his AMA status.

They met J.T. at Avis and caravanned back to the Lower Keys, stopping for the night in Marathon. White-hall's information arrived about 11:00 p.m. It contained the names and ages of eight men, along with the hospitals and prisons where they had resided before entering the program. Arthur Benetti showed up among the eight, as expected. Twenty-years-old at the time, he would be twenty-four now. The state prison in Starke had him on death row when someone in the federal government plucked him out to kill people for his country. Only two other men had been recruited from places in Florida, the rest from places as far north as New Jersey and as far west as California.

Sam zeroed in on the two from Florida. Marlon Knox came from a mental institution in Miami named Wind-haven. Leonard Ousley from the Florida State Prison in Starke.

"I'll see what I can dig up on those two," J.T. said.

"If we had photos," Sam said, "we could show them to a reporter I met at the newspaper, see if she recognizes them."

They were in J.T.'s room, having a drink, J.T. clicking the keys on his computer.

"I can probably get a pic for the guy from the prison," J.T. said. "Not too sure about the other guy."

Remembering their earlier conversation, Sam said, "Oh yeah, did you ever find out about the guy who organized all this?"

J.T. stopped work and turned around. "Yeah, it was Senator Blaine, from Florida. He came from a wealthy family, graduated West Point, and became a war hero. Good credentials for politics."

"Whitehall told us he's the one who got his medical ticket pulled," Simone said.

Sam gave her a slow nod. "A guy like Blaine would have the kind of juice to get the psychiatrist blackballed."

THE NEXT MORNING, they had breakfast in the hotel restaurant. As the server poured a second cup of coffee, Sam's phone chirped. He took it out and peered at the display.

"It's Lora Diamond."

"Who?" J.T. asked.

"His reporter friend," Simone said. She made a face.

"Oh." J.T. gave Sam a grin and nodded approval.

Sam opened the phone and said, "Hello."

"Hey, it's Lora. Where are you?"

"Why, what's up?"

"The police are looking for you." She told him that

three more people had been killed, two of them at the funeral home.

"Lonnie said the coroner told Chief Boozler that the murders were all linked somehow, and that it looked like they had all been killed by a professional."

"A professional?"

"Yes. As in hit man."

As in Black Palmetto.

"How were they killed?"

"Howard Tim, the undertaker, was stabbed with a trocar. You know what that is?"

"Yes, it's used for embalming."

"That's right. I had to ask Lonnie what it was. Anyway, the other person, Mr. Tim's bookkeeper, died of a broken neck."

"You said three. Who was the other?"

"Morton Bell. Jake's father. They found him in his car in a strip mall parking lot."

Sam waited for her to say somebody had seen him dump the body, but she didn't.

"Huh, how'd he die?"

"He was stabbed, too. They arrested a man named Ted Carter, after finding a bloody knife at his home."

"Then what do they want with me?"

"Lonnie said something about of a hearse getting blown up with a body in it."

"What body?"

"You remember when we met at the diner the other night, I mentioned a murder that happened two months ago?"

Though only a couple of nights before, it seemed like a long time ago.

"I showed you the clippings of my stories about it when we went to my house."

"Yeah, I remember."

She told him that Lieutenant Cates had said someone called the funeral home a few days ago and asked for the murder victim's body to be exhumed and transported to Fort Lauderdale for a funeral. It had happened the night before a parole officer was due in town to examine the body.

"The hearse got blown up on a bridge over Blackwater Sound, north of Key Largo. And it wasn't an accident. A military bomb was used. That's what led them to Ted Carter. He's a war vet, and they knew he had explosives out at his place."

"That's when they found the knife with blood on it?"

"Yep. They're checking it for prints."

"Okay, then, back to my question. Why are the police after me?"

"Oh, yeah. Lonnie said you have a background with explosives."

"Why would he think that?" Sam asked, though he already knew the answer.

"He said they did some research on you. Something to do with the Navy. He wouldn't tell me any more than that."

So the murderer destroyed any evidence the parole officer might have found on the two-month-old corpse, and had killed the funeral home folks to cover his tracks. Very thorough. If the knife at Carter's place turned out to be a murder weapon, Sam doubted they would find any prints.

Silence on the line stretched into several moments.

"You still there?" she asked.

"Yeah, I'm here."

"Well, you never answered my question. Where are you?"

He wondered if she might be funneling information to the cops.

"Not in Iguana Key, that's for sure."

Another silence.

"It's okay if you won't tell me, but you need to call your lawyer. I guess you didn't give him your phone number. He called me asking about you."

"What does he want?"

"He wants to keep you out of jail."

THIRTEEN

Sam hung up the call with Lora and dialed Charles Ford.

"You need to make yourself scarce for a while," Ford said. "The police don't really have anything on you, but they can make your life pretty miserable. I have a cabin on the back side of the Key that few people know about. You're welcome to stay there if you want."

They left the restaurant a few minutes later and Sam drove, with J.T. following in his rental.

"Did he say how big this cabin is?" Simone asked.

"No, but we can take a look. If it doesn't work out, we can always come back up here."

They met Ford two hours later in the parking lot of Chopin's, and he led them to his place. The trip took them over a state road through pines, palmetto and marsh, with a narrow waterway along one side as they neared their destination. Cranes and egrets fed at the water's edge, their bills spearing unseen prey beneath the surface.

When they finally turned off, they followed a shell-and-sand driveway, bordered on both sides with live oaks, to a home constructed of cypress and limestone. Less than a hundred feet through the trees lay the blue-green of the Gulf of Mexico.

Ford killed the engine and motioned for Sam to join him.

Inside the car Sam said, "Some cabin."

"Yes, there should be plenty of room," the attorney said, glancing at Simone and J.T. in the other cars. "Did you hear about the funeral home murders?"

"Lora mentioned it." He added that she'd also told him about the police finding Morton Bell's body and arresting Ted Carter.

Ford sighed. "His mother called before I left the office and hired me to represent him."

"Do you think he did killed those people?" Sam asked.

"Of course not. Carter's no fool. He would've disposed of the knife and explosives had he been guilty. Arresting him takes the heat off the police for a while, but he's just a pawn." He glanced at Sam. "They probably see you as the chess master."

Chess master. Sam wondered if Ford really believed Carter to be innocent, or just said so because they were paying his bill. He also wondered if the jailed suspect might be one of the two Palmetto men from Florida, either of whom might be a champion game player.

"I told you before," Sam said, "I didn't kill anybody."

"Oh, I know that."

After a few moments of silence, Sam said, "You have any idea who the killer might be?"

"Yes, but an idea is all it is at this point."

Sam waited, but the attorney didn't say anything else.

"If you know something, you need to tell me."

Ford shook his head. "Sorry. Maybe after I confirm my suspicions. I'm headed to Miami to do just that as soon as I leave here. I'll let you know how that turns out."

He started the car, and Sam got out and watched him drive away. The guy might know even less than Sam did, but at least they had a good place to stay, hopefully without the cops nosing around.

Using the key Ford had given him, he unlocked the cabin door and they went inside. Carrying their bags, they passed through a living room with tan leather furniture and prints on the walls of sailboats and marsh scenes. It also had a limestone fireplace, and Sam wondered if the weather ever got cold enough to use it. Down the hall they passed two bedrooms and a bathroom and ended at the room where Ford probably slept. It had a private bath and a walk-in closet.

Simone dropped her bag on the bed. "I call this one."

"Fine with me," Sam said.

J.T. grinned, a look that said, *Guess you two are on the rocks.*

"You get those mug shots yet?"

"Hey, give me a chance," J.T. said, moving back down the hall.

Taking one of the other bedrooms, Sam tossed his bag atop a trunk. He took off his shoes, lay down on the bed, and stared at the ceiling.

"You napping?" Simone asked from the doorway.

"Nah, just thinking about Spanner's car."

"Yeah? What about it?"

"While J.T.'s running down those photos, I thought we'd ride around and make another search for it. I noticed the road outside follows the shore on this side of the island, and we didn't cover that area before."

"I'm game."

She climbed onto the bed and lay on her side. Propped on her elbow, she kissed him on the cheek. He could feel her warm breath on his neck.

"How about sleeping in my room tonight?"

"Sure." Sam felt his heart kick into high gear.

"Just to sleep, nothing else."

He tried to hide his disappointment, but it must have shown in his face.

"I just don't want J.T. to get any ideas," she said.

"You think he'd do that?"

"Maybe." She got up from the bed and stood there. "I'd hate to have to shoot him. He'd bleed all over everything."

"That's considerate of you."

She studied him for a moment, smiling at his sarcasm. "Your lawyer would probably appreciate it."

BOOZLER SAT WITH his eyes closed and his elbows on the desk, massaging his temples. He looked up as the mayor ambled past the empty desk of the chief's secretary and rapped on the doorjamb.

"Did you get the message that I called?"

The chief scanned across his desk and picked up a yellow note.

"Yeah, I've been busy. I guess you heard about the murders."

The mayor shook his head and took a seat. "It's bad about Morton Bell." His feet didn't quite reach the floor. Boozler had never noticed that before, the mayor normally in his own office behind the desk when they talked.

"He stopped by here last night. Wanted me to arrest Mackenzie. I told him I couldn't, and he left here on his way to your office."

When he didn't say anything, Boozler wondered if he had avoided the old man.

"I heard you found a murder weapon at Ted Carter's place and brought him in."

"We found a knife with blood on it. The technicians are examining it now. Could be a murder weapon. He swears he doesn't know how it got there."

"You think he did it?"

"Maybe, but I thought I'd question Mackenzie again, if we can find him. He didn't answer the door at the motel. We called his lawyer, and he said he didn't know where he was."

The mayor shifted in his chair and crossed his legs.

"I'll bet Madame Zena was beside herself, finding Morton's body like that. I heard they had a thing going at one time."

"That was the rumor."

"It'd be a real shame if his company closed down. We'd lose a lot of jobs."

Boozler shrugged. "Yeah, I suppose. Hadn't really thought about that, yet."

"Did you call in Tallahassee or the FBI?"

"What?" The chief felt his face flush.

Dale Edison stepped into the office. "Got a minute?" Then he apparently saw Boozler's face and turned to the corner where the little man sat. "Sorry, I didn't mean to interrupt."

"No problem," Boozler said. "We're just talking about Morton."

Edison clicked his tongue. "Yeah, that was a shocker. I thought I'd watch behind the glass while you interrogate Carter, if that's okay with you."

"Fine. It'll be a while. His attorney just got here and he's in with him now."

Boozler pointed at the chair next to the mayor, and Edison sat down.

"Let me guess. Charles Ford?"

"You got it."

"What about the state guys, Rich?" the mayor asked.

The DA frowned. "Huh?"

"Oh, he was just asking about bringing in the Florida Department of Law Enforcement or the FBI," Boozler said, flipping his hand as if shooing a fly.

The mayor didn't seem to notice his brushoff. "It would be better if we called them, rather than them finding out from the newspaper. Could be a problem."

"There's no problem," Boozler said, his voice rising. "We have everything under control."

"Yeah," Edison chimed in, "Those guys would be in our hair for a month."

"Okay, I want to go on record that I suggested calling them."

The chief just stared, thinking the guy should go work on the garbage contract, or city PR, and stay out of the business of law enforcement. The little man seemed to read his mind. He frowned, hopped down from the chair, and hurried out of the office. Without Morton Bell around, he probably knew he wouldn't be mayor long.

Edison remained in his chair. "What's his problem?"

"He's probably getting nervous since his sponsor is gone."

"Oh, yeah. Hadn't thought about that. On a different note, did you get any more information on Mackenzie?"

"No, why do you ask?"

Edison had a strange expression on his face. Boozler had seen it before, recently, when the powder had puffed out of the Bible.

"I've just been thinking, about the SEAL connection you mentioned, and I wonder if he might be here for something other than what he told you."

"Like what?"

"Well, I don't know, but maybe we could sweat it out of him if you brought him in."

The chief wondered what Edison was hiding, and if it was something he himself should worry about.

"We're trying to find him now. I'll let you know when we pick him up."

SAM AND SIMONE rode out of the driveway onto the state road that followed the Gulf coastline of Iguana Key. The area turned out to be more developed than Sam had thought. Most of the houses along the road were as opulent as Ford's, but some were basic dwellings that appeared to have been there for fifty years or more.

Moving about thirty miles per hour into the sun, they scanned the driveways for Spanner's vehicle, and paid special attention to the undeveloped wooded and marshy areas between the homes for any unusual colors or reflections that might indicate a ditched automobile. After an hour or so of searching, they reached a bend in the highway and what appeared to be an abandoned marina. The old place seemed to signal a dead end of the coastal area, the road then heading back toward town. Sam turned the car around in the empty, weed-choked lot. A dock house sat at the head of several empty boat slips, and a faded tin sign nailed to its front wall read *Captain Short's Marina*. An aged cruiser about forty feet long lay berthed against the dock at the far end of the marina. Painted white, except for a sea-blue stripe around the top edge of the hull, it appeared as though it been well maintained. Maybe Captain Short's home. A shiver ran across the back of Sam's neck, but he wasn't sure why. Just a boat.

They headed back up the highway, the sun now at their backs. Though moving faster than before, they continued to scan the landscape.

As they crossed a bridge over a creek, Simone, said, "Stop. I saw a reflection over there through the scrub." She pointed toward the Gulf side to a spot through marsh grass and palmetto. He eased the car to the shoulder. They got out and crossed the road.

Something glinted through the reeds, maybe thirty feet into the undergrowth. Could be glass or the bright trim of a car. Twin tire tracks led down the slope, getting progressively deeper into the marsh.

They trampled through reeds for several feet until the soil turned spongy. Water glistened ahead, and about twenty feet beyond that Sam got a closer look at what they had seen from the road: the rear edge of a car roof. The creek fed into the large pool around the vehicle, and floating weeds covered much of the surface.

"I'll probably need a light to see anything down there," he said.

He hurried back to the car and got a diving light from the trunk. As an afterthought, he stretched on a pair of latex gloves, and went back and shed his clothes, down to his underwear.

"Watch out for snakes," Simone said.

Sam raised an eyebrow. "Thanks, I never would've thought about that."

"Yeah, well, you're the diver, not me."

The mud bank descended after a couple of feet, dropping him up to his neck in the weeds. After filling his lungs, he flipped on the light, submerged, and swam down through the underwater jungle. The driver's window had been partially lowered, probably so the car would sink faster. He peered inside through the greenish water at the front seats. No body. A quick scan of the rear seat revealed the same there. Shining the light back in the front, he spotted keys in the ignition and a large rock by the accelerator pedal. The engine had run wide open until the car hit the water and sank. He opened the door and pulled himself over the seat to the glove box, which hung open. Nothing remained inside it. A Florida map and an owner's manual floated in the water above it. A tire gauge, two ballpoint pens, and a gadget that included several miniature tools in one, lay on the seat. Someone had raked out the contents of the glove box searching for something. Sam's lungs felt as if on fire, and he surfaced for a quick breath. Returning, he found the trunk lid release and popped it.

He made his way around the rear bumper, which sat a few feet beyond the drop-off, and saw that the license plate had been removed. An unzipped overnight bag lay inside the trunk, clothing and toilet articles strewn around it. Though his lungs began to ache, he examined the bag, using the light and found no identification of any kind. Something slippery brushed against his leg and he jerked and bumped it with his knee. It came to life and wriggled against him as if electrically charged. A pain shot through his leg from a fin or a tooth, and a tail slapped him as the creature sped away.

Sam thrust to the surface and gulped in air, his heart pounding. His leg ached where the creature had cut him. Maybe a barracuda or a garfish. Either could have done him a lot of harm. Getting his breathing under control, he decided he'd seen enough. He closed the trunk and got out of the water. Using a stick, he stirred away his footprints in the mud as best he could.

"Hey, you're bleeding," Simone said, concern in her eyes.

Blood oozed from a superficial cut on his upper leg.

"Yeah, something scraped me. It's nothing." He put on his dry clothes and shoes.

Back behind the wheel, he said, "Whoever ditched that car might be close by, unless he had a helper to drive him back."

"Are you thinking about that boat we saw back there?"

"Yeah, it could be our guy."

They went back to the marina, but the cruiser had disappeared.

Sam got out and hurried to the dock, but couldn't see the boat in either direction. Getting back in, he sighed. "I should have paid more attention. At least got the hull number."

"You didn't know. Besides, it could have been somebody just stopping for a break."

"I think I knew something wasn't right about it."

"Forget it. It's no big deal."

Sam started the car, drove out onto the highway headed back, and took out his phone.

"Who're you calling?" Simone asked.

"Lora Diamond."

She turned and peered out her window.

"She's our only link to what the police have," Sam said. "We need to keep her in the loop."

"I didn't say anything."

Lora answered. He told her about the sunken car and described its location.

"You think it belongs to the guy you were looking for? Spanner?"

"Probably. I can't imagine any other reason someone would have ditched a car like that. Probably did it on high tide and thought it wouldn't be found."

"Could you see the license plate?"

She didn't need to know he'd already examined the vehicle. That could cause him some trouble with the police.

"No. The bumper was underwater."

He left out the part about the cruiser. It could have been a coincidence that the boat had left the marina in the short span of time between their two visits, but Sam didn't think so "Get whatever you can out of the story. Just keep me out of it."

"Okay. I'll go out there before it gets dark and scope it out."

When he hung up, Simone said, "Too bad we didn't find anything connecting Spanner."

"That's okay. I'm pretty sure it's his vehicle. The way it looked down there, someone had done a search, probably for the information about the Black Palmetto. If that person had found it, Spanner's body would've also been down there. So the fact that it isn't tells me he's still alive."

"Maybe. But that's one conjecture on top of another. It could be that some thief just wanted to get rid of a hot car."

Sam supposed he had wanted it to be Spanner's ve-hicle. That alone surely didn't make it true, and he really hadn't found any concrete evidence. "Yeah, you're right. We need to keep an open mind."

Still, he knew it had to be Spanner's car, and they were onto something.

FOURTEEN

SAM TOOK A quick shower and put on fresh clothes. When he entered the living room, J.T. sat in one of the leather chairs, his computer and a beer on the coffee table in front of him.

"I got the pics on the two guys," J.T. said.

"Let's take a look."

Simone entered the room. "Where'd you get the beer?"

"The lawyer has about a case of it in the fridge," J.T. said as he oriented the computer so Sam could see it from the sofa.

Simone got two beers and handed one to Sam. They took a seat and studied the images of Marlon Knox and Leonard Ousley. Knox looked about eighteen-years-old, with longish blond hair and glasses. The image had come from a Miami Police Department drug arrest about seven years before. The charges were later dropped.

"What about the mental institution Whitehall had on his list for this guy?" Sam asked. "You find anything on that?"

"Windhaven? No, that place is a ghost. They don't have a website, or even a phone listing, which probably means it's very exclusive and expensive."

"So this kid came from a wealthy family. That might

explain the charges getting dropped on his drug arrest. Did you search for a birth certificate?"

"Yeah, didn't find one. Somebody got it expunged. Same for the other guy. Ousley."

"Huh."

Ousley looked older, but not by much, and meaner. He had short brown hair, dark eyes, and a smirk on his clean-shaven face. J.T. had gotten the photo from the state prison in Starke, Florida where the convict lived on death row until the government program picked him up.

Both photos were several years old, but maybe somebody in town would still recognize one of them.

"Did you notice the name of the officer who arrested the Knox kid?" Simone asked Sam.

Turning back to the computer, Sam said, "No, who?"

She pointed at the screen. "Richard Boozler, Miami PD."

"Huh, that's weird. What do you think it means?"

Simone shrugged. "It isn't a coincidence, that's for sure. Miami has millions of people, and these two names popping up together...what are the odds?"

J.T. chuckled. "Too high."

"Yeah," Simone said, "This kid has an influential father or mother who talked Boozler into dropping the charges."

"When was he at Windhaven?" Sam asked.

J.T. brought up the e-mail from the doctor. "According to what Whitehall sent us, Knox entered Windhaven about two years later, and the Palmetto picked him up a few months after that. He would've been about twenty at the time."

"Well," Sam said, "he must've killed somebody, or the government wouldn't have been interested in him.

Boozler probably got him out of that, too. That would explain how our local cop could go from an officer position in Miami to chief of police in Iguana Key, in seven years. I wish we knew what the kid did."

Simone spoke up. "Miami probably had tons of serious crimes committed during the month he entered that mental facility. There wouldn't be any easy way to narrow them down."

"He didn't pop up on any other arrests," J.T. said.

"It would have to be something that would cause the guy to track Boozler here after the Black Palmetto collapsed and risk getting caught."

J.T. leaned back in his chair, his eyes aglow. Sam watched the gears click inside the mercenary's head.

"That would be cash," J.T. said. "A lot of it."

"Yes, or maybe a big drug score, which could be turned into cash. Maybe Boozler got paid off for keeping the Knox kid out of jail, but he might also have ended up with whatever it was the kid killed somebody for. We need to find a big drug bust. One where the money or the drugs went missing."

"You might have put your finger on what happened," J.T. said, "but how does any of that help you find Spanner and what he stole from the research lab?"

Simone spoke up. "If we find the assassin, we'll find Spanner."

Sam pointed at her with his index finger, his thumb up, like an imaginary gun. "That's right. All this is connected. I'm convinced of it." Remembering his first conversation with Lora that morning, Sam said, "The reporter mentioned something about a parole officer coming to town. He wanted to examine the body of a man who was murdered here a couple of months ago. I don't think he got a chance, because it got blown to bits on the bridge over Blackwater Sound. I'll bet his missing parolee served time for whatever happened back then, and he got out of prison and came here to settle up with our guy."

"Why don't you ring up Lora," Simone said, "and see if you can get something useful out of her."

"Can you send these photos on e-mail?" Sam asked J.T.

"Sure. I just need to know where."

Sam called the reporter and asked for her e-mail address.

"What've you come up with?"

"I'm going to send you photos of two guys. See if you recognize either of them."

"Okay. You think one of them is the killer?"

"Could be."

"How would you have a picture of the guy?"

"It's just an idea. I'll tell you more if you recognize one of them."

Silence.

He asked if she knew the name of the ex-con the parole officer had been after.

"No, but I can ask Lonnie."

"Yeah, let me know." He didn't want to place too much emphasis on it because she would launch into a lot of questions he didn't want to answer. "You find the sunken car yet?"

"Yep, I'm here now, waiting for the police to show up. Send the photos, and I'll check them out."

SAM CALLED JACKSON CRAFT, a confidence man he'd known for years. Jack had a long history of fleecing crooks, and had never been fingered as the bad guy, at least not by anyone who remained alive to tell about it.

"Samuel, how's it going?"

"Not bad, Jack. I wondered if I could ask a favor."

"Anytime, my friend. Just name it."

Jack sounded chummy, but he could bare his fangs when things turned sour, and Sam had seen that side more times than he could count. Though never sure whether or not he considered Jack a friend, they had helped each other from time to time in tough situations. Unlike J.T., though, he had all the money he would ever need. He ran his elaborate schemes only because he liked the life, and because he could.

Sam described the situation in Iguana Key. Simone had cautioned him about saying anything about the Palmetto, given its black ops classification. So he left that part out, but wouldn't have been surprised if Jack already knew about it.

"There's this psychiatrist who got blackballed by the AMA, and I wondered if you might know anybody who could help get his medical license reinstated."

"He's important to your case?"

"Could be. Plus, I think he got a raw deal."

"You have any ideas who this killer might be?" Jack asked.

"We have a couple of names, Marlon Knox and Leonard Ousley, and we have photos, but they're several years old. They might not look the same, now."

"You got them from the psychiatrist?"

"He gave us the names. J.T. came up with the pics."

"How's J.T. doing?"

Sam glanced at J.T. clicking keys on the computer. "Ah, you know."

"I take it he's there now."

"Sure thing."

"If there's any money involved, don't tell him about it."

Too late. Jack had never trusted the man, maybe for good reason.

"Gotcha."

"What other information do you think this psychiatrist could give you?"

"I don't know. Maybe some current photos, and some personal information that'll help us track them."

"These guys wouldn't have been associated with a black ops program in Homestead, would they?"

So, Jack did know about it. Sam supposed a successful confidence man had to have a good network.

"Could be."

Ice cubes tinkled in a glass, Jack probably having a gin and tonic. He remained silent for a couple of moments then said, "Okay, give me his name and I'll make some calls."

SAM AND SIMONE got fresh drinks and carried them through French doors to the deck outside the living room.

"Pretty nice layout," he said, leaning against the rail.

"Yeah, let's go down to the dock and check out the waterfront."

They descended the deck steps and strolled in the soft shade of the palms, along a wooden walkway, the late-afternoon air now balmy. Beads of condensation glistened on the glass surfaces of their cold beers.

The walkway led onto the dock and Sam saw a boathouse that had been concealed from the cabin's view by surrounding mangroves.

"The water is beautiful here," Simone said.

"Yes, it is." It looked cool and clear, a blue green even brighter than that off the Miami coast. On the dock, they went into the boathouse and found a late model Boston

Whaler in its single slip. A white runabout with a wide blue stripe on each side, it sported a 170 horsepower outboard motor.

Sam thought about the cruiser they had seen down the coast and felt a tingle at the nape of his neck.

The sensation must have been noticeable, because Simone said, "What is it?"

"Nothing," he said, walking back out onto the dock with her following behind him. He scanned the water as far as he could see. "I just thought about that boat down at the marina."

She shielded her eyes from the sun with her hand and gazed across the Gulf.

"I don't see anything out here."

"Yeah, me, either. I wonder if Ford left keys to the Whaler in the cabin. Maybe we could take a ride."

They strode to the cabin and found boat keys hanging from a hook next to the door. Back in the boathouse they got into the Whaler. Sam checked the gas tank and found it almost full, so he started the motor, unwound the ties, and backed the craft out of the slip. About an hour of daylight remained. That would be plenty of time to go beyond the marina and return.

The Whaler rose easily to a plane on the smooth water, and they cruised along the coast about a hundred yards from shore. Boats dotted the neighboring docks, but none resembled the cruiser. About a mile past the abandoned marina, Sam thought he heard the ring tone of his phone. He took it out of his pocket, saw Lora's number on the display, and backed the throttle down to a quiet idle.

"Hey, it's Lora. You sitting down?"

"Why, what's happened?"

"When the police showed up at the sunken car site,

Lonnie pulled me to the side and said they'd found prints on the knife from Ted Carter's storm cellar."

"Did they get a match?"

"Yeah, and you're not going to believe this. They belong to Chief Boozler."

Boozler? How could that be? Had they been wrong about the Black Palmetto? Had it sounded so good that they'd followed blindly down its path?

"Did they confront him about it?"

"Yes, and he said he had a break-in a few weeks ago, and that the burglar must have stolen the knife from his garage."

"That sounds pretty flimsy."

"I'll say. Lonnie said the chief hadn't been too thrilled to go out to Carter's place. Lonnie pushed the issue, so he relented, and he looked sick after they found the knife."

"Did they arrest the chief?"

"No, Lonnie didn't know what to do, Boozler being the top-ranking police official, so he went to his desk to call the Monroe County Sheriff for direction. By the time he got off the phone, Boozler had slipped away without anyone noticing. They went to his home, and his wife said he had come home early, went up to the attic and got a bag she didn't recognize. He left again without saying where he was going. Lonnie said he wouldn't answer his phone, either."

"Do they think he's the killer?"

"Lonnie wouldn't say any more. He was really upset, I could tell. I don't think he wants to believe the chief would do something like that, but it doesn't look good with him running away."

"Don't they have GPS trackers on the police cars?"

"Yes, but the chief left the cruiser at his house and took his personal vehicle, a Range Rover."

Range Rover? Pretty rich for a police chief in a place like Iguana Key. He probably didn't clear enough in a year or two to pay for one of those.

"Huh. Did you find out about the parolee?"

She paused then said, "No, I completely forgot, with all the talk about the fingerprints and the chief."

"Try to find out. I think it might be important."

Another pause. "Okay, but this has been a one-way conversation, so when I call back, I expect you to have something for me, and it better be good, or this source is going to dry up real quick. *Comprende*?"

"You got it. I'll tell you everything."

They ended the call and he relayed to Simone what had happened.

Simone shook her head. "I had the feeling the guy was dirty when we saw his name on that arrest report."

"Yeah, well, looks like you were right."

She raised an eyebrow. "What was that about you telling her everything? You're not going to do that, are you?"

Sam chuckled. "Are you kidding? She's the last person I'd tell. I'll give her just enough to keep her out of our hair."

He cut the wheel, arcing the boat back toward Ford's dock, and opened the throttle.

FIFTEEN

THE PHONE WOKE Sam the next morning around 8:00 a.m. Lora Diamond.

"I found out about the parolee. And by the way, his parole officer never made it to Iguana Key. Lonnie called his office and they said they haven't heard from him since he left there."

"Yeah?" Sam rubbed sleep from his eyes.

"You sound like you just woke up."

"Yeah, I did."

He glanced at Simone. Still sleeping like a baby. They'd gone to bed about midnight, and she had cautioned him about staying on his side of the bed. That worked fine until an hour later when he awoke with her arm across his chest and her lips next to his cheek, her breath warm on his face. After that, he tried his best to blank out thoughts of this exquisite woman clad only in a t-shirt and snuggling him. It didn't work, and the red display of the clock bore down on him like a tyrant, until sometime after 6:00 a.m. when he finally drifted off to sleep again.

"You have the parolee's name?"

"I do, but it's put-up-or-shut-up time. You get my drift?"

"I think so."

"Okay, tell me what you know, and I'll tell you his name."

"Hold on a minute."

He got out of bed, put on his pants, and padded down the hall to the kitchen. With the phone pressed between his ear and shoulder, he made coffee while he told her a story.

"We found a news item from about seven years ago where Richard Boozler arrested the blond-haired kid in the photo I sent you. It was a drug charge and they released him shortly thereafter. We think the kid killed somebody two years later, and Boozler got him another free pass. The parolee I asked you about might have taken the fall for the killing."

A few moments of silence, then, "How do you know that? You don't even know the parolee's name yet."

"Yeah, we're guessing about that part. But Boozler being in the wind fits pretty well with that scenario, don't you think?"

"Wait a minute. You asked me to get the parolee's name before you knew about the chief running off, so the only thing you told me is about the arrest seven years ago. I can check that out, but I want to know how you got the Knox kid's name in the first place."

He could just say, *Sorry, that's classified,* but that would only make her dig deeper. A reporter loves a government conspiracy better than anything. She'd never leave them alone.

"He's a friend of the man we're trying to find. Sean Spanner."

"Oh, yeah, who told you that?" Hostility in her voice.

The coffeemaker hissed and burbled, and he poured a cup and stirred in cream and sugar.

"Our client."

Silence.

"So you've had this Knox kid's name for several days, and you didn't tell me?"

"No, we just got it last night, right before I talked to you."

"You talked to your client last night?"

"Yes."

That seemed to take the wind out of her sails just a little. "Huh. I don't know if I believe you or not."

After a few moments of silence, Sam said, "Well, that's what I've got. You going to give me the name?"

She sighed. "I guess so. I just hope you're not leading me on."

Her tone had a slightly romantic quality that made him wish he hadn't had to lie. But then, that's probably how she got most of her information. He took a sip of the coffee and remained silent.

Sighing again at his reticence, she said, "His name is Fletcher Spikes. Lonnie pulled his case and found that he was sentenced to life for killing a drug distributor in Miami, but was released recently because of a DNA mismatch."

Sam found a pen and wrote down the name. "By the way, did you recognize either of the photos I sent?"

"No. The younger guy seemed vaguely familiar, but not enough for me to put a name on him. I'll show them around and see if I get a hit."

SAM TOOK HIS coffee cup into the living room and sat on the sofa, mulling over the phone call and the revelation from the night before about Richard Boozler's prints on the bloody knife. Could he be the killer? The ex-con that the parole officer had lost probably was the man killed a couple of months before. If Richard Boozler had done the deed, that meant he accidentally left the knife in the storm cellar when he stole the bombs. Fletcher Spikes probably came to see him, right out of prison and told him he knew the score. But why tell him? Maybe the chief had something the man had wanted, like a pile of cash from a drug deal gone south. The same thing Marlon Knox came back to Iguana Key to collect. If Boozler got Knox off on a murder charge, he probably set Spikes up for it. Then, to keep his mouth shut, the policeman had killed him.

The parole officer had inquired about Fletcher's body, and the dominoes began to fall. First the explosion on the bridge, then the funeral home employees who might have recognized the chief's voice. In the meantime, Jake Bell must have seen something, and got killed for it. Then Jake's father, who happened to be in the wrong place at the wrong time.

So Boozler could be the killer. Nothing in their assumptions so far would preclude that. Although, if the bloody knife hadn't been found, they would never have thought about him, and it actually could have been stolen as the chief had said. That had been the only incriminating evidence against him, and it could have been planted. Or the killer just got sloppy and left it by accident. The last part didn't seem likely.

J.T. came into the room and mumbled something unintelligible, then went into the kitchen and came back with a cup of coffee. Sam told him about Lora's call. His eyes widened, and he sat down and got busy on the computer, searching for information on Fletcher Spikes' arrest.

"By the way," J.T. said, "I got into the DMV's system last night after you went to bed and found Boozler's

Range Rover. It was pretty easy after that to trace it back to the dealer and then to the GPS tracking system."

"Why didn't you wake me?"

J.T. grinned. "Didn't want to disturb you and Simone."

Sam let the comment drop. "So where did the Rover go?"

"He drove it to a place a mile or two down the coast." J.T. brought up a computer screen and studied it for a moment. "It's still there now."

"On Iguana Key?"

"Yeah, see for yourself."

J.T. turned the computer to the side and Sam got up and stepped over to it. A close-up of a map displayed on the screen, and J.T. pointed at a flashing spot. After orienting himself on the scale of the map, Sam estimated the location of the vehicle to be somewhere around the abandoned marina where he and Simone had seen the old cruiser.

"Maybe the cruiser belongs to him," Sam said, "and he went down there to board it and left the Rover at the marina. He knows the police would catch him if he goes up US-1, because there's only one road to the mainland, but if he had a boat, he could go anywhere."

"You said it's about a forty-footer? Probably wouldn't be very fast."

"No, but if he left before dark yesterday, he could be well on his way to the Caribbean by now."

J.T. cocked his head to one side. "Yeah, you're right."

"I'm going down to see if I can find the vehicle."

Back in the bedroom, he heard the water running in the shower. He put on his shirt and shoes and went outside to the car.

It took about ten minutes to reach the marina. From the road, he didn't see any vehicles in the lot, including the Rover, which didn't make sense, so he drove in and continued to the far end where a dirt road led off the corner of the lot into the trees. The edge of a structure rose in his view, partially obscured behind a palmetto-and-mangrove thicket. The place hadn't been visible from their vantage point the day before. A vehicle he assumed to be the Range Rover sat behind a large tree with a dark green cover over it. Also parked close by were two other vehicles, one a plain dark sedan and the other an Iguana Key PD cruiser. Two men in suits stood there with Lieutenant Cates, who was also dressed in civilian clothes, along with a policeman in uniform. They all seemed to be looking Sam's way.

Too late to turn around and run. Sam pulled in next to the cruiser. They all wore sunglasses. Sam took his own black shades from the console and put them on. No need to let them see his eyes if he couldn't see theirs.

Lieutenant Cates and the uniformed officer stepped over as Sam got out of the car.

"What are you doing here?" Lonnie asked.

Sam peered beyond him. "I saw the cars and wondered if you'd found something."

The other officer, whose nametag read Dudley Crew, turned toward the driveway and then fixed Sam with a stare. "You can't see down here from the road."

Crew stood an inch or so taller than Lonnie, but otherwise had a similar build. Another gym junkie.

Ignoring the remark, Sam said, "Lora Diamond told me what happened with the chief of police. I thought maybe you'd found him."

"And your interest in the chief would be what?" Crew asked.

Nodding toward Lonnie, Sam said, "The lieutenant knows. I'm trying to find a man named Sean Spanner. He was probably abducted by the person who murdered all those people in town. If that was the chief, he could lead me to Spanner."

One of the suits, the older of the two with graying hair and FBI written all over his ivy-league presence, said, "Chief Cates, can we get back to the job here?"

"Acting Chief," Lonnie corrected, glancing at Crew and Sam with a smile on his face, as if pleasantly embarrassed by the miscue.

"Whatever, let's get this over with. He's probably been gone all night."

Lonnie's smiled leaked away. "Certainly, Agent Crease."

Officer Crew turned to Sam. "Stay close. We want to talk to you before you leave."

The agents and policemen eased toward the wood structure, which turned out to be a boathouse, and Sam followed. The door stood ajar, an open padlock on the ground next to it, as if whoever had entered had been in a hurry. Inside, Sam saw a long, empty boat slip, the water level at least six feet below the dock boards. It looked like a grave. Though fairly large, it wouldn't accommodate the cruiser Sam had seen the day before.

"He purchased a Cigarette boat a few weeks ago," Officer Crew said, "and we suspect he had it moored here."

"Did he tell you about the boat?" Crease asked.

"No, no," Lonnie said. "Dudley here is something of a computer genius."

Eyes turned to Crew, and he smirked behind his shades. "I wouldn't go as far as to say that." His tone sounded more about making fun of Lonnie, than about his own modesty. "I just checked with the Florida Department of Transportation and found the boat registered in the chief's name."

Agent Crease nodded. "Boozler didn't tell anyone about buying it?"

The two policemen exchanged glances. Crew shook his head and Lonnie said, "Not that we know of."

"Then how did you learn about this place? You find that on the computer, too?"

Lonnie grinned. "No, that might've taken a crystal ball." Neither Crease, nor anyone else, smiled at his joke, and his face turned serious. "Chief Boozler's wife told us about it. She said she suspected him of cheating on her with another woman and followed him here a couple of nights ago."

"He was probably getting ready to flee," Crew said, "and wanted to check out the Cigarette."

One-half of Crease's face smiled, an expression that said, *No kidding?* Then he stared down at the empty space in the water, as if awaiting a clue to bubble to the surface. "Okay, here's what we'll do. I'll alert the Coast Guard to check any Cigarette boats they see, and in the meantime, we'll dispatch a couple of choppers from Key West with some spotters aboard. Unless he's holed up somewhere with a covered berth, we'll find him." He headed toward the door. "We'll be in touch." The younger agent followed.

As Sam and the two policemen walked toward the cars, a large Mercedes with dark glass all around, pulled into the lot and eased their way. The two agents slowed their gait and waited for it to get closer. When it stopped, Agent Crease stepped over and the back passenger window lowered. Crease stooped to see the person inside, then squatted to talk at eye level. Someone important.

"Forget about them," Officer Crew said. "We told you to stay in town and you skipped."

Sam stopped and turned to face him. "I don't know what you're talking about. I'm still here."

"We went to your motel and you were gone. The chief wanted to bring you in for questioning."

"Nobody said I had to wait at the motel until the police wanted to see me. Besides, your chief is the one on the run."

Crew cocked his head. "You're hiding something, Mackenzie. Let's go, we'll talk downtown."

Sam couldn't believe his dumb luck, walking right into their hands.

"Are you arresting me?"

"Not yet," Crew said.

"Then I'm outta here."

"You're not going anywhere." He grabbed Sam's wrist.

Glancing down, Sam said, "Better take you hand back if you want to keep it."

Lonnie bowed up, his elbows rising, as if readying to draw two six-shooters.

"You can't talk to an officer of the law like that, Mackenzie," Lonnie said. "Cuff him, Dudley."

Dudley tightened his grip and pulled the cuffs from his belt with his free hand. Sam's face felt hot, and his wrist ached from Crew's fingers digging into his skin. Without thinking about all the grief the situation could bring down on him, Sam spun his wrist inside Dudley's fingers, grasped the policeman's wrist underneath with the same hand, and twisted downward, leveraging the man's elbow with his other hand. The officer screamed in pain and dropped to one knee.

"Stop where you are!" Lonnie said, pulling his Glock. "Hands in the air! Now!"

Uh oh. Sam released the man and stepped back, his pulse pounding in his ears. Why hadn't the guy moved his hand when he told him to?

"I said hands in the air. You're under arrest for assaulting a police officer."

You've done it now.

From behind them, Agent Crease said, "Hey! Coats! Put down your gun and let him go."

"What?" Lonnie said, glancing from Crease to Sam and back.

"You heard me. Let him go. He's with us."

The acting chief appeared dumbfounded, but so was Sam. Why would they do that for him?

"We'll take it from here," Crease said. "You two can go back to whatever it is you normally do around here. Obviously, it isn't catching killers."

Dropping the gun to his side, Lonnie cast his eyes down at Officer Crew, still on one knee, rubbing his wrist. "Are you okay?"

"He nearly broke my arm."

Lonnie turned his stare to the FBI man, his lips tight, and said, "It's Cates, Agent Crease, not Coats."

The FBI agent snorted a laugh. "Whatever."

The Mercedes backed out and drove away.

"Better watch yourself," Dudley said, massaging his upper arm. "This can be a dangerous place." He kept his eyes on Sam as he and Lonnie got into the cruiser.

They sped away, the tires throwing gravel and sand against the side of Sam's car.

Before the agents could pull out, Sam went to the driver's window and motioned for Crease to lower it.

"Who was in the Mercedes?" Sam asked.

Crease smirked. "Don't press your luck. Friendly piece of advice? Stay out of our way."

The agent raised the window as he eased the car past Sam and left the marina.

SIXTEEN

J.T. STARED WITH DISBELIEF. "You're telling me the FBI got you off the hook?"

"Yeah," Sam said. "But the guy wouldn't tell me who was in the Mercedes."

Simone raised an eyebrow. "Had to be somebody with some juice."

"I guess, but I don't know why they would want to help me. Anyway, we need to check out the Cigarette and see if there was any kind of GPS tracker on it. The acting chief said this Crew guy is a computer whiz, so they might have checked that angle already."

"Yeah, well, anybody can do a computer search," J.T. said. "Doesn't take an Einstein to figure that out."

"You're right," Simone said to Sam. "An item as expensive as a Cigarette should have a tracker on it."

Already clicking the keys on his computer, J.T. said, "If it does, I'll find it."

"Did you find anything on Fletcher Spikes?" Sam asked.

"Oh, yeah," J.T. said, glancing at Simone and back to his computer. "He killed a guy in a drug bust, just like we thought. Stabbed him with a knife that was never found."

"This is news to me," Simone said.

J.T. grinned. "I was about to tell you when Sam got back."

"Sure you were."

"That's right, I was." J.T. frowned, held her stare for a few moments, then turned to Sam. "The police recovered the drugs, but no cash."

"What was the street value of the drugs?" Simone asked.

"I don't think it mentioned anything about that."

Simone turned to Sam. "See what I'm saying about this guy? They *always* mention the drug value. That's big news, especially if it was high enough to get somebody killed."

Sam smiled. After seeing the story, J.T. probably had the idea he would take off on his own and try to find Boozler. Now, if he came up with GPS coordinates, he probably planned to keep those to himself, too. Classic J.T. thinking.

"Come on, man, it's easy enough for us to check out. Besides, we're going to stick to you like glue until all this is over, so you might as well tell us right now."

J.T. went silent for several beats then shrugged. "Okay. They estimated the street value to be around four million dollars. But you know the wholesale price wouldn't be that much."

"Yeah, maybe a couple of million," Sam said. "All of a sudden, a Range Rover and a secondhand Cigarette boat don't seem all that extravagant."

HARPO FELT TIRED to the bone, as if a load of lumber rested across his shoulders. He'd walked for two hours in the sun before the kindly truck driver had stopped to give him a ride.

"This is the place up ahead," Harpo said.

"You sure?" the driver asked as he gazed at the funeral home sign and pressed the brakes.

"Yep. Thanks for the ride."

When the vehicle came to a full stop, he opened the door and climbed down, singing along with the choir performing inside his head. Harpo slammed the door and stepped to the curb. The driver gave him a concerned look, then shrugged and drove away.

He trudged up the driveway, past the hearses and limos to the back door. Yellow tape crisscrossed it, and he wondered what that was all about. Mr. Tim had given him a key after he'd been working there for two years, so he used it, ducked under the tape, and went inside.

Nobody seemed to be there, the lights off in all the offices and the hallway. He called out for Mr. Tim, but got no answer. Feeling weak, worn out and hungry, he stepped into the bookkeeper's office and flipped on the light. She always had food in her desk, and shouldn't mind if he took some, as long as he replaced it later. Upon finding a bag of pork rinds in the bottom drawer, and a can of soda in her personal refrigerator, he took the items to the big broom closet, where he had a cot. Mr. Tim had let him sleep there for the past several months, since he'd gotten kicked out of the old construction trailer where he'd been squatting without the owner's permission. Wouldn't be doing that kind of thing in the future. Once he accomplished his mission— maybe tomorrow, or the next day, way too tired right now—everything would be completely legitimate, and he would even help others when possible, his path to heaven now clear.

Sitting on his cot, he ate the pork rinds and drank the soda, then lay back and closed his eyes. He listened to

Dr. Worth talk about the devil, and prayed for what he had to do that he knew would be awful, but necessary. It seemed like something Satan could be behind, but he knew in his heart that wasn't the case. Still, he also prayed that the sickness hadn't clouded his judgment about it. At some point the Sandman flowed like a thick fog under the door of the closet and swept him away.

"No DICE ON the Cigarette tracker," J.T. said.

As he spoke, Simone stepped into the room. "Couldn't find it, huh? I thought so." She took a seat on the sofa with Sam.

J.T. frowned and gave her a sidelong glance, then said to Sam, "The manufacturer installed one, but I found the invoice for Boozler's purchase, and it contains an order for removing the tracker before delivery. Guess he bought the boat specifically for his getaway and wanted to make sure it was untraceable."

"Huh," Sam said. "That's too bad." They were all silent for a several beats. "You know, maybe we've been going about this the wrong way. I've been tossing over some things in my mind and keep coming back to that stolen flash card. It has to be something potentially devastating to Knox, or he wouldn't have gone to all the trouble he did to get it. The people at the facility where it was stolen probably didn't have a clue about what Spanner—Benetti—took, because it was left over from the Palmetto group, but they contacted Whitehall and he told them what it was. Benetti probably knew Knox came down here to retrieve that lost drug money, so he shows up with this card. He tells Knox he has it and offers to sell it or destroy it for a big chunk of the money. Knox doesn't go for it, and somehow he subdues Benetti. He searches him and his car and tosses his motel room, and still doesn't find it."

"What makes you so sure he didn't find it?" J.T. asked.

"If he'd found it, he would've disposed of Benetti's body with the car."

Nodding, J.T. said, "Yeah, I guess so, but what difference does it make? Nobody knows where it is. That's what you two came here for, and got all wrangled up with these murders. If we knew where to find the thing, we'd be gone. You could collect your fee."

"That's right," Sam said, "but I have an idea where it is. I should've thought about it before now. If Benetti had it with him when he got to Iguana Key, and he didn't hide it in his car or the motel room, he had to stash it somewhere between the time he was at Chopin's bar and when he left to meet with Knox."

Simone smiled. "I'm following you, now."

SEVENTEEN

SAM DROVE THE three of them to Chopin's. Sitting in the drive next to the building, the engine idling, J.T. accessed the computer system inside.

"Buttoned up pretty tight. The wireless connection was easy enough, but the system security is more sophisticated than I expected. It took a few extra minutes to crack. Maybe I'll poke around a little and see what he's hiding."

"Just get the address," Sam said. "You can do that another time."

"Okay, okay, give me a minute. Going into the administrative system now…and here it is. Only one woman on the payroll, so it has to be her." He read the information from the screen and Simone wrote it down.

As Sam put the car in reverse to back out, Chopin rounded the corner of the building.

"Hey!" the wide man said, approaching the car. "What are you doing?"

Sam lowered his window. "We wondered if we could talk with your barmaid again," he ad-libbed.

Chopin folded his tattooed forearms against his chest. "She's busy. Besides, she already told you everything she knows about that guy. All he did was drink beer and use his telephone, and then he left. End of story."

"I thought we could go over it again, see if she remembered anything since we talked."

The bar owner dropped his arms to his side, snorted a chuckle, and turned to walk away. Over his shoulder, he said, "She gets off at one in the morning. You can talk to her then."

A FEW MINUTES after 10:00 p.m. Sam parked the car in a vacant lot behind a stand of volunteer mimosa trees. He, Simone, and J.T. got out and ambled down the dark street. Home air conditioners groaned against the heat. They didn't see anyone in the yards or sidewalks. Probably too late and too hot. A drop of perspiration slid down Sam's neck into his shirt.

At the house they eased around the left side to the back door, and Sam used his pick to open the lock. His pulse droned in his ears. If they found the flash card, did that mean the case would be over? Maybe, but he had to wonder what it contained, and if finding it could help find Marlon Knox or Richard Boozler, or whoever the killer might be. *And the two million dollars.* Inside, a light glowed above the stove, and they found their way to the small living room.

"The barmaid said they had drinks in here," Sam said, "and Benetti kept trying to reach someone on the phone. When he finally got through, she said she left the room so he could talk privately. When she came back a few minutes later, he said he had to go but would be back later. She's a pretty girl, and I believe he really planned to come back. So he must have stashed the flash card somewhere in this room to keep it safe."

They searched the sofa and easy chair, under and inside the zippered cushions, and the upholstery folds. Even turned them over and checked underneath. Found a tear in the cloth on the sofa bottom, but no flash card.

Simone checked around the large-screen television and the sound system in the corner. A couple of artificial plants sat on tables at each end of the sofa with pebbles at their base. Sam took one and J.T. took the other, digging their fingers into the pebbles. No luck.

"I'll check the bathroom," Simone said, "in case he went in there."

"We should check in the bedroom, too," J.T. said. "They might have gotten in the sack, and she just didn't tell you about it."

Two doors stood open down the hallway, the first one for the bathroom. Sam and J.T. moved on to the second. The room had clothes strewn on the floor by a closet, and the bed hadn't been made since she'd last slept in it, so they started there. They searched under the mattress and around the frame. In the bedside cabinet Sam found a couple of old magazines and a stack of papers, mostly receipts and utility bills.

The closet contained a lot of clothes and shoes, but nothing else of interest. Simone had come up empty searching the bathroom. They gave up about midnight and left.

When they got back to the car, Sam said, "I would've bet a thousand bucks we'd find it there."

"What if she found it, or Benetti gave it to her to keep for him?" Simone asked.

Sam started the car, eased it out of its hiding place, and pulled into the street. "You're right. That has to be it." His disappointment slid away, replaced by a renewed adrenalin rush.

THE TOYOTA SAT behind Chopin's bar where it had been before. Sam pulled in beside it. They'd already discussed how it'd play out, and Simone called the bar-maid's phone.

"This is Simone. We talked to you about Sean Span-ner a couple days ago. Yeah, well, we think this killer might be coming for you next, and we need to talk again, like right now. We're parked next to your car out back. Hey, I don't care what you tell him. If you want to stay alive, you better get out here."

She closed the phone. "Piece of cake."

A few minutes later, the blonde came out the door, spotted their car, and headed over. Simone got out and opened the back door on the passenger side. The woman saw J.T. in the back seat. "Who's that?"

"Nobody to worry about."

They got in and Simone turned around, flipped on the dome light, and said to the woman, "We know Span-ner gave you the computer flash card."

Sam had turned in the seat so he could watch her face when she answered.

The barmaid's eyes widened, and she waited a beat too long before saying, "What are you talking about?"

"You lied to us. Just give it up, and we'll let that slide and be gone."

"He didn't give me anything. I told you, we just sat on the sofa and had a few drinks. He kept making calls, and when he finally got through, he left."

"We're not leaving until we get that flash card," Sim-one said. "And if you think you can sell it, think again. It's valuable only to the guy who's killing all those peo-ple around here. You'll be next when he realizes you have it."

"But I don't have it. I don't know how I can con-vince you."

Simone remained silent for a few moments then said, "Okay, if you want to play it that way." She glanced at the clock display on the dash. "It probably isn't too late. Sam will call his friend at the news office, and she'll write a nice little story for the front page of the morning paper with your name in it. You'll be glad to turn it over then."

The barmaid gasped. "No, you can't do that."

"Sure we can."

She wrung her hands, and moments dragged by before she said, "All right. But I didn't lie to you. Like I said, he didn't give me the thing you're looking for. I found it on the floor this morning under the edge of the sofa where he must have dropped it."

Sam didn't think so. Benetti would have been more careful than that. Likely, he had stuck it under the edge of the cloth covering of the bottom of the sofa, and it had slid through the tear in the fabric.

"Do you have it with you?" Sam asked.

"Chopin has it. I told him the guy gave it to me at the bar and asked me to hold it for him, but it didn't look like he was coming back. Chopin said he'd check it out."

"Didn't he plug it into a computer?" J.T. asked.

"I don't think so. I just gave it to him tonight, and we've been really busy."

"Where is it now?" Simone asked.

"In his office safe."

The four of them left the car and eased to the back door of the building. Sam saw no security cameras anywhere. Upon entering Sam peered down a long, dimly lit hallway.

"First door on the left," the barmaid whispered. "He might be in the office."

It stood ajar about twenty feet away, light spilling out around the edges. They eased that way and Sam peeked around the jamb. There was a desk, but nobody sat behind it, so they stepped inside.

Several framed photographs hung from one wall. One pictured Chopin, sporting the long ponytail, sitting at a piano on a stage. He appeared to be in his twenties and much thinner, his hair a dark brown. The long sleeves of a tuxedo covered his elaborate ink, if he had any at that time. "At the Lincoln Center" had been handwritten across the top of the picture. The others displayed a more current and far heavier Chopin sitting on his Harley Davidson motorcycle, standing with biker friends, standing and pointing to the sign above his bar, behind the bar, drawing a mug of beer from the tap. Sam wondered if he belonged to a biker gang. That could cause them some trouble if things went badly.

"The safe is under the desk," the blonde said.

Sam stepped over and watched as J.T. rolled a leather executive chair out of the way, got down on his hands and knees, and lifted a piece of carpet-covered wood. The safe rested in the hole underneath.

J.T. dropped the wood cover back into its spot and stood up. "It has a combination lock. You can probably open it."

Sam shrugged. "Yeah, maybe, but it'd be easier just to get him to do it." To the barmaid he said, "Go get him."

She shook her head. "He'll fire me. I told him I was going for a smoke. Can't you leave me out of it? Maybe tell him a lie about how you know he has the thing?"

After a beat, Sam said, "Okay, go back to work. If you warn him, though, I'll make sure he knows everything."

As she started to leave, Sam said, "Is there a phone extension behind the bar?"

"Yes," she said and disappeared out the door.

He punched the number from the desk phone into his cell and handed it to J.T. Chopin hadn't heard his voice before.

"Press the call button and tell him you have a beer delivery at the back door."

Nodding, J.T. took the phone and made the call.

After a pause, he said, "All I know is the order says Chopin's. Okay, but if you don't want the shipment, you got to sign the paper to refuse it. Just come to the back door. Won't take a minute. I'll be here." He closed the phone.

Sam eased over to the door and listened. When he heard footsteps, he swung the door open and pointed his gun at the short round man. Chopin tried to retreat the other way, but Sam grabbed him by the collar and stopped him.

"Get in here," Sam said, nodding toward the office.

Chopin eyed the barrel tip. "You going to rob me?"

"Just do as I say."

The round man smirked. "Or what, you'll shoot me?"

Simone moved so he could see her through the doorway, her gun at the ready. "If he doesn't, I will. Just give me a reason."

Chopin stared at her gun for a moment, then sighed and stepped into the office.

"Who's this?" Chopin asked, nodding toward J.T.

"None of your business, fat boy," J.T. said. "We'll ask the questions."

To Sam, Chopin said, "I don't think you know what

you're doing. I've got connections in Miami. They'll track you down and kill you."

"Yeah? I'll keep that in mind."

"We want the flash card Spanner gave you," Simone said.

"What are you talking about?" Chopin's eyelids fluttered.

"This is the only place he could have left it."

"He didn't leave anything here. Can you put down the guns? Please? I told you, he just had a few drinks and left. He kept making calls, but it didn't look like anybody answered." He turned to Simone, probably hoping for some sympathy. Wrong place to look for that.

Sam pointed the gun at the round man's head. "Hey, we know you have it, and we already found your safe, so just open it up, and we'll be on our way."

He glanced at the desk and frowned. "Okay, okay. Just cool it with the gun. I couldn't see what was on it, anyway." He stepped behind the desk and knelt to lift the wood cover. Sam stood over him in case he had a gun stowed inside the safe. The lock snapped open after a few moments, and Chopin lifted the steel door and eased it back on its hinge to rest against the carpet.

J.T. pulled him from under the desk by the collar. "That's good, we'll take it from here."

"Hey, I've got other stuff—"

"Just get out of the way."

When Chopin stood up and moved aside, J.T. reached into the safe and pulled out a thin black item about the length and width of a postage stamp. "It's an SD memory card."

Simone took it, studied it for a moment, and handed it to Sam.

ON THE WAY back to the cabin, J.T. plugged the card into his computer. "The files are encrypted. Might take me a while, but I think I can open them."

"We don't have to do that," Simone said. "All we have to do is take it back to Homestead, and we're finished."

Sam glanced at her. "You sure? Once those guys have a look at it, they might find it's something they don't want anybody to know about. And maybe they wouldn't want us knowing about it, either. They could send somebody."

"But it's encrypted. They should know we wouldn't be able to open it."

Nodding, Sam said, "They might think that, but they might think we were able to take a peek. I don't want to take that chance. We need to know what's on it."

The phone chirped and Sam looked at the display. Lora Diamond. He wondered what she would be calling about at this time of night.

"Charles Ford is in a hospital in Miami. Somebody stabbed him and left him for dead."

"Was he robbed?"

"I don't know. He was in the parking lot of a place called Windhaven."

The place where Knox spent some time before the Black Palmetto. Sam wondered how Ford would know about it. He did say he wanted to confirm his suspicion of someone.

"What's his condition?"

"They have him in the ICU. He lost a lot of blood before somebody discovered him."

"I wonder if he's conscious."

"I don't know. A Miami PD detective called me because they found my card in his car. I asked about his condition, but the detective said I'd have to call the hospital. The only thing the hospital would tell me is that he just got out of the ER. I'm headed up there now if you want to go."

Ford might be able to identify his attacker. Had to be Marlon Knox, and he could be waiting outside the ER to finish what he'd started. He might also kill Lora in the process.

"Hold on." He covered the phone and told Simone and J.T. what had happened.

"We can handle this," J.T. said. "Go with her and see what you can find out."

Simone glared at J.T. for a moment, then shrugged. "Do whatever you want."

EIGHTEEN

LORA DIAMOND MET Sam in Chopin's parking lot. After stopping at an all-night convenience store for coffee, they headed for the Overseas Highway.

"What were you doing out riding around at this hour?" Lora asked.

"We went back to see Chopin."

"Oh yeah? Did he give you any more information about this Spanner guy you were looking for?"

"Not really, but it was worth a try."

"Why so late?"

She asked too many questions, and saying the wrong thing could end up in the newspaper. He didn't know this woman well enough to decide if she could keep a secret or not. His intuition told him she couldn't.

"What was it the policeman said about Ford?" he asked, changing the subject.

"I told you everything on the phone."

"Tell me again, in case I missed something."

Sighing, she repeated, verbatim, what she'd said before.

"You're from Miami," she said. "You ever heard of Windhaven?"

"It sounds familiar."

"The detective said he thinks it's some kind of rehab center. He talked with the nurse who found Charles in the parking lot, but she was pretty close-mouthed about the place."

"Did he find out what Ford was doing there?"

"I don't know. He got tired of me asking questions and told me to come by the police headquarters in the morning if I wanted to know anything else."

A few minutes after turning north on US-1, headlights appeared in Sam's side mirror and grew larger by the second. As the vehicle passed under highway lights, it appeared to be a black SUV. He thought it would go around them, but it slowed about twenty feet from their rear bumper, and a flashing red light burst on inside its grille.

"What's going on?" Lora asked. "I wasn't speeding." She started to slow the car.

Sam turned and peered through the rear window and saw two men who didn't appear to be in uniform.

"Speed up," Sam said.

"What?"

"They're not cops. Floor it. Now!"

Lora pressed the accelerator and the car picked up speed again. Sam knew they wouldn't be able to outrun them, but he needed time to think. Sure enough, the big engine roared up behind them and started around Lora's car. When it got alongside, the man in the passenger seat motioned for them to pull over.

"Are you sure they aren't the police?"

"Yes. Pretty sure."

"Pretty sure?"

The man in the other vehicle motioned again, this time with a handgun.

"I'm sure now, okay?" He glanced at the speedometer, which indicated almost eighty miles per hour. An intersection appeared up ahead. "We need to lose them. Keep it on the floor, and when I tell you, hit the brakes and turn into that road on the left."

This time she didn't ask questions.

"Now! Hit the brakes and start turning!"

The car slowed to about sixty within a couple of seconds and the SUV kept going. Lora's tires skidded and then caught traction as she slowed more and cut into the turn. The SUV was pulling to a stop a hundred yards ahead when Sam lost sight of its brake lights.

"What are we doing?" Lora asked.

"Just go! We'll talk about it later."

A dirt road appeared on the right, and Sam told her to turn onto it. They pulled in about a hundred feet, cut to the left through the undergrowth, and circled back behind a stand of palmetto. Brittle shrubs scraped the bottom of the car until they stopped. She killed the engine and lights, and he opened the door to get out.

"Stay here, and be ready to go again."

"I'm scared. What are they going to do to us?"

After a moment's hesitation, he said, "Don't worry, I'm the one who's going to be doing things."

He eased the door shut, pulled his gun, and stepped to the edge of the palmetto cover. The conversation from a half hour before with Simone flickered into his head. Had their employer sent these two to kill him because he'd found the flash card? Maybe they were just here to retrieve it. Then, knowing that hopeful thinking had little power in a situation like this, he decided to assume the worst case.

Headlights from the SUV appeared and stopped at

the mouth of the dirt road. A moment later the vehicle turned in and moved slowly past the palmetto thicket for about eighty more feet before stopping. Probably saw their tracks turn into the brush. Sam picked up a baseball-sized rock and threw it, striking the rear hatch. They cut their lights, and Sam took cover again. He watched as two moonlit silhouettes exited and made their way toward the rear of the vehicle. Each held a handgun, ready to fire.

"What do you want?" Sam asked. "I have a gun, and I'll shoot you if I have to."

"Put down your weapon," one of the men said, "and let's talk."

"Forget it."

Moments passed.

"We want the computer card. The fat man told us you took it. Turn it over, and we'll let you be on your way."

They were triangulating on his voice, moving closer.

"I don't have it. You come any closer and you're dead."

"Are you going to force us to take it?" Still closer.

Sam thought he'd said enough, and had given them their chance. All he could see was an occasional shadow, but he could hear their footsteps as they crushed dead grass and twigs. It sounded as if they were moving apart.

Easing down to the ground on his stomach, he wondered if he would run into any snakes or spiders. The noise of the men's footfalls stopped a couple moments later, and Sam picked up on their shadows about a car length away. He grabbed another rock that his knee had bumped and tossed it to his right, away from the thicket. A beam of light flashed on from the driver's side and pointed toward where the rock had rolled through the bushes. Two shots followed. *Bam! Bam!*

Sam squeezed off his own shot. The light dropped to the ground, and Sam thought he heard the body of the man drop with it. The driver screamed a string of obscenities and moaned with pain. Two reports then came from the other man's gun, the projectiles *zinging* a couple of feet over Sam's head. He fired back at the muzzle flares and heard the other man fall.

Moments passed.

"Larson!" the driver said, "you okay?"

"I'm hit, but I don't think it did much damage."

"I'm bleeding all over the place, man. You got to get me to a doctor."

"What about the flash card? We can't just leave it."

"Forget the flash card. We'll get it later."

"But—"

"I said we're leaving."

Sam heard the two men struggling into the vehicle. He got up and almost bumped into Lora. She had gotten out of the car without him hearing her, and could have been shot had she been there a few moments before.

"Are you okay?" she asked.

"I'm fine. Let's get out of here."

"What about them?"

He sighed. "They'll probably live."

Back in the car, she started it up and sped around the palmettos, onto the dirt road and back to the highway.

"What do we do now?" she asked.

"Just head on to Miami."

Sam thought about Simone and J.T., pulled out his phone, and called.

"Where are you?" Simone asked.

"On the highway. Two guys in a black SUV tried to waylay us on US-1."

"You get hurt?"

"No."

He could hear her breathing into the telephone. "How about them?"

"They'll need medical attention."

"You know, I saw a vehicle like you described pull out of the parking lot right after you left, but I didn't think about it following you. There were a lot of cars coming and going. You think it was the people we talked about earlier?"

"I don't know. It might have been somebody else."

"Yeah, but who?"

"I've got an idea. We'll talk when I get back. Just be on the lookout."

"Okay. Sam?"

"Yeah?"

"I'm glad you're all right."

The words hung in the air for a moment before they said their goodbyes. Simone had sounded more worried and sentimental than usual.

"Who were those guys?" Lora asked, bringing him back to the present.

"I don't know."

"I heard you say you had an idea about them, though."

He really didn't know anything for sure. Agent Crease had told the cops, *He's with us*, referring to Sam, right after talking with someone in the big Mercedes. It became pretty clear a few minutes later, though, that Crease didn't really mean it, and had just said what he'd been told to say. But Sam hadn't thought of the reason until now. *Mr. Mercedes wanted to let the pigeon fly and they would follow him home.* Only one problem: they followed the wrong pigeon.

NINETEEN

LORA KEPT ASKING questions he didn't want to answer.

"What did they want?"

"They wanted what Spanner stole."

"You mean the flash card?"

She must have heard the guy ask about it.

"Why did they think you had it?"

"Someone told them I did, but they were wrong."

She paused for a moment. "That was your girlfriend you spoke with?"

"Simone is a business partner."

"Tell that to somebody who'll believe it. I saw the way she looks at you."

"The way she looks?"

Lora chuckled. "The way you look at her, too."

Well, they actually had been pretty tight at one time.

"Let's drop it, okay?"

She shook her head. "You men."

It got quiet as the miles peeled away. Then, as Sam's eyes began to droop, she said, "Tell me about this flash card they were looking for."

"I don't know anything about it."

"I don't believe you. And you know what else? I think you know a lot more about this killer than you're saying. You gave me those photos and made up a story about your client giving them to you."

"Believe what you want."

"I'm going to find out, one way or another."

"Listen, the less you know about this, the better. Most of it is classified."

"Do they have something to hide?"

Sam looked at her. "Of course they have something to hide. That's why they call it classified, and it would be very dangerous for you to know about any of it, much less put it into print."

"You know about it. That means you're in danger, too."

"Yes, I am." Though he hadn't thought much about that aspect yet, the target on his back seemed to be growing by the minute. The threat from the guys on the highway was just the beginning. They probably wouldn't stop until they got the flash card and killed everyone who knew about it. Unless somebody killed them first.

Lora quieted then, leaned back in her seat, and stared through the windshield.

The white noise of the road droned, and after a few more minutes of highway lull, she sighed and said, "You might as well take a nap if you want. I'm wired. All this is going to spin around in my head for hours."

"Okay, I might catch a few winks."

THEY ARRIVED IN Miami a few minutes after 4:00 a.m. and went straight to Jackson Memorial. After locating the Intensive Care Unit, a policeman standing guard at the nurses' desk told them that Ford had lost a lot of blood and hadn't awakened since surgery. The cop wouldn't have given Sam the time of day, but never even asked Lora for identification. Just volunteered the information after she told him why she was there.

Deciding to stay around for a while and see what happened, they took a seat in the visitors' room outside the unit, along with about fifty other people. After a half-hour or so, a man who looked like a detective entered the room and headed through the door to the ICU. Probably looking for the policeman. A few minutes later, Mr. Detective came out and looked over the crowd, his eyes settling on Sam and Lora. He walked over and asked if they were the couple asking about Charles Ford.

"We are," Lora said. "He's a friend of mine from Iguana Key. Someone from Miami PD called me about him a few hours ago."

"That was me." He pulled out a card and handed it to her. "Mr. Ford had your card in his wallet. He also had money in his pockets, so we don't believe he was a robbery victim. We're hoping he can identify his assailant when he wakes up. Do you have any idea who would do this to him?"

The detective sat down next to her and opened a pocket notebook.

"No, but Charles is a defense attorney, and he's representing a man in a murder case."

"You mean he might have run across the real killer, trying to prove his client's innocence?"

"Yes, that could be it."

Sam wondered about her reticence. Maybe she just didn't want to get embroiled in a Miami investigation.

"The officer inside said you work for the newspaper down there?"

"That's correct."

The detective stared for a couple of beats, maybe waiting for more, which didn't come. "Okay, I'll touch base with the PD in Iguana Key and see what they have."

Good luck with that, Sam thought.

The man's eyes drifted toward Sam. "And who are you?"

Sam introduced himself.

"What's your interest here?"

Sticking to the story he'd given the police in Iguana Key, he said he'd been hired to track Sean Spanner and retrieve money he had stolen. "I think Spanner might be mixed up somehow in this case."

"You think this Spanner could be the guy who stabbed our vic here?"

"Maybe." *Anything is possible*, he thought.

"Where do you live?"

"Here in Miami, at a marina."

"Oh, yeah? Which one?"

Though the man seemed to ask the question offhand, Sam knew he would check him out. He couldn't think of any reason to worry about it, so he told him.

The detective got Sam's phone number and made more marks in the notebook. "Okay. It looks like you might be in for a wait." Getting up, he said to Lora, "If you think of anything that might help in the meantime, call me at the number on the card."

"What do they say about his chances?" Sam asked, nodding toward the ICU.

"About fifty-fifty, I think. But you know, they're just guessing." Turning to Lora, he said, "Don't forget. Call me if you think of anything."

Lora eyed the card and gave it a thump. "Don't worry, I will."

"Okay, I've got some other cases to look into, so I'm out of here."

He forced a smile at Lora, but lost it as his face turned to Sam, and then he went back into the ICU. Sam assumed he wanted to tell the officer about the murders, and to be watchful for anyone who seemed interested in seeing Ford. A minute or so later, he came out and left, not even glancing their way. Other things on his mind.

They decided to get coffee in the hospital cafeteria, and after a few sips, Sam said, "I'll be right back." He headed toward the restroom down the hall, kept going, and pulled out his phone.

Jack Craft didn't answer, and Sam wondered whether he might still be sleeping or just had his phone turned off.

Back at the table, he said to Lora, "I need to leave and take care of something, but I should be back in a couple of hours."

Lora touched the napkin to her lips, her reporter eyebrow elevated. "I could take you."

"Sure, if you don't mind."

With Sam navigating, they took the Dolphin Expressway and continued east on the MacArthur Causeway. The sun's rays burned through the horizon as they rode into Miami Beach and headed toward his marina.

When she turned the car into the parking lot, Lora said, "Is this where you live?"

"This is it. I need to talk with a friend who lives here."

Jack's new BMW sat in its parking spot. He'd traded the Mercedes a couple of months earlier. Said the big luxury liner projected a cooler image. It did look good.

"Does this have something to do with Spanner?"

"Maybe indirectly."

They got out and strode down the dock. Sam noticed the newspaper on Jack's walkway.

"I don't think he's up yet. Why don't we go to my boat and have a cup of coffee?"

She linked her arm in his and smiled. "I bet you use that trick on all the girls."

The post-dawn sun shone on them with a pleasant warmth and hue, and electricity seemed to flicker in Lora's eyes.

He smiled and led the way down the dock. "Seemed worth a try."

Chuckling, she pulled her arm away.

As they approached *Slipstream,* his forty-foot cruiser, Lora let her eyes roam over the vessel. "How do you like living on the water?"

"It isn't much fun when a storm comes along, but other than that, it's good."

"My dad had a boat. It wasn't this big, but it had a cabin. We would take it out on the Gulf for day trips."

"Oh, yeah?"

"Yeah, this brings back some good memories."

Sam stepped aboard and opened the door, and they went into the lounge.

"Have a seat and I'll make the coffee."

"Okay if I look around?"

"Sure, if you don't mind the mess."

She came into the galley a few minutes later as the java machine finished brewing.

"Nice setup."

"Thanks. It serves its purpose."

He poured the cups and they each stirred in cream and sugar.

She took a sip and peered at him over the cup. "Umm. Good."

They stood there, only a couple of feet apart. She moved closer and Sam set his cup down. He touched her hand, and Lora's eyes zeroed in on his lips. Then the coffeemaker sputtered and popped, and she gave him a sad smile, turned around, and stepped away. Sam flipped off the offending machine.

The moment had passed, and he felt an uncomfortable silence taking its place. He pointed at the door. "Let's go outside on the deck."

They exited and ambled aft to the chairs under the awning. Fog rose off the morning water, and skipjack and mullet broke the surface, feeding and playing. A pelican with part of its foot missing sat on a timber nearby. It eyed the fish and scratched underneath its wing with the tip of its long beak.

"That's Pete," Sam said, nodding toward the bird. "I think he's pretty old. I usually feed him when there isn't much fishing activity. Sometimes he'll take the food out of my hand."

"You're kidding. I've never heard of a tame pelican." She looked around as they took a seat. "I could get used to this. So calm and peaceful."

"Yeah, everyone is asleep right now. Give it a few hours and you'll hear music and boat motors."

"Still, pretty nice. I kinda had you figured differently."

"How so?"

"Well, more like military. A cabin in the woods, dogs patrolling the perimeter, security systems." She glanced at him, her expression sober. "From the way you shot those men in the dark, maybe also doing a lot of target practice."

"Maybe I should look into that. A cabin in the woods."

Smiling, she said, "No, I like this better." She took a sip of coffee and set the cup on a nearby table. "And I like you better, too."

Sam grinned. "What? Because of the boat?"

"No, not just that. I liked the way you handled that situation back on the highway. Most guys would have just tried to outrun them, but you knew what to do." She touched his arm and smiled. "Feeding the pelican out of your hand sounds kind of cute, too."

"Yeah, the ladies seem to like that part."

Lora slapped lightly at his arm and made a mock frown. "Oh, I should have known!"

"Hello over there!"

Sam turned to see Jack Craft standing on the dock, a cup of coffee and a newspaper in his hands.

"Jack, I was just coming to see you."

"I hope you were bringing that lovely lady with you."

Glancing at Lora, Sam said, "Yeah, we'll be right down."

"Wonderful. Bring your coffee. I have some fresh pastries."

They followed him along the dock to where *The Clipper* rested in its oversized slip.

After holding the main hatch open for them, Jack went into the galley. He took a plate from the refrigerator, removed a piece of foil covering it, and put it into the microwave.

"Have a seat at the table," he said as he punched buttons.

By the time they sat, and Sam introduced the two, the oven beeped, and Jack took the plate out and set it on the table.

"These have caramelized apples inside."

"Didn't know you could bake," Sam said.

Jack smiled. "A lady friend made them for me." He laid out napkins before them.

"They smell delicious," Lora said as she took one.

"Believe me, they are."

Sam picked out one and took a bite. "That is good."

Jack smiled, helped himself to a pastry, and leaned back in his chair.

Lora's phone chirped, and she pulled it out of her purse and looked at it. "I need to take this." She got up and went out on the deck.

"Okay, what was it you needed to see me about?" Jack asked.

"I wanted to know how you did with that favor I mentioned," Sam said.

"Oh, the doctor. It went okay. I think the fix is in."

"Who did you talk to about it?"

Something in Sam's face must have put Jack on the alert, because his smile slid away. "Why, what happened?"

"Somebody in a big Mercedes came around. Whoever it was seemed to outrank the FBI agent investigating the cases down in Iguana Key."

"That cause you some trouble?"

"Not right away. As a matter of fact, it was the opposite. The local cops were trying to roust me, and the agent told them to lay off. This was right after he spoke with the person in the Mercedes."

Jack shrugged. "So what's the problem?"

"The problem is, I think the same person had two thugs follow Lora and me and hold us up outside Iguana Key."

Something changed in Jack's eyes, the gears turning over.

"Who did you talk to about the problem?" Sam repeated.

"A lobbyist in Washington who knows a lot of important people. He said he thought he could reverse the ruling on the doctor's case."

The lobbyist might have called the person in the Mercedes, but that seemed like a long shot. "What did you tell him?"

"The bare minimum, just that the doctor got the shaft and didn't deserve it."

"Huh." Maybe it was time to revisit the doctor and see who might have contacted him. "You ever heard of a place called Windhaven?"

Jack chuckled. "Sure, I know a couple of people who vacationed there last year."

"Vacationed?"

"Well, you know…"

Lora came back in and sat down. "That was just my boss looking for me."

TWENTY

Sam's phone sounded off and he looked at the display. He didn't recognize the number. "Hello."

"Mackenzie, this is Lieutenant Cates. A detective in Miami called and told me about Charles Ford being stabbed. Is Lora there with you?"

"Yes, hold on."

He handed the phone to her. "Lonnie Cates."

She put it to her ear. "Hello, Lonnie. I was probably on the phone when you called. He's in a coma. We thought his assailant might be the same person who killed the people in Iguana Key... Because Ford was up here investigating somebody. Maybe it was the killer, and he found out about it. Okay, I'll let you know if he wakes up. By the way, is there any progress on finding the chief?" Nodding for a moment, she said, "Okay, I'll let you go, then." She said goodbye and handed the phone back to Sam.

"What did he say about Boozler?"

"They got an anonymous call from a man saying he saw him, and he was on his way to check it out."

They finished the pastries, and Sam said he needed to get something from his boat. "I'll be back in a few minutes."

"Take your time," Jack said with a smile.

Lora gave Sam a look that said she wondered what he was up to.

When he neared *Slipstream*, Sam dialed up Simone and told her about Cates' call. "He got a tip on Boozler. You think you could catch up and follow him?"

"I can give it a try."

"How's J.T. coming along with the encryption?"

"Pretty close to breaking it. He has a call in to one of his contacts to verify something to do with the code. Hold on."

Sam heard her relay their conversation to J.T. and tell him she would be back later. "Okay, I'm headed for the car. What did you find out about the lawyer?"

Sam brought her up to speed on the coma situation. "I'll drop by the hospital again later and see if there's been any change."

"Where are you now?" she asked, the sound of the car starting in the background.

"I left Lora at Jack's place and came over to my boat to call you."

A couple of beats passed, and he wondered if she believed him.

"Okay, I'll try to pick up Cates' trail."

SAM WENT BACK to *The Clipper* and told Lora that something had come up that he needed to attend to. "I'll meet you back at the hospital later. Jack will give me a lift. Right, Jack?"

The confidence man didn't miss a beat. "You bet."

She frowned. "I'll be glad to drive you—"

"No, that's okay, it might take a while."

Lora grudgingly agreed, thanked Jack for the pastries, and left.

JACK TURNED HIS BMW into the driveway of Windhaven. The place looked like a business office, though there were no signs of any kind. It had minimal landscaping, and the drive led to a small parking lot to the side of a covered front entrance. Picking a space in the shade of a cluster of palms, Jack parked and they got out.

A small entrance hall lay directly inside the door, and a woman sat there behind a desk, reading a book. "Can I help you?"

"We're here to see the director," Jack said, handing her one of his many business cards. He cast his eyes around the room, as if inspecting for vermin.

The woman studied the card for a moment and looked him up and down. He had donned a suit that probably cost three thousand dollars and carried a polished leather portfolio. Sam had showered and put on a dress shirt and a pair of khakis.

"Do you have an appointment with Dr. Schuller…" She looked at the card again. "Mr. Bane?"

"No, but it's imperative that I speak with him immediately. My client is a very wealthy man, and he has it on good authority that this facility recently violated his son's patient confidentiality."

She stood up and glanced at the card again, her eyes wide, as if there might be something there that she didn't see the first two times. "Please have a seat and I'll tell him you're here."

Returning a few minutes later, she escorted them through a doorway with an electronic lock to a hallway and finally an office on the left. Unlike the exterior façade and the foyer, it reeked of opulence. A massive desk, constructed of a rich wood, dominated the space. It squatted atop an oriental rug that extended the length of the room. What appeared to be original paintings hung from the walls, interspersed with framed certifications from prestigious colleges and universities.

A very large man stood behind the desk with Jack's card in his hand. Well over six feet tall, he probably weighed in excess of three hundred pounds. His hair resembled a snowcap atop a mountain, and the skin on his face had a rosy glow, no doubt from high blood pressure and alcohol.

"Mr. Bane, come in, please," he said, rounding the desk. After shaking with Jack, he reached for Sam's hand. "And you are?"

Sam smiled. "Mr. Bane's investigator."

"Ah, well then, let's go over here where we can chat."

He led them to the side where a loveseat sofa sat facing two leather chairs. Jack and Sam took the chairs, so the big man went to the sofa and lowered his bulk, taking up two thirds of its width.

"Now, Mr. Bane, what is it you wanted to see me about?"

Jack opened his portfolio. "I understand you were visited yesterday by an attorney named Charles Ford, and you divulged private information about a former Windhaven patient."

Schuller frowned and leaned back on the sofa. "You're talking about the man who was stabbed in the parking lot last night."

"Yes."

"I didn't give him any private information. Windhaven handles some of the most sensitive cases in the Southeast. Discretion is our code of honor. Who made this accusation?"

Jack closed his eyes and shook his head. "Sorry,

unlike this establishment, I don't divulge information about my clients."

"But I didn't do what you are saying. I gave out no information to Mr. Ford."

Jack slapped the portfolio closed and dropped it on the rug with a thump. He took a deep breath and sighed as he let it out. "Then, tell me, what exactly did you say to the man? My client has threatened to go to the psychiatric board, and he wants me to file a civil suit."

The big man ran his fingers through his white hair, and his face turned a deeper red. He stood up and said, "Can I get either of you a drink? Scotch or bourbon?"

Jack seemed to consider that for a moment. "Scotch sounds lovely. Straight up is fine."

Sam said he would have the same.

After a couple of healthy slugs of Scotch, Schuller sat back down and described the conversation he'd had with Charles Ford.

"The attorney said he just needed to confirm something. He said it was critically important, a matter of life and death. He had a recent photograph of a man and wondered if he had been a patient here several years ago. The picture seemed familiar, but I certainly couldn't put a name to it. Then Mr. Ford described an incident that happened here a long time ago, and I remembered the man. It had been several years, and he had changed a lot, but I was pretty sure it was the same person. I could tell by the eyes."

"So you confirmed it for Ford?" Jack asked.

"No, I did not. I told him I wouldn't be able to help him because of privacy concerns. I suppose he took that as an affirmation, because he smiled and left."

Schuller got up and poured himself another drink.

"Did he leave the photo with you?" Sam asked.

"No, he put it in his pocket."

After a couple of moments, Jack said, "That doesn't sound like you violated anybody's privacy to me." He turned to Sam. "Do you have any other questions?"

"Just a couple. Did Mr. Ford say how he came to know about this person?"

Schuller eyed Sam with the slightest expression of condescension, his eyes glistening from the scotch. "Yes, he said he worked on Windhaven's legal team several years ago when the incident occurred that I mentioned earlier."

"What was the incident?" Sam asked.

The big man glanced at Jack. "I don't know if I should—"

"This is important," Jack said, a stern tone to his voice. "I'm willing to make a favorable report to my client and encourage him to drop this action, but please answer the question."

"Well, I suppose it will be all right, since the man gave me this information, and not the other way around. He said he remembered that the patient had stabbed a nurse in the neck with a ballpoint pen. The nurse survived, but she left her position and sued Windhaven."

"Do you have a photo of the patient?"

"Oh, no. We never photograph our clientele."

Sam hadn't expected that they would, since many of the patients probably were celebrities who avoided cameras on their personal time, especially when checking in for detox.

"Okay, can you describe the man in the photo that Mr. Ford had?"

"Well, he seemed kind of nondescript. As I said, the

eyes were what I recognized, and I don't know how to describe them, other than that they were blue. The man seemed heavier, more mature than I remember, but that's about all I remember about him. Ah, and he had short hair. The patient had long hair when he was here." He took another belt of the Scotch, and his eyes narrowed. "Something just occurred to me. If you are who you say, then you would know what this person looks like."

Jack chimed in. "Oh, believe me, we know our client's son, but we wonder if he really is the man in the photo, and we wonder why Mr. Ford wanted to know all this, since he is a criminal defense attorney. It's just a good thing you didn't say any more than you did."

They deposited their drinks on the desk, untouched, and walked out the door, leaving a greatly relieved and slightly drunk Dr. Schuller behind. Back in the car, Sam gave Jack directions to Dr. Whitehall's apartment and took out his phone.

Lora answered with, "Where are you?" Her tone bordered on irritation.

"I'll be on my way in a few minutes. Any change in the patient's condition?"

"No, still in a coma."

"I just thought of something. Ford seemed to think he knew the identity of the killer, but wouldn't say until he confirmed his suspicions. It occurred to me that he might have had a photograph of the suspect with him when he got stabbed, and maybe that was his method of confirmation."

"Huh. If he did, the police would have it now, unless the killer took it."

"Yeah, my thinking exactly. You seemed to be pretty

chummy with the detective at the hospital. Why don't you call and ask him?"

"Chummy?"

"Seemed that way to me. He wasn't too interested in what I had to say."

"Okay, I'll give it a shot. Get over here pretty soon, though. I need to get back home and get some rest. I'm about to fall asleep here."

Now that she'd reminded him of how long they had been up, fatigue began to grip the backs of his eyes. "Don't worry, I won't be long."

Jack turned into the parking lot at Whitehall's apartment and Sam got out.

"I'll be back in a few minutes."

Upstairs, he knocked and waited. A minute or two passed before the door opened a crack.

"You again."

"I got someone to check into your case, and you should be getting your license back pretty soon."

"Okay." He stared at Sam through rheumy eyes, said, "Thanks," and started to close the door.

Sam stuck his foot in and stopped it. "I need to talk."

The man stared again, and then shrugged, as if he didn't have any choice, or didn't really care one way or the other. After leaning out and scanning the hallway, he swung the door open. Sam went inside and sat on the sofa, Whitehall dropped into his chair. Two empties sat on the table beside his chair. He'd started early.

"So, what is it now?" the doctor asked.

"Did you get any other visitors talking about the Black Palmetto?"

"Yes, I did. And I didn't like it one bit."

"Who was it?"

"The man who hired and fired me."

"Senator Blaine?"

Whitehall gave him a nod.

"What did he want?"

The doctor picked up one of the cans and shook it. "Hold on." He stepped into the kitchen, returned with a fresh beer, and sat down with a sigh. After a long swallow, he said, "Where was I? Ah, yes, I suppose it doesn't matter now. Blaine had spoken with the people who hired you and wanted to know what had been stolen from my closet at the center in Homestead."

"Did you tell him?"

"Sure, why not?"

"The flash card?"

The man's eyes widened a fraction. "Yes, how did you know?"

"We found it. It's encrypted, but I'm pretty sure we can break it."

As if on cue, Sam's phone chirped. He took it out and looked at the display: J.T.

"I need to take this," he said.

"I figured out what's on the card," J.T. said when he got on the line. "It's some sort of tracking system, and its range seems to span the globe. I see pulse points with numbers on them in Europe, the Caribbean, and across the U.S."

"Huh, a tracking system," Sam repeated, primarily for Whitehall's benefit. "How many points in all?"

"About fifteen."

"You know what they are?"

"No, but I'm still working on it."

Sam glanced at Whitehall as he said, "Okay, excellent," and hung up. He had an idea what the program might be about.

Smiling, Sam gestured with the phone. "The technical person working on the flash card."

The doctor rolled his rheumy eyes. "I surmised as much."

"I just wonder how you accomplished it."

"Accomplished what?"

"Implanting GPS transmitters in the operatives at the Black Palmetto."

The doctor took a deep breath, guzzled the rest of the can of beer, and wiped his mouth with the back of his hand. "I put them under hypnosis and placed the transmitters under the skin just below the shoulder blade. The incision was so tiny it probably seemed like an insect bite when they awoke."

"Did you develop the system yourself?" Sam asked, wondering how he might have acquired the skills to do something like that.

"Heavens, no. A defense technologist did all that for me and somehow hooked the system into their network. I just did the medical part."

The idea made sense. Given the doctor's apprehension with the program, this had been his fail-safe device, in case any of the operatives went off the reservation. He would be able to pinpoint their locations, and the Palmetto could send someone to terminate them. The only problem was, he got canned before any of that happened, and nobody else knew about the system. Until now.

Whitehall continued. "Blaine was furious when I told him about it. I might have mentioned the capability at the time, if security hadn't ushered me out like a traitor. The senator wanted terribly to get his hands on that flash card, and I'm not sure why, now that the program has been decommissioned."

Sam wondered about that himself. Why would Blaine want the card enough to send two thugs with orders to kill to get it?

The doctor staggered into the kitchen again and Sam waited for him to return. All this talk had been too much for the old guy. Or maybe he just started every day with a six-pack.

When he returned, Sam said, "How can we identify someone on the tracking system? My technician said he just saw pulse points on the screen."

"It's complicated. Ring him up, and I'll tell him how to do it."

After getting J.T. on the line and telling what he'd learned, Sam handed the phone to the doctor. Whitehall explained something about a hidden table that cross referenced names with pulse-point numbers.

When he got the phone back, Sam said to J.T., "You have what you need?"

"Yep. I found the table the guy mentioned. Marlon Knox is number six." He clicked the keyboard a few more moments and said, "The coordinates indicate he's on US-1 below Key Largo, traveling south. Maybe heading back to Iguana Key."

Knox probably had hung around long enough to see if Ford survived, intending to finish him off if he had to. The cop posted at the ICU might have put the kibosh on that. Sam thanked Whitehall and left.

Back in the car, he told Jack about the tracking system and J.T.'s call. "You want to take a ride to the Keys?"

"Sure. I could give the new car a good blowout."

Sam called Lora and told her she could go ahead and leave, that Jack was going to take him back to Iguana Key.

"Thanks for letting me know. I could have been gone an hour ago if I'd known that."

"Sorry. I'll call you tonight."

"Don't bother." She hung up.

Two hours later, they were well past Marathon, nearing Bahia Honda. Sam spotted Lora's car in the side mirror. How did she do that? He remembered the look of suspicion she'd given him when she left Jack's place. Had she followed them from the beginning, to Windhaven, and then to Whitehall's, and just told him she was at the hospital? She could easily have arranged to meet him in the hospital parking lot, and he wouldn't have known any difference. Ever the reporter, after the story.

J.T. called to say that Knox had turned off on Big Pine Key and was traveling inland.

"How about Benetti?" Sam asked. "Does he show up on the map? That could be where Knox is headed."

"Hold on." A few moments later J.T. said, "Here he is, at a spot on the tip of Big Pine, on the Gulf side. He's a few miles farther down The Keys from where Knox is heading."

"Okay, we'll deal with that later. You think you can intercept Knox from where you are?"

"Yeah, I do. I got in the car a half hour ago."

When they hung up, Sam turned to Jack. "I thought you said something about a blowout. You're barely breaking the speed limit."

Jack gave him a cool, sidelong glance, and the BMW surged, pinning Sam's back to the seat.

Sam called Simone and brought her up to date on the tracking system and on following Knox.

"You catch up with Cates?" Sam asked.

"Yes, he's been all over the place. Now he's headed up US-1. I'm trailing a safe distance behind his car, about twenty miles north of Iguana Key."

"Okay, stay with him. He might know something we don't." He thought about asking if she'd brought her gun and ammo, but decided she'd be insulted if he did.

TWENTY-ONE

HARPO WENT TO the funeral home tool shed and found the machete. He had used it to clear brush at a cemetery a few months before. In his younger days, he had cut cane with a blade like this one, and was skilled in throwing it at a target.

Using the bench grinder in the corner, he shaped the tip to a sharp point. When he finished, he turned and threw it at the wood door. It spun a couple of times, bounced off, and clattered to the floor. Next try: same result. On the third attempt, the tip found its mark with a satisfying *thud*. He pulled it out and thought he could feel a pulse racing down the handle to his fingers. It would do just fine.

The key for the maroon hearse hung from the wall in the garage. He pushed it into the ignition and fired up the big machine. Sitting there, listening to the engine hum, he thought about what he had to do. The bad dude had killed Alton, and nearly killed him, too. There had to be a reason why he'd done that, and it probably had something to do with the body they were transporting. Probably had killed that poor guy, too. The law did a great job of rousting homeless people, but they stunk in the criminal-catching department. No matter. Harpo planned to put things back on track.

One morning a month or so ago, he had come out of the marina tool shed where he'd slept the night be-

fore and had seen the dude getting onto a nice old boat.
That's where he would go first. He put the vehicle into
gear and eased it out of the mortuary's carport and down
the drive to the highway. Dr. Eddie Worth belted out a
sermon inside Harpo's head, telling the flock just how
hot brimstone would get for sinners who didn't listen.
The program faded as another frequency tried to horn
its way in. Harpo tapped his temple with his knuckle
and the doctor returned, loud and clear. A couple minutes later the holy man's voice trailed off to a whisper
as he eased into a rendition of "Come Home." Harpo
hummed along with the slow, sad song, and when it
ended, a news program came on. He tuned it out, having learned how to do that over the last couple of days.
The trip took about an hour, and Harpo arrived to find
the cruiser moored at the spot where he'd seen it before.
He pulled the hearse into a thicket of mimosa trees, got
out, and eased through the brush toward the water, the
machete hanging from his hand by his side.

"WHERE ARE YOU?" Sam asked J.T.

"A couple of miles inland. According to the GPS,
Knox is going about fifty, so he probably doesn't know
anybody is after him yet. How about you?"

"About thirty miles from the turn-off. Jack's got his
BMW on ninety."

"You're with Jack? Tell him I said hello. On second
thought, put me on the speaker."

Sam punched the button on the phone and told him
to go ahead.

"Jack, how's it going, buddy?"

Jack smiled. "Going okay, J.T. And you?"

"You know me. I'm doing great. I hope you'll let me know the next time you have something big cooking."

"You got it." Jack glanced at Sam and ran his fingertip across his throat.

Sam turned off the speaker and put the phone to his ear. "Okay, call us back when you spot the guy."

HARPO STOOD BEHIND a mangrove trunk for ten minutes, waiting to see if the guy would come out on deck. When nothing moved, he eased his way down the dock and climbed aboard the cruiser. He didn't hear a sound. No cars, birds, nothing. It occurred to him that he also didn't hear the radio, so he tapped the spot that usually brought it back. Still quiet. That wasn't good, not good at all. Though unsure what he should do about it, he pressed on.

Reaching the main hatch, he twisted the handle and found it locked. Probably wouldn't take much to break it, but that would make some noise. So he stepped alongside the cabin to the rear and found another hatch. Peering through a window that made up the top half of the door, he could see that it led below deck, probably to the sleeping compartments. This boat was at least forty feet long, so it probably had rooms for two or three beds, maybe a bath. He twisted the handle. Locked. The machete had a thin blade, so he inserted it into the gap between the door and the jamb, and the door popped open.

What if the guy was sleeping? Would he be able to slay him in his sleep? What if he had a camera on deck and saw Harpo, and he waited down below with a gun or a knife. *All these questions!* He tapped his temple, trying to get the signal back. Nothing. How could he do this without the signal? That's what brought him here in the first place. Tapped again. Still quiet. His head went into a spin, and he leaned against the wall until it passed.

He drew a deep breath, swung the hatch open, and pushed inside to a landing and a ladder leading down. The top step groaned when he put his weight on it, and he stopped and listened. Something squawked outside. Retreating to the corner of the landing, he squeezed in as tight as he could.

Just a bird outside. A droplet of perspiration ran down the side of his face and into his collar. He drew another deep breath, let it out, and descended the ladder. At the bottom, he stepped down a short passageway and turned right, where he found the captain's cabin. It occupied the entire space from that point to the rear of the boat. Its door stood wide open, the edge of a king bed visible. Inching closer, he could see into the entire compartment. It was tidy; bed made, clean wood floor, no clutter. About to head inside for a closer look, he heard another noise. It sounded like a muffled voice. He ran back up the steps and peered out a porthole on the wall at the top.

A man stood beyond the dock, on land, yelling, "Come on out. Nobody has to get hurt."

Was it him? He wasn't sure. This guy had the height, but leaves on the tip of a mangrove limb hid part of his face. The gun in his hand tipped the scales, though. It had to be him, and he must have seen Harpo board the boat.

"Okay, I'm coming in," the man said. "If you're there, you better drop your weapons or there's going to be some bloodshed."

Harpo gripped the machete and wondered what he should do. If he went out, the guy would kill him, of that he had no doubt. He'd already tried to kill him once, and would surely hit his mark given a second chance. The machete would be no good against a bullet. And now his beacon had forsaken him. That had to be a sign. A bad one.

He squeezed into the corner, hopefully out of the line of sight from the porthole or the window in the hatch. Noise came from the forward hatch knob, the guy, probably forgetting he locked it. Then the sound of footfalls trailed down the side of the cabin, stopping at the rear hatch. Harpo wanted to look, but the guy probably stood there trying to see inside. The lock handle twisted, and he squeezed tighter into the corner. Maybe the guy would just go down the ladder and not look his way.

But no. As the man entered, he turned, saw him in the corner, and swung the gun toward his face. Harpo's heart felt as if it might explode, and he could hear the roar of blood coursing through his ears. He swung the machete toward the gun hand, felt steel clash against steel, and the gun fired. It sounded like a bomb in the close quarters, and then it clattered to the deck. Harpo rammed into him, and the man's eyes went wide as he lost his balance and tumbled end over end down the ladder.

Harpo sped out of the open hatch and back to the dock. He seemed to fly over the boards and across the ground like a swooping bird, not remembering his feet ever touching down. When he got to the hearse, and jerked on the door handle, someone said, "Hey, you there, drop the knife and turn around."

Looking over his shoulder, he saw a beautiful woman with long black hair. She wore tight jeans and a T-shirt. And held a gun pointed at his head. Police? No, he didn't think so, but she had an expression on her face that said she would shoot him where he stood if he didn't do as she said. He tossed the machete to the ground and turned to face her.

"Who are you?" she asked.

"I'm Harpo. I work at the mortuary. Call 'em, they'll tell you."

"I don't think they'll be telling anybody anything. They're all dead over there. Did you kill them?"

Dead? He'd just seen Mr. Tim a few days ago. Tears poured from his eyes and streamed down his face. Wiping them with his sleeve, he said, "I didn't kill anybody. How could they be dead?"

"Somebody broke the girl's neck and stabbed the old man with a trocar. You do that?"

"Did they die because of me?"

The woman's face changed, softened, and she dropped the gun to her side "Probably not. I heard the shot a minute ago. Did you shoot the policeman on the boat?"

"Policeman? No, I thought he was the man who killed my friend, and he tried to shoot me. I hit him and he fell down the ladder."

Glancing toward the boat, she sighed and said, "Let's go take a look."

She motioned for him to lead the way. He didn't want to, but didn't think he had any other choice. They reached the ladder where the man had fallen. He lay at the bottom, unconscious.

"You first," she said. She followed him down and checked the man for a pulse.

"He'll live," she said. She took a quick scan around and came back. The policeman's head twitched, and he seemed to be waking up.

They climbed back up the stairs, past the policeman's gun on the deck, and went back to the hearse.

"I need to talk to you," she said as she eyed the vehicle. "Get in this thing and follow me." She started to walk away and turned back. "If you try to lose me, you'll be sorry." Smiling, she headed into the woods and drove out in a late model car going toward the highway.

Harpo started the hearse, backed out of the mimosas, and followed. Wind stirred the trees and water droplets sprinkled the windshield. On the highway, they drove for a couple of miles, and she turned into the parking lot of a convenience store. She parked close to the street, away from customers' cars, and he pulled in next to her. When she motioned for him to join her, he got out of the hearse and into her car. The rain had gotten heavier, and she had the wipers going.

"Okay, now, tell me about this guy killing your friend."

"He shot me and Alton and blew up the hearse. The Lord spared me, but Alton wasn't so lucky." He gave her the details of that night and what had happened in the days since.

"So you recognized this guy and thought he might be on that boat?"

"Yeah. I saw him there not long ago. I don't think he saw me, though, so he probably blew up the hearse because of the body."

"That's the John Doe they found murdered a few months ago?"

"Yeah, how'd you know?"

She narrowed her eyes, staring at his face. "Turn your head and look at me."

He did as she asked and she said, "What's that?" and reached toward the tender spot where the antenna had been.

A spark raced from her fingertip to his face, lightning flashed outside, and a clap of thunder shook the car. Then, Dr. Worth came back on line.

SAM'S PHONE CHIRPED and he thought it would be J.T. calling again. When he answered, Simone said, "Cates led me to the cruiser, but nobody was on it. It's tied up at a marina on Big Pine Key. The place seems to be closed down for the season, maybe permanently."

"We just turned onto Key Deer Boulevard, the main highway on Big Pine. J.T. should be close by. He was a few minutes ahead of us trailing Knox."

"I'm next to the highway at a convenience store, so I'll watch for him. On another subject, you remember the hearse that got blown up on a bridge over Blackwater Sound, and the cops didn't think anybody survived?"

"Yeah?"

"Well, one of the guys did, and he's here with me now. He saw Knox that night, and remembered him from the marina we just left."

"What's he doing there?" Sam asked.

"I think he planned to kill Knox for what he did, but he ran into Cates, and Cates is unconscious on the boat. Hey! I just saw J.T. go by."

"Go after him, and keep the line open so you can give me directions."

"I'm pulling out now," Simone said. "He's maybe a quarter mile ahead."

Sam brought Jack up-to-date on what Simone had said. Big drops of rain blew against the windshield, so Jack turned on the wipers and slowed down. They turned onto it a few minutes later and passed a convenience store. Soon after that, Sam saw Simone's car. J.T. had probably slowed to keep Knox from suspecting a tail. The convoy traveled another mile or so before turning toward the northeastern coast of the island into a posh subdivision. Flowing front lawns led down to modern Mediterranean mansions, with swimming pools and boathouses in back.

J.T. had turned into a wide driveway of one of the homes that had a For Sale sign in the front yard. Simone turned in behind him, and Jack followed. Sam got out and hurried to catch up with J.T., who was already trotting into the yard of the house next door.

"Where is he?" Sam asked as he ran alongside, rain pelting his face.

"He's on a motorcycle. Turned into a driveway a couple of doors down and headed toward the back yard. I think he saw me, because he sped up the last mile or so."

They cut behind the house all the way to the water's edge, skirted it over to the property where Knox had turned in, and stopped behind a thicket of palmetto. The place appeared vacant, maybe a vacation home for somebody with a lot of money. A pool lay directly behind the house with a cover over it, and a boathouse large enough for someone to live in sat at the edge of the water. A dock ran about forty feet out. Knox wasn't anywhere in sight.

"You sure he didn't go inside the house?" Sam asked.

"No, but I thought he probably came all the way back here."

Sam caught a whiff of gas-and-oil smoke, a giveaway for a two-stroke engine. He wiped rain from his eyes with his sleeve. "He's back here. Let's check the boathouse."

A double-wide door secured the structure on the house side. With their guns out, one on each side of the door and under the boathouse eave, Sam checked the lever handle. Wouldn't budge. He took a pick from his wallet and worked it for a couple of minutes before the mechanism snapped. Assuming their positions again, Sam twisted the handle and swung the door inward. Leaning around the edge of the entranceway, he saw a wall about five feet high with a stairway at its center leading down to a lower level.

An engine started up somewhere beyond the wall. It sounded large and powerful. Sam motioned for J.T. to follow and led the way to the stairway. By the time he reached it, the engine roared, and a boat shot out of a slip down below traveling away from them into open water. It was a Cigarette racer, and the man piloting it wore a motorcycle helmet with a tinted face shield. It had to be Knox. A small motorcycle stood atop the rear deck, strapped to a transport rack. The front end of the boat rose about a foot above the water before bouncing back and reaching a plane. Knox peered back over his shoulder, swung his arm around, and fired a shot that hit the corner of the wall next to Sam's face. Sam returned fire, and Knox spun around and fell to one side when the round struck him in the back. The racer kept going, putting distance between it and the dock. More shots by Sam and J.T. missed their target, the Cigarette now more than a hundred yards away and gaining speed.

TWENTY-TWO

THE PHONE SOUNDED off and Sam looked at the display: Simone.

"You better get out of there," Simone said. "I heard a siren, probably the Big Pine PD."

They put their guns away, opened the door, and stepped out into the rain. Retracing their steps along the back of the property, they headed toward the cars. Sam gazed out at the water. Knox had disappeared into the Gulf, leaving only ripples in his wake. A Cigarette might go sixty or seventy knots and could already be a mile away.

At the cars, Sam told Jack that he would ride with J.T.

"Okay, unless you need me for anything, I'm going back to Miami."

"Sure. Thanks for the ride."

J.T. suggested that Sam drive. He backed out and pulled away, and Simone followed within a few seconds. Spreading out, they maintained a lawful speed. When they got a few blocks outside the neighborhood, two cop cars flew past, their blue lights flashing. Neither of the occupants looked their way.

"Something's wrong," J.T. said.

"What do you mean?"

"I can't find Knox. He disappeared from the monitor."

"Keep looking. He's got to be there."

"No, he isn't. I've restarted the program a couple of times, and all the others show up, but he's gone."

Something gnawed in Sam's stomach as he thought back about the scene in the boathouse. "Maybe I damaged the transmitter when I shot him."

"Aw, man, that was the only way we had to track him. Why didn't you go for a head shot? At least he'd be dead, and the money might be on that boat."

Blood pulsed in Sam's ears, his face hot. "Hey, I did go for his head. That boat bounced out of the dock like a bucking bronco."

"Okay, okay, forget about it. No big deal. We'll get him."

"What about Benetti? He still on the monitor?"

"Yeah, he's right where he was before."

"Okay, tell me how to get to him. Maybe Knox headed that way."

A few minutes later, J.T. said, "You spend the night with the babe?"

Sam glanced at him. "Yeah, on the road and at the hospital."

"Simone was jealous."

"What do you mean?"

"She fussed and fumed after you got out of the car. I asked her what was wrong, and she said, 'Mind your own business.'"

"News to me. According to her, she's heavy into some guy named Karl."

J.T. clicked keys on the computer and said, "Huh," his attention already turned back to the monitor.

When they reached the main road where they'd entered the island, J.T. told him to turn right. The others stayed behind them. Sam had a hunch they were headed toward the old cruiser where Simone had been.

They turned into an abandoned marina, obscured from the road by mossy oaks, and rode down a sandy road overgrown with weeds. About fifty yards ahead, Sam saw the old cruiser, tied up at a dilapidated dock. No sign of the Cigarette, but the rear end of a maroon hearse shone from the edge of a mimosa thicket.

Simone came over as they got out. "Cates' car is gone. He was waking up when I left the boat earlier."

"We lost the signal on Knox," Sam said. "I think I damaged the transmitter when I shot him."

She gave a slight eye roll, but didn't say anything.

"Benetti is here somewhere, though," Sam added.

"Maybe he's tied up on the boat. I didn't have time to search all the compartments."

The man who had been sitting in the car with her got out. He stood about five-five, had curly brown hair going gray, and hadn't shaved in a week or so. Though he might be homeless, he appeared to be wearing a fresh change of clothes, and he looked as if he'd recently bathed. One side of his face was swollen and bruised, probably from the explosion, and his eyes seemed dreamy, faraway. Maybe not a terrific witness, but if he had seen Knox, he might be helpful in finding him.

Sam asked Simone to pop the trunk, and he retrieved a pair of field glasses. He hurried to where the boat sat and gazed up and down the coast. No Cigarette. When he turned around, Simone and J.T. stepped onto the dock.

"You want to search the boat?" J.T. asked.

"Yeah, hold on a minute." Sam glanced back at the cars and saw Lora drive in and stop. She had been better at tailing them than Sam had expected. He didn't see the homeless man. "Where's the guy who was with you?" he asked Simone.

She pointed toward the hearse. "He said he wanted to lie down in his car, that all this activity has worn him out."

"You think he's the real deal?"

"Oh, yeah, he's real, all right. Maybe your friend at the newspaper knows an artist who could do a sketch from his description."

"Good idea." He turned toward the parking area. "Lora just pulled in. I saw her following us on US-1. Why don't you go over and talk to the two of them about a sketch? J.T. and I will look for Benetti."

Simone narrowed her eyes. "Why can't you do that, and I'll stay and search?"

"C'mon, you've been talking to the guy. He might clam up if I go."

She sighed. "All right, but you owe me for this."

After finding the main door on the boat locked, Sam and J.T. entered by the rear hatch and descended the ladder.

Sam made a quick search of the Captain's quarters and aft closets, and J.T. did the same for the forward spaces.

Within a few minutes, they met back and J.T. said, "I don't think Benetti's here."

"Yeah, let's check out the marina buildings."

They left the boat, stepped to the abandoned office that stood a hundred feet away and found it padlocked.

"Stand back," Sam said. He stood a few feet to the side of the lock and fired his 9mm at it. The mechanism burst apart and fell to the ground.

When he swung the door open, J.T. leaned around its edge and called out, "Benetti, you in there?" No answer. He called again. Still quiet.

They both entered. Sunlight stretched only a few feet inside the doorway. Sam flipped a wall switch, but nothing happened. After a few seconds, his eyes adjusted, and he saw a cot against the far wall. They edged closer. A man lay there on his side, his wrist attached to the bed-rail with a nylon tie. Spent syringes littered the floor. Without the three-day beard, he would be the man in the Spanner/Benetti photograph.

J.T. felt for a pulse. "He's alive."

Sam cut the tie with his pocketknife as the man opened his eyes.

"Who're you?" he asked.

Ignoring the question, Sam said, "We're going to get you out of here, Benetti."

With some effort, he sat up on the side of the bed and rubbed his wrist. "Where's Knox?"

"Long gone," J.T. said. "Do you know the name he's using on Iguana Key?"

"No. He slugged me, and the next thing I know, I'm lying here tied to this bed." He slurred his words, maybe groggy from the drugs.

"You try to shake him down?" Sam asked.

"What?" He frowned. "No, I just called him up. I guess he held some grudges I didn't know about."

"Get off it," J.T. said, sticking his gun tip in the man's face. "We have the flash card with the tracking system on it. That's how we found you, so let's start again."

"Right," Benetti, said, eyeing the gun.

Sam motioned for J.T. to put the gun away, and said, "You offered to sell him the card?"

"Well, yeah, for a fair price. But he wanted it for free. I wouldn't tell him where I hid it, so he's been pumping me full of something he thought would get me to talk. Didn't work, though, at least I don't think it did."

"What about the money you stole?" J.T. asked.

"Knox got it. He gloated about finding it in my hiding place at the motel."

TWENTY-THREE

AFTER PICKING UP a bag of burgers, Sam, J.T., and Benetti headed toward Ford's place.

Their captive gobbled down two of the sandwiches on the way. When Sam asked him about Knox's appearance, he described the man as maybe five-ten and about two hundred pounds, clean shaven, with longish black hair. And he always wore sunglasses, even inside. It didn't sound like anybody Sam had run across in Iguana Key, but it might to Lora. They still needed to find the money, and if they could believe Benetti, Knox had it.

When they got to the cabin, Sam said, "Go take a shower. Bathroom's on the right down the hall." He eyed the soiled shirt and pants. "And toss those clothes. I'll get you some clean ones."

Wondering if he might try to escape, Sam stepped to the bathroom door and peered at the window. Too small for him to go through.

When he got back to the living room, he and J.T. ate the burgers. By the time they finished, Simone arrived and came inside.

"We found Benetti," Sam said. "He's cleaning up in the bathroom."

"Oh yeah? He tell you anything?"

"Nothing we hadn't already guessed."

J.T. pointed at the food bag. "We brought you a burger."

She smiled and grabbed a sandwich. "Oh, man, I'm starving. I haven't eaten since yesterday."

"You get the drawing done?" Sam asked.

"The guy was still working on it, said he'd send it to J.T.'s e-mail."

J.T. opened the computer and punched some keys. "Huh, it isn't here yet."

"Give him a few more minutes," she said around a bite of burger. "Harpo wasn't very good at describing Knox, so I don't know how it'll turn out. I think something's seriously wrong with the guy. He kept tapping the side of his head with his knuckle, as if that might help him remember."

"He was in the vehicle that exploded, right?" J.T. asked.

She took another bite of the burger and shrugged. "Yeah, I guess he's lucky to be alive. And who knows, maybe he was already a little crazy."

Benetti ambled down the hall, wearing clothes Sam had given him. He looked like a different person, after the shower and a shave. Sam introduced him to Simone.

"So, you guys going to let me go?" Benetti asked. He still looked a little groggy.

Simone chuckled. "Sorry, our orders were to recover what you took and bring you back."

Benetti ran his fingers through his damp hair and sighed. "What if I won't go?"

Sam smiled and pointed his gun at him. While the guy might still be under the influence of the drugs, he had been an assassin and could be dangerous. "Oh, you'll go, one way or another. Knox might have given you a hard time, but you opened that door with your blackmail scheme. Your welfare isn't on the top of our list of priorities." Their guest turned to Simone, probably hoping for sympathy.

"Hey, the picture's here," J.T. said, clicking the computer keys.

The other three huddled around so they could see the screen.

"That's not him," Benetti said. "Doesn't look anything like him."

The face looked nondescript, except it had pointed ears and short hair brushed up on each side...sort of like horns. As a matter of fact, it bore a strong resemblance to artists' renditions of Lucifer. Maybe the sketch hadn't been such a great idea.

Benetti had described Knox as having long hair. Maybe the homeless guy just wanted to lead them down an empty trail with the drawing and kill Knox himself. On the other hand, Benetti could still have hopes of catching up with him and taking the money.

"You left Harpo at the newspaper office?" Sam asked Simone.

"Yes. Lora said she'd get someone to take him back to the hearse."

"We should try to catch up with him and see where he goes. Maybe he can lead us to Knox and the money our man Benetti here stole."

Shrugging, Simone said, "It's somebody else's turn on bum duty."

Sam glanced at J.T., who gave a thumbs-up and said, "I'll go."

"I can help you find Knox," Benetti said, eagerness in his voice.

"How could you help?" she asked. "You were tied up the whole time you were in town."

"But I know what he looks like and he said some things." The last part sounded like an afterthought.

"What things?" Sam asked.

"You got to promise to let me go if I tell you."

Sam smiled. "Okay, I promise. Tell us what he said."

"No, you got to be serious about it."

"He is serious," Simone said.

"Then I guess I'll have to trust you." He seemed to think for a moment, then smiled and said, "When I first woke up, after he'd drugged me and put the cuff on me, he said he was closing in on the two million dollars that belonged to him, and he wasn't going to let me get in the way of that."

"Yeah, we knew about the money," Simone said. "What else?"

The smile leaked away. "Huh. Okay, one time he came in stressed out, said he'd just killed two people at a funeral home."

Simone huffed a chuckle. "We know that, too. You're going back to Homestead." She turned to Sam. "Put him in the car with the cuffs. I'll take him up there, and you and J.T. can stay here and search for the guy."

"No, I'm telling you, I know things!"

Staring at him, she narrowed her eyes. "Fine, but it better be good. The people where I'm taking you won't be too interested in due process."

Benetti's face turned crimson. He was probably remembering some things he'd done to prisoners as an assassin.

"But the Palmetto's gone!" he blurted. "All they have there now is a bunch of scientists."

"Don't kid yourself," Sam said. "An organization like that never goes away. It just puts on a different mask."

"Aw, man." He frowned for a moment. Then an ember of hope seemed to flicker in his eyes. "He said something about his father being an important man, that he would bust him out if he got caught."

The words lay there for a moment.

"Did he mention a name?" Simone asked.

"No, but he said he's in Washington."

Sam said to J.T., "We didn't ever find a birth certificate for Knox, did we?"

J.T. shook his head. "Nope."

"Has to be Senator Blaine," Sam said. "His name keeps coming up. You ever check out his family?"

"Yeah, he's married and has a daughter who's a heart surgeon in California."

"Knox could be an illegitimate son," Sam said.

"Yeah, could be." J.T. stood. "I'll go back over to the marina and see if I can locate the bum."

"Okay, go ahead." After J.T. had gone, Sam turned back to Benetti. "Did Knox ever hint at what he does in Iguana Key?"

"He never said anything like that, but I got a glimpse of a car one day before he closed the door of the shack. It was dark, maybe blue or black, and had plain hub caps, like government issue."

"You think he's a cop?" Simone asked.

Benetti shrugged. "Nah, I don't think they let cops wear long hair."

"Could it be a wig?" Sam asked.

"I guess, but he had hair like that the last time I saw him about a year ago."

TWENTY-FOUR

J.T. CALLED AND said he'd caught up with Harpo at the marina and followed him to a beach neighborhood.

"He parked in a vacant lot with a lot of foliage and walked down the street to a house."

"Did you look up the owner?" Sam asked.

"Not yet. The bum is carrying a machete, so if Knox is in there, somebody's going to get hurt. I guess I need to follow him in."

Didn't sound like J.T., but Sam had to read between the lines: *If Marlon Knox is in there, the $2 million probably is, too.*

"Okay, keep us posted."

J.T. called back a few minutes later. "Nah, the place must have been empty. The homeless guy broke in the back door and came back out a couple of minutes later. I'll find out who owns the place as soon as I get a chance."

"You following him again?"

"Yep. He's headed back toward town."

HARPO DIDN'T KNOW where else to look. That day he'd seen the guy at the marina, he'd described him to Alton, and Alton said he thought he'd seen the same man outside the beach house Harpo had just left. But Harpo's memory had been fuzzy since the explosion, and he wasn't absolutely sure he had the right house. Alton had gone on to the great paradise in the sky, so he couldn't ask him. He tried to concentrate. Dr. Worth had finished his afternoon sermon, so he tuned out the rest of the program. They were just advertising cars and fancy restaurants and sporting events, things he couldn't afford anyway.

He had a vague recollection of seeing somebody that looked like the guy park behind Chopin's late one night and go in the back door. Maybe he would head over there and hang around, see if the man came back.

AN HOUR PASSED before J.T. called again. "Harpo parked a block away from Chopin's bar. He walked through the trees toward the place, and now he's just sitting there near the back door like he's waiting for something to happen. One thing's for sure, Chopin isn't the guy we saw on that motorcycle."

"No, but there could be a connection."

J.T. sighed. "Okay, I'll keep an eye on him, but we're probably wasting our time."

"Did you find the owner of the beach house yet?"

"Yeah, it belongs to a man named Dale Edison. Do you know that name?"

"Hmm. Not offhand. I'll check with Lora, she probably knows who he is."

Something nagged at Sam, something he'd thought about earlier, but in the confusion had never gotten around to asking J.T. about it. Then it came to him.

"I don't suppose you wrote down the address on the place where we shot at Knox, did you?"

"Nah. It's probably just a house he found empty and decided to use the boathouse."

"Yeah, maybe, but it could be somebody who knows

him, too. You think you can figure out the address without going back up there?"

J.T. snorted a laugh. "You're kidding, right? Course I can. I'll check it out while I'm waiting."

"Okay, I'll check on Dale Edison."

Sam called Lora and thanked her for arranging the sketch.

"Sure, no problem." She sounded cool. "I guess you had more important things to do in Miami than hang around with me."

"Sorry about that. I got a call from somebody who thought he had a bead on the killer. It turned out to be a bust. Looks like you didn't have any trouble following us, though. Where did you pick us up?"

She paused for a couple of beats, maybe making up her story. "I think I might have blown my engine trying to keep up," she said, ignoring his question. "Who called you with the tip, the homeless man?"

"Uh, yeah," he lied. "I had circulated the photos of the two guys. Like I said, it didn't pan out. I have a question for you. You know a guy named Dale Edison?"

"Sure," Lora said, "he's the local prosecutor. Why?"

He told her about Harpo breaking into the house.

"You think Edison is the killer?"

"Don't know yet. I just wonder why Harpo went there."

Sam decided to tell her about finding Spanner/Benetti in the shed, and about his description of Knox. "Does Edison have long hair?"

"No, more on the short side, kind of a careless, trendy look, like he's trying to look as if he doesn't comb it."

The hair really didn't matter. As they'd decided before, he could have worn a wig when he talked with Benetti.

"Does he look like the sketch your guy made from Harpo's description?" Sam asked.

"Huh, I don't know, maybe a little."

Sam's pulse rate picked up a few beats. "Has he been in Iguana Key long?"

"Only a few months, I'd guess. The editor of the paper said he didn't expect him to be here long, like he might be on his way up. Where are you, anyway?"

Could be him, Sam thought. "I gotta go." He hung up and told Simone about Edison.

Her eyes widened. "Let's get the address and check it out." She cut her eyes toward Benetti, who'd been quiet, maybe wondering how he could get away, or just content that he'd gotten a decent meal and a hot shower after days in the shed. "What do we do about him?"

Sam thought for a second. "Let's tie him up until we get back."

Benetti had been listening, because he jumped up from his chair. "Hey, man, no way. What if all of you get killed? Nobody'll know I'm here."

"You better hope that doesn't happen," Sam said. He pointed his gun at him. "Hands behind your back."

The former assassin did as instructed, and Simone bound his wrists with nylon ties.

"Feet, too," Sam said.

The bound man continued to protest as she tied his ankles together.

When they got in the car, Sam called J.T. on speakerphone and got Edison's address. "He could be our man. See what you can find out about him."

"I already did. He attended a private law school up north a few years ago."

"You get a birth certificate?" Simone asked.

"Yep. His parents are Roy and Cynthia Edison. No brothers or sisters, at least when he was born."

"Could it be a fake?"

"Well, sure. It looks legit, but anything can be faked."

Sam tried to put that information together with what they knew about Marlon Knox.

"What's his age?" Sam asked.

"About thirty."

"That would fit with the law school and his position, but it would be a little old for our man Knox. That is, if it's authentic."

"Yeah, big if, though," J.T. said.

"Well, see what else you can find, just in case."

"Will do, but if you're headed over there, maybe I should drop the tail on Harpo here and help you out. Might be some big trouble."

J.T. probably wanted to be there when they went inside, in case they found the money.

"Better stay with Harpo. Why don't you ask him why he's staking out Chopin's?"

J.T. sighed. "Guess that's your call. You want me to get him coffee and doughnuts, too?"

SAM AND SIMONE rode by the house. No vehicles sat in the driveway. He kept going, past several vacant lots, and turned into the yard of the next home down the road. It had a For Sale sign close to the curb. The place looked as if no one had been there for a while; weeds a foot tall, the sale sign leaning to one side, old junk mail on the front stoop.

"Here, put these on," Sam said, handing her a pair of latex gloves.

They strode around the house to the edge of the sand dunes and turned back toward Edison's property.

The rain had stopped, and the sun shone full on the side of Sam's face. Perspiration beaded under his shirt. The breeze from the Gulf felt tepid, no help at all.

When they reached the house, they found the back-yard bordered by a wood fence. They opened the gate and went through to the back door. It stood ajar, the jamb splintered. A large dog portal with a clear plastic flap had been installed at the bottom. He pointed to it and Simone nodded. Sam entered first and she followed.

They eased through a little entrance hall to the kitchen. Though neat, it appeared to be unused, with dust on the stove and counter tops. Light poured through a window over the sink to the tile floor. A shallow pet dish filled with water sat there, alongside an identical but empty dish.

A dining and living room lay to the right. No sounds, except the hum of the refrigerator and the central air. They moved through the spaces. A large-screen TV sat next to the wall opposite a sofa and an easy chair. Sam wondered if the dog might be in the yard, or sleeping somewhere in the house. From the size of the food dish, it would be big, something that might put you in the hospital, or worse.

The hallway off the living room led to a bath and bedrooms. They went down it and checked each room. One had been converted into an office, and had a desk with a computer. They found nobody.

Simone drew a deep breath and let it out, dropping her gun by her side. "Okay, let's search the place."

Back in the living room, Sam said, "I want to check the office first. Can you take the front of the house, in case he comes home?"

"Yeah, that's fine."

Something made a clicking noise beyond the kitchen.

They both stopped and listened, and then peered out the double windows to the front yard. No cars had arrived, and Sam didn't hear any footsteps, then he realized the source of the noise.

"The dog door," he whispered.

"Oh, man." Simone worked the action on her 9mm. "I hate shooting a dog."

"Yeah, but be ready, in case it's a Pit Bull or a Doberman."

They waited a moment, and when the animal didn't come for them, they eased through the dining area toward the kitchen. Sam peeked around the corner.

The animal rushed toward him, but stopped short, as if realizing he wasn't who it thought he was.

"Huh," Sam said, easing into the kitchen. The creature would stretch out about three feet long and had two-inch spikes down its back, like something from *Jurassic Park*.

Simone came in and peered down at it. "What is that?" She backed up and thrust the gun out in front of her.

Sam held up his hand. "Hold on. I think it's a pet."

"You sure? It looks like a dragon."

"It's an iguana. You saw a picture of one on the brochure in the motel, remember?"

She seemed to relax, but not much. "Yeah, but I thought they were little and cute."

The animal sat there on the tile, its head moving from Sam to Simone and back, looking confused.

"Some people probably think so."

"Well, what do we do now? I'm not staying in here with that thing staring at me."

"Maybe it's hungry."

"Don't tell me they eat meat?"

"No, I think they're vegetarians."

Sam eased by the creature to the refrigerator and opened the door. It turned its head as he passed, but didn't offer to run. Edison had probably raised it from a baby, and it trusted humans to not harm it. He found several bundles of some kind of lettuce and took one out. When he dropped them into the food dish, the iguana edged over to it and chomped on the greens.

"It's harmless," Sam said.

"If you say so."

Leaving her there staring, he headed to the office and checked under the desk and behind two hanging prints. No safe. In the bedrooms he searched the closets for any signs of the money. Edison had some nice business wear; eight suits that looked like new, more than a dozen long-sleeve oxford shirts, several Italian ties, and three pairs of dress shoes with trees inside. He didn't have much in the way of casual clothes.

Sam didn't find any money, but he did uncover a stash of cocaine in a box on the shelf of one of the closets. It amounted to several ounces, and probably had cost the guy a lot of money. Unless he was Knox and had it left over from drug dealing a long time ago. The nightstands yielded nothing but some months-old magazines. The spark Sam had experienced earlier about Edison had diminished to a flicker. Even with the drugs, this man didn't sound like assassin material.

Back in Edison's office, Sam sat down at the desk. The computer seemed to be running, so he punched a key and the screen lit up. A click on the e-mail icon brought up the in-box and a list of junk mail. Sifting through them, he found nothing that caught his interest and closed it. There were no word processing documents, other than samples that came with the computer. On the browser, he checked the favorites and found one for webmail. Opening it brought up a different mail system altogether, and the inbox list gave his pulse a spike. All the messages appeared to be sent to the chief of police. Edison's name didn't appear anywhere as a copy recipient.

Most of the messages were about mundane administrative issues, or newsletters from police organizations from which he had subscribed. A couple of them caught his eye, from the parole officer Lora had mentioned, but they didn't tell him anything he didn't already know. Sam wondered how Edison could have copies of all this. He would ask J.T. about it.

In the drawers he found a file folder containing house receipts for utilities, all but one dating back to about a year before, maybe when he had moved into the house. The one exception was a rent receipt for an apartment in Miami, dated about six months before the others began. Sam knew that particular apartment complex. Most of its renters were low wage, so Edison might have been down on his luck at the time, maybe jobless.

A second folder held documents that pertained to his position in Iguana Key, one of which indicated that he'd been hired into the job a little more than a year before. Another document was his latest performance appraisal, signed by the mayor. The man gave him an average rating, citing weaknesses in initiative and reporting timeliness. Seemed odd for a professional person, like somebody not really paying attention to the job. The cocaine might explain that, but the guy might have other things on his mind, too.

When he got to the back of the folder, Sam found a small piece of paper, a corner that had been torn off an official document of some kind. Part of a government seal was still visible, but he couldn't identify it. He put it into his pocket, closed the drawers, and went back to the living room.

"I didn't find anything," Simone said.

He told her about the cocaine and the computer.

"You mean like a mirror image of the chief's e-mail?"

"That's what it looked like. I'm wondering what it means that he has access to them on his computer."

"Maybe he was just investigating the guy. He's the prosecutor, and he might've gotten a court order. Boozler did disappear under a cloud."

"Yeah, maybe. But if Edison is Marlon Knox, he could have been waiting for something to show up that pertained to the two million, too."

He pulled out the paper fragment and showed it to her.

"Huh. Looks like the DEA seal to me."

TWENTY-FIVE

A CAR DOOR slammed outside and Sam peeked through the curtains.

"It's a man in a suit, probably Edison."

"Okay, quick assessment time," Simone said. "Do we take this guy down?"

Sam shook his head. "I don't have a good feeling about it. If we're wrong, we could go to jail."

"Yeah, I agree. Let's go."

They stepped around T-Rex, as Simone had named the iguana, and went out the back door. When Edison ambled toward the front stoop and out of their view, they headed through the gate and retraced their steps to the car.

Back behind the wheel, Sam said, "Let's wait out by the street for a while and see what happens."

About ten minutes later, two police cruisers approached Edison's house from the other way and turned into his driveway.

"If he was Knox," Sam said, "I don't think he would call the police about the break-in."

"Yeah, but he still might be connected. He did have the cocaine stash. Not exactly your average prosecuting attorney."

Sam turned the car onto the street and pointed it back toward Ford's cabin.

"Call J.T. and see if he talked to Harpo," Sam said.

Simone got him on the line and put the phone on speaker.

"He said he thought he remembered seeing our man going in at Chopin's one night," J.T. said, "but lots of people go into a place like that, especially if it's the only game in town."

"That's all he said?" Sam asked.

"Yep. You find anything at Edison's place?"

"Not much," Sam said. He told him about the cocaine, the e-mails, and the rest.

"Huh, I don't know. What if he's helping Knox, hoping Boozler would say something on his e-mail about the two million?"

"Why would he do that?" Sam asked.

"Well, I don't know. I'm just trying to fit this guy into the equation. If he isn't Knox, he might be a friend or a relative."

Sam hadn't thought about that. He'd assumed Knox to be a lone wolf. In his kind of business, he probably wouldn't have many friends, but Edison could be a relative.

"That might explain what we found," Simone said.

Sam shook his head, not too sure they had hit on any plausible answer. He said to J.T., "Can you dig a little deeper on him and see if he had any family that would fit Knox's description?"

"Sure, soon as I get back to the place."

"Okay, see you there."

Simone broke the connection. They rode in silence for a few minutes and passed Chopin's bar. The rear end of the maroon hearse hung from the edge of a pine thicket about fifty feet down the road. When they got closer, Sam saw Harpo nearing the big vehicle. J.T. had already gone.

Sam had an idea. "Why don't we take Harpo back to talk with Benetti? Both of them have seen Knox, but they have different takes on his description. Maybe something will click."

Shrugging, Simone said, "Worth a try."

They pulled in next to the hearse and the homeless guy stopped and turned around, probably ready to run. A guy like him wouldn't like all this attention.

"I'll go get him," Simone said.

When the car stopped, she got out and called his name. He waited for her to catch up.

They talked for a minute or so, saying things Sam couldn't hear, the guy smiling and nodding. He obviously liked her looks. Who wouldn't? She turned around and headed to the car, with him following.

Back on the road, Simone said, "Listen to this." She turned in her seat to face Harpo sitting behind Sam. "Tell us again why you went to that beach house."

"I told the other man, and he said you wouldn't put me in jail because of the door."

"No, we're not the police. Nobody's going to tell them you broke the door open. But why did you go there?"

"I told my friend Alton—he's dead now—about the man I saw at the marina, and he thought he'd seen him at that beach house. But I don't know if it was the right one."

"What do you mean?"

"Alton said it was the house next to the one for sale. But after I left and had a chance to think about it, I decided he could've been talking about the one on the other side."

Simone took out her phone. "I'll call J.T. and ask him who lives there."

Sam slowed the car, made a U-turn, and headed back toward the beach houses.

After a few moments, she said, "He doesn't answer."

"That's okay. We can check out the place."

They drove by the home for sale and kept going past a couple of vacant lots. Sam stopped the car in front of the next house down the road. This one looked older than Edison's, and its stucco walls had vines growing up the sides. The screen door appeared to be warped, maybe from water damage, and stood ajar. Several tiles on the roof were missing. A fifty-seven Cadillac convertible sat under a metal awning. It had a flat tire, and its poor condition gave Sam the impression that it might have been parked there like that for a long time.

"You think anybody's home?" Sam asked.

Simone shrugged. "That old car doesn't look like it runs. I'd guess whoever lives here has gone somewhere in another vehicle. Let's check it out."

He backed up and hid the car in the yard they had used before.

"Wait here," Sam said to Harpo, who sat with his head bowed, eyes closed. "We'll be back in a few minutes."

Harpo never looked up. His lips moved without sound, as if lip-syncing a song…or saying a prayer. A man lived inside there, but Sam wondered about his sanity. And at that moment, the idea of following his directions searching for a killer seemed pretty insane, too.

They got out and tracked to the rear of the property.

No fence, just a back door with peeling paint. Wearing the gloves again, Sam stepped onto the stoop and twisted the knob. To his surprise, the door opened. The owner might have left it unlocked, but someone could be inside, too. He pulled his gun and glanced back at Simone. She motioned for him to go ahead and followed him in.

Unlike Edison's home, the kitchen here had been used a lot. Dirty dishes and pans cluttered the sink. Empty paper bags from fast-food restaurants lay on the counter among wadded burger wrappers and unused napkins. They pushed through to a dining room. The table had been pushed to one wall, and a single chair sat under it. A flat-panel TV about twenty inches wide sat on one corner. Empty beer bottles and more fast-food bags kept it company. A roach raced across the table surface and down one leg.

Sam listened for noise, but didn't hear any. Simone touched his arm and pointed to a door swung back to within a foot of the wall. He pointed the gun toward it and nodded for her to pull it back. She did, and its hinges squeaked, but nobody stood behind it. They moved through the room to the hallway, down past an empty bathroom to one of two bedrooms. The door stood open. No bed. Boxes littered the floor space.

A few feet farther, the door to the second bedroom hung ajar. As Sam reached to bump it with his toe, he heard a noise. He stepped to the side and flattened himself against the wall. Simone did the same on the other side of the door. They waited for a couple of moments and nothing happened.

With his gun at the ready, Sam said, "I hear you in there. Come out with your hands in the air!"

All quiet.

His pulse pounded in his ears as he eased back to the door and kicked it open. It swung back and banged against the wall inside. From the doorway he could see that the window stood wide open in the empty room. They entered and he went to the window and peered out. A cheap aluminum screen lay in the shrubbery, its frame bent as if someone had stepped on it. He climbed through to the ground and ran to the edge of the yard. Nothing moved up or down the street. Then a car careened onto the street from the vacant lot next door and sped away. Sighing, he relaxed, and even laughed to himself.

Simone met him at the front door and let him in.

"Did you see who it was?"

"Yeah, it was J.T."

"What?" Her eyes narrowed. "I told you about him. He could have shot us."

"Yes, he could."

Then a hint of a smile twitched at the corner of her mouth. "Ran like a baby. What are you going to say to him?"

"Maybe nothing. He knew it was us, even before I spoke."

"What makes you say that?"

Sam shrugged. "If he hadn't, he would've shot us through the wall and never given it a second thought."

"You think so?"

"Yeah, I know so."

Simone sighed. "Okay, he must have thought this place belonged to Knox, or he wouldn't have been here. He didn't have time for much of a search, so let's see what we can find."

He took the front of the house this time, and Simone took the rear. Tossing the cushions on a worn sofa, he found only food crumbs. A stand next to a recliner yielded a couple of skin mags, along with a periodical for classical pianists. An odd combination. The TV in the living room sat on a cabinet with doors. Sam found nothing inside but a couple of instruction manuals for the television and a video player. In the kitchen he searched through the cabinets and found a mismatched set of dishes and a couple of pans with spider webs inside.

A drawer next to the sink contained bills, going back six months, for utilities and cable, all in the name of C.R. Crowne. Sam sighed. Didn't ring any bells.

He strode to the bedroom where he found Simone on one knee, her head inside the closet. Eight or ten pairs of shoes and their boxes covered the floor around her, along with a pile of dirty clothes.

"We need to get going," he said. "Probably been here too long already."

Simone stood and shook her head. "This guy's a real slob. You find anything?"

"Not much. Only this." Sam handed her one of the bills.

"Crowne. Huh. I don't remember that name ever coming up."

"Yeah, me, either."

She pointed to the closet. "He has a big box full of shoes in the corner. But I found a stack of heavy books in the bottom. Let me thumb through the books for a minute and we'll go."

"You check the junk room?" Sam asked.

"Yeah, nothing but junk."

"How about the chest of drawers over here?"

"I looked in that, too. There're some photos I didn't get a chance to sort through."

The pictures were in the top drawer, along with some mismatched socks, a couple of old wrist watches with broken bands, an owner's manual for a cell phone, a pair of tarnished silver cufflinks, and an old baseball. There were eight photographs, all old. Sam scanned through a couple, but the people in them didn't strike a chord. He stuffed them into his pocket and checked the other drawers. All were empty.

"Okay, here's something," Simone said from the closet. Down on her knees, she had the box pulled all the way out. "The baseboard is loose in the corner. I pulled it out and there's a hole in the wall behind it. It has cash in it."

Sam leaned in and saw a hole about the length and width of a brick. "How much?"

"Hard to tell without pulling it out. It's in bundles like at the bank, and they're stacked up inside the wall."

She extracted a couple of the bundles and two more dropped down into their place. "They're hundred dollar bills, about fifty in each stack." As she pulled them out, more kept dropping down. It took a few minutes, but when she finished she had thirty-nine stacks.

"About a hundred and ninety-five thousand," she said. "This might be part of the money Benetti stole. Even if it isn't, it's illegal or he wouldn't have it in the wall."

"Okay, let's take it and get out of here."

He found a shopping bag in the junk room and dumped a bunch of old clothes from it onto the floor. They filled the bag with the money and went out the back door.

Back in the car, Harpo still looked as if in a trance. Sam started the engine and thought about the pictures. Before driving off, he took them out. One snapshot caught his eye. It looked old and worn, as if carried in a wallet for a long time. Two men sat at a table in a bar having a beer. The flash and age had bleached out their faces, but both men had long hair and beards, one dark and one sandy colored. The darker one appeared to be in his mid-twenties, the other several years younger. Despite the difference in coloration, their faces had what appeared to be a family resemblance.

"They're brothers," Sam said, holding it up for Simone to see.

"Yeah, and the younger one is Marlon Knox."

Sam remembered seeing an image of the other man the night before. A thin Chopin seated at a piano, resplendent in a tuxedo, playing to the crowd at the Lincoln Center.

TWENTY-SIX

SAM DROVE THE car into the bar's parking lot and pulled into a space on the side where he could see Chopin's car. The clock digits on the dash registered 6:25 p.m. Two other cars had followed them in and parked close to the entrance, part of the early happy-hour crowd. He turned off the engine and took out his phone, but before he could dial, the phone chirped. Jack Craft's number flashed on the display.

"Jack, what's going on?"

"I'm almost back to Miami, and I wondered what you found down there."

Sam told him about them finding Benetti, but that he didn't give them anything they could use. "We did learn that Knox has a brother in Iguana Key, though. His name is Chopin Crowne. Owns a bar, and we're about to go in and roust him."

"Crowne. Huh," Jack said.

"You know him?"

"Well, no, I don't know him, but I remember a movie actress in the eighties named Ava Crowne. She was quite a beauty."

Sam didn't remember anyone named Ava Crowne, and didn't have time to hear Jack reminisce about an old silver-screen heartthrob.

"Let's talk about this later, Jack. I need to call J.T. and get him over here to help us."

"Wait, let me finish. Ava Crowne had a fling with our friend the senator. They got caught together in a hotel in Cozumel. It was all over the tabloids for a month or two. Blaine's wife threatened to leave him, then the buzz died, and I never heard anything else about it. I believe she had a young son at the time."

"So you're saying she could be Knox's mother?" Sam said.

"Maybe. I'll check it out for you."

"That would be great. Thanks, Jack."

"You bet."

Sam broke the connection and looked up to see Chopin getting into his car.

"This might be easier than we thought," Simone said. "Maybe he'll lead us to Knox."

Chopin backed the car out and headed toward the highway. Sam started the engine and waited a moment before following.

"What was that about Knox's mother?" Simone asked.

He relayed Jack's side of the conversation.

"Never heard of her."

"Yeah, me either, but if she is his mother, she might be in contact with him."

Chopin headed inland toward the Iguana Key downtown area. Sam called J.T. and brought him up-to-date, including their visit to the second beach house and the conversation with Jack.

"You didn't happen to go to Chopin's house after we talked, did you?" Sam asked.

"Uh, you mean the beach house?" J.T. asked.

"Yeah. The reason I ask, somebody was there ahead

of us and went out the window. I caught a glimpse of the guy, and he looked a little bit like you."

"Oh, yeah? Was that you? Huh. Well, I went by there, but I didn't get a chance to search the place. See, Harpo told me the same thing he told you, about maybe mistaking which house to go to. I checked it out and found a guy's name I hadn't heard of before. Turns out, it's a rental, and I didn't find a name for the renter. You saw the place. Whoever lived there had been there a long time. Probably not our guy. But I thought, what the heck, I'd take a look around." He kept talking about the house without saying anything important, and Sam knew he was just trying to postpone dealing with why he had gone there and tried to conceal it from them.

"That's okay," Sam said, "just wondered if it was you. By the way, did you ever find out who owned the property up on Big Pine Key, where you followed Knox to the boat house?"

"Oh, yeah," J.T. said, relief in his voice, "I was working on that a few minutes ago and got sidetracked. Hold on a minute and I'll get it for you." Keys clicked, and within seconds, he said, "Wow, you won't believe this. It belongs to Ava Crowne."

Too bad he hadn't done that when Sam had first asked him about it. Maybe they would have been further along. Then again, they might not have known what to do with the information if they'd had it. Jack had only mentioned the affair a few minutes before, and that had been sheer luck.

"See what you can learn about her. Particularly if she had two sons, or was ever married to someone named Knox."

"Already ahead of you, brother," J.T. said, the bravado back. "It says here that she married a millionaire named Adam Crowne when she was twenty and had a child named Chopin. Made several movies, and the last couple bombed. Divorced a few years later, stayed single a couple of years and married her second husband, a struggling writer named David Knox. They had another son, Marlon, and that marriage lasted only a year. She's been a recluse ever since."

She'd probably gotten a fortune in a divorce settlement from Crowne, and stayed with Knox just long enough to give her new son a name other than Blaine.

"Okay, so now we know. How's Benetti doing?"

"He's doing a lot of whining. Says the ties hurt his wrists."

"Well, let him whine. I'm hoping we'll be back in an hour or so."

When he hung up, Chopin slowed ahead and turned into the parking lot of an apartment complex. He got out of his car and went into the lobby. About ten minutes later, he came out rolling a large metal suitcase. He struggled getting it into the trunk and took off again.

"That case looks heavy," Simone said. "Maybe weapons or cash."

"Yeah, I'm guessing weapons. He probably took the Cigarette boat from Boozler, and I assume he got the money at the same time. I can't see him bringing the cash back here, so he probably has that with him already."

Sam followed the killer's brother through downtown and onto the road leading to Ford's cabin, but when Chopin reached the coastal highway, he turned south toward the marina where Sam and Simone had first seen the old cruiser.

"Knox is probably waiting at the marina with the Cigarette boat," Sam said.

"He's making his getaway, and like you said, he has the money with him. So we take him dead or alive."

"Okay, but keep the collateral damage to a minimum."

She huffed. "What? You're worried about Chopin getting hit?"

Shrugging, Sam said, "Well, you do have a reputation."

She grabbed his arm and squeezed in a playful tease. Her fingers lingered a moment or two longer than necessary. Or was that his imagination, maybe wishful thinking? Then she pulled her hand away and turned in the seat.

"What about him?" she asked, nodding toward Harpo in the back seat. "He might get hurt if he gets in the way."

Sam had forgotten about him. In the rearview mirror, he saw the homeless man watching the car up ahead, seemingly oblivious to their conversation, maybe thinking about what he would do to Knox when they caught up with him.

"We should've left him back at the hearse."

"Too late now." Turning back to the front, she said, "The big boy's slowing down." She put the field glasses to her eyes. "He's talking on the phone."

"Maybe the plans changed, and Knox wants to meet him somewhere else."

The speedometer read fifty-two mph. They kept getting closer to Chopin's car, so Sam put his foot on the brake and lagged back.

Several minutes dragged by at the slow speed, and

then they passed a side road where several men sat on motorcycles, their engines running. Sam watched the rearview mirror and saw them enter the highway.

"That's the reason he slowed down," Sam said. "He spotted us and called his friends."

Simone turned to look.

"They're right behind us. I think they're going to pass."

Engines thundered as the bikers cut around the rear of the car. There were six of them. When they got even with the car, the one next to Sam's window yelled for him to pull over.

Chopin's car picked up speed and began to put distance between them.

"I'm going to try to outrun them," Sam said as he floored the accelerator. "If we get waylaid, we'll lose Chopin."

They sped ahead, but their lead lasted only a few seconds before the bikes caught up. As the men passed, the last one to go by pulled a sawed-off shotgun from a scabbard mounted under the handlebars. He swung it around and fired. Even with the window closed, it sounded like an explosion, and the steering jerked to the left as the car slowed, the front tire blown.

Sam wrestled with the wheel, steered to the side of the road and stopped. His face felt hot, and his pulse beat like a bass drum in his ears. A bead of perspiration tickled the side of his face. Chambering a round in his 9mm, he said, "Call J.T. and tell him to go to the marina. He should be able to get there before Chopin."

"What are you going to do?"

"I don't know, yet."

The bikers had stopped in front of them and dismounted. None of them wore helmets. Half of them wore bandannas on their heads. All of them sported week-old beards and aviator shades, and looked as if they could stand a shower and a change of clothes.

Chains appeared in the hands of a couple of the men. One of them looked older than the others, and Sam thought he might be the leader. He stepped up to the car, the man holding the sawed-off right behind him.

"Get out," the leader commanded.

Sam swung the door open and stuck the gun behind his back into the waistband of his pants as he got out. He eased around the corner of the car toward the men.

The leader held his hand up, palm facing Sam. "Hold it right there and tell us why you're following that car."

"He's headed to meet with the man who killed all those people in Iguana Key. We're after the killer, not your friend."

The leader turned to one of the bikers to his side, a questioning expression on his face. The other guy shrugged. They probably didn't know anything about it.

Sam gazed beyond the bikers up the highway. Chopin's car seemed to melt into the horizon.

"Hey, pay attention!" the guy with the shotgun said. "We're talking to you!" He stepped up close to Sam and stuck the muzzle to within inches of his head.

Sam's face felt as if on fire. The decision about what to do crystalized in that moment. He smacked the barrel of the saw-off away with the heel of his left hand, drew the 9mm, and shot the biker.

The shotgun fired wild as the man screamed and fell backward. On the ground, he let go of the weapon and clutched what was left of his kneecap. Blood ran between his fingers. Sam stepped over and kicked the gun out of range.

"Who's next?" Sam asked. He extended his arm and moved the sights of the 9mm over the faces of each of the five bikers still standing.

The men dropped their chains on the pavement. No one said anything.

"No takers, huh?" He pointed the gun at the leader. "Okay, I'll make it easy for you guys. If I don't have the spare tire on my car in five minutes, I'm shooting your friend here."

TWENTY-SEVEN

SAM CALLED J.T. "Are you at the marina, yet?"

"Yeah, since about ten minutes after Simone called. Chopin came rolling in a little while later and wheeled a suitcase into the boathouse where the Cigarette is tied. Knox arrived on the speed bike right before you called, and I guess they're powwowing in there now. What happened with the bikers?"

Sam told him about the tire and shooting the man with the sawed-off. "They changed my tire and I let them go."

The wounded man had moaned and begged the whole time for somebody to take him to a hospital. As Sam drove away, they helped the guy onto the back of one of the bikes and sped off in the other direction.

"Did you get a look at Knox?" Sam asked.

"No. He wore the helmet into the boathouse."

Pretty bold of Knox going back to the place Boozler had kept the boat, after the FBI and the local lawmen had showed up there. Of course, he might not have known that.

"You get a chance to search the Cigarette boat?"

"Yeah, I had a few minutes before Chopin got here. Didn't find anything, though. Unless Chopin brought the money in that suitcase, Knox must have it stashed somewhere else."

"I don't think he would have entrusted it to Chopin. Could be back at that house on Big Pine that his mother owns, though."

"Yeah, maybe. I stuck a GPS transmitter into the corner of one of the boat's pockets so we can track him."

"Where did you get that?"

"I carry one in my bag. Never know when you'll need to follow somebody."

"You can bring it up on your computer?"

"Sure, I already have it blinking on the screen."

"Ah, man, you're a genius."

Simone huffed a laugh.

"I thought you'd like that. Listen, the fat boy is coming out of the boathouse, and the Cigarette engine just started up. Why don't you call your pilot friend Randy and get the seaplane? We can let Knox go on his merry way and catch up with him later, after he's had a chance to pick up the cash."

"That sounds like a good plan. I'll head back toward Ford's place and try to touch base with Randy."

Randy flew a seaplane for a wealthy businessman in Key Largo, and occasionally did favors for Sam, as long as Sam paid him well. They had met a few months before when Randy worked for a loan shark in Miami who was trying to kill Sam, and Randy got caught in the middle.

In the end, he landed the sweet deal in Key Largo.

"Okay, I'll see you back there."

WHEN SAM REACHED the cabin, they found the door standing ajar and Benetti gone.

"That's just great," Simone said. "Back to square one."

The wooden chair where their captive had been tied lay on the floor in pieces.

"Don't worry about it. We have the computer card and most of the money he stole. If we get Knox, we'll have it all."

She sighed. "I guess you're right. I wasn't looking forward to riding back to Homestead with him droning on in the back seat."

They had bought Harpo a burger and dropped him off at the hearse. Though he seemed disappointed, he got out of the car, pointed a finger at Simone, and smiled. "Be seeing you," he said.

Something about his expression gave Sam a feeling of unease, like the guy still might know things about Knox that they didn't.

J.T. arrived a few minutes later and looked down at the broken chair. "What happened to the whiner?"

"He got away."

"Yeah, well, we can still follow him on the scope. Knox headed north when he left the boathouse. I'll bring up the monitor and check his location as soon as I get a beer." He asked if anyone else wanted one and got no takers.

Sam sat down on the sofa and called the pilot's number. It rang several times before Randy answered.

"I hope you don't want your money back," Randy said. Sam had dropped a lot of cash on him a couple of weeks before when he'd flown Sam and J.T. to the Caribbean and back in a matter of hours.

"Nah, I've got another job for you. You still piloting for the guy in Key Largo?"

"Yeah, but I have to take the plane up to Miami in

the morning for maintenance." His voice sounded a little slurred.

"You drinking, Randy?"

A couple of seconds passed before he answered. "Just a few short ones after work."

Sam glanced at Simone and J.T. and shook his head. "Can you fly?"

"Course I can fly! What kind of question is that?"

"What's wrong with the plane?"

"We're getting an instrument error, and I need to get it checked out. It could cause a problem."

So now the seaplane option didn't sound so good, with a drunk pilot and a sick plane.

J.T. came back in with his drink and sat down at the computer.

Sam held his hand over the phone and said to J.T., "You think you could fix the electronics on a seaplane if you had to?"

J.T. shrugged. "I don't know. Never tried."

He could do it, Sam thought. He put the phone back to his ear. "I've got ten thousand dollars for you if you can pick us up on Iguana Key in an hour."

"Yeah, okay. What'll I have to do for it?"

"Just pick us up and I'll fill you in. Shouldn't take more than two hours." He gave him their coordinates and hung up.

"Is this guy a drunk?" Simone asked, her eyebrow askew.

"Yeah, a little bit. Should be okay, though."

She frowned. "If you say so."

Pointing at a blinking dot on the computer screen, J.T. said, "I figured Knox would be headed to the Caribbean, but he's tooling up the coast. Maybe he needs to gas up. That boat has a big tank, but it guzzles the fuel."

"Yeah," Sam said, "but we should be able to catch up if Randy gets here on schedule. Oh, I almost forgot." He showed J.T. the paper fragment. "I found this in Edison's desk. Simone said it looks like the DEA seal."

"Maybe. I'll check with my DEA contact and see if he knows anything about the guy."

They readied to meet the pilot at the dock, and after about twenty minutes, J.T mentioned that Knox had stopped in Marathon. "That would be a good place for him to top off the tanks."

Sam's phone chirped. Before answering, he glanced at the display and saw Lora's number. He opened it and said, "Hello."

"I called about Charles Ford, and he's still asleep."

"That's too bad. I hope he makes it."

"Yeah, me too. But I think things are about to break loose on these murders. I'm rolling onto Marathon now, and I just got a call from a reporter who works for the paper up here. He said he's been following my stories and thinks he knows who the killer is. I'm meeting up with the guy in a few minutes."

"Do you know anything about this guy? He could be the killer. Knox is in Marathon now. We have a tracker on his boat."

After a brief hesitation, she said, "You're breaking up, and I gotta go. I'm turning in at a marina, and I think I see the guy over there waiting for me."

"Wait!"

The connection died. A feeling of dread swept over Sam. He punched in Lora's number, but it went to voicemail after the first ring. A second try yielded the same result.

"What was that about?" Simone asked.

"I think Knox just kidnapped Lora Diamond."

TWENTY-EIGHT

SAM CALLED RANDY BACK. "Where are you?"

"I'll be landing in about ten minutes."

"Okay, we'll be waiting at the dock."

He hung up and they headed out the door and down the pathway to the shore. Turboprop engines droned in the distance, and a moment later the plane appeared above the tree line and began its descent. Randy made one pass, banked a wide turn back, and aligned the craft with the shoreline. The pontoons touched down on the surface of the Gulf and the plane taxied to the dock, the props fanning a salty mist in their faces.

Sam hurried over to the door and opened it. "Don't shut down the engines. We're ready to leave."

Randy gave him a thumbs-up. He appeared hung over, his face and eyes red.

The plane had accommodations for eight passengers, configured with four rows of seats behind the cockpit, one on each side of the aisle. J.T. took the co-pilot spot up front, Simone sat in the first row behind Randy, and Sam sat behind J.T. As they buckled their belts, a figure came out of the woods onto the dock. Harpo. He stepped over to the plane and popped the door open.

"Let me go with you. I can help."

His eyes were wild, as if they belonged to somebody else hitchhiking inside his head. Maybe he *could* help. His information had led them to Knox, albeit indirectly.

"C'mon, you need me," Harpo added. "I know places he might go."

"Okay, get in."

"You're kidding," J.T. said.

Simone shot J.T. a frown. "I agree with Sam. Maybe he knows something."

Harpo stepped around Sam's feet and down the aisle. The edge of the machete blade shone through a hole in the elbow of his baggy long-sleeved shirt. He sat on Simone's side near the back.

The pilot throttled the engines and the plane eased away from the dock. They were airborne a minute later, and J.T. read off Knox's coordinates. Randy entered them into the autopilot system, and the aircraft banked and climbed to cruising altitude.

"Knox is on the move," J.T. said. "He's continuing up the east coast."

Sam wondered if Knox had Lora with him or had left her in Marathon. She hadn't answered her phone on several additional attempts, and that could mean he had the phone, or something even worse. So far, it looked as if he had killed only to protect his identity and further his goal of obtaining the misplaced fortune in drug money. From all appearances, he had located the money. Chopin had probably mentioned them following him, so Sam hoped Knox had taken Lora only as protection.

The plane caught up to within a few miles of the Cigarette about forty minutes later.

"He's stopped at a place south of Key Largo," J.T. said.

Sam put the field glasses to his eyes. From that distance, he saw only trees and a rough shoreline. When the plane descended to a hundred feet or so above the treetops, a serpentine canal appeared, leading inland.

"He's in that canal," J.T. said. He told the pilot to head that way.

Within a couple of minutes, Sam spotted the Cigarette docked next to an old cabin. He tried to spot Lora, but palms obscured his view.

"I saw the boat," Sam said, "You need to take us down."

"I can't land in the canal," Randy snapped. "It's too narrow." He looked fidgety, his face florid, like he needed a drink.

"Then go back to the mouth. I think we can make it on foot."

"That's old man Sherman's place down there," Harpo said.

Sam turned to him. "How do you know that?"

Harpo shrugged. "I lived around here when I was young. Went up to Okeechobee to cut cane. Got pretty good with a machete." He smiled, and Sam wondered what might be going through his mind; cutting cane, reliving good memories of his youth or using the machete on Knox.

"You think Sherman still lives there?" Sam asked.

"Nah. I guess he's gone now. Had to be eighty back then."

If the cabin was abandoned, Knox might have set up a hideout there.

The sun lay on the horizon in the west, a great ball of orange. The Key Westers would be having cocktails on the docks, cheering it on, making a party out of it, thankful for another wonderful reason to have a few more drinks. Sam wished he could be there, rather than here facing the specter of yet another kill by Knox, this one much more personal than the previous ones.

"How long is this going to take?" Randy asked. "You said two hours. That's just about up, and it'll be dark soon."

"I don't think it'll be much longer. Maybe another hour or so."

"Yeah, well, I need to get back before too late. I told my boss I was going out for a quick spin to check out the electronics before I take the plane in tomorrow morning for maintenance. He'll get suspicious before much longer. I'm kind of on probation, already."

"Probation?"

"Yeah. I had a little too much to drink a few weeks ago on a trip taking some clients to the Bahamas. I flew the plane fine, but he saw the bottle I was nipping on. Said if he catches me with booze on the plane again, I'm gone. I come in late, he'll be checking my breath and inspecting the plane. That's one of the reasons I took this job today. If he cans me, I'll at least have something to tide me over 'til I get another gig."

That didn't sound good. He had been pretty handy when Sam needed a quick flight somewhere. If he lost that capability, Sam would have to find somebody else.

Randy glided the plane to the surface, and the pontoons smacked the water unevenly, one, then the other. Sam's bag fell from the overhead compartment into his lap. As the taxi smoothed out, Simone turned to him and frowned.

The mouth of the canal didn't have a place to dock, so the pilot eased the plane in under an outgrowth of mangroves. J.T. jumped out with a rope and tied up to a limb.

Sam, J.T., and Simone jumped out onto soft earth. Harpo followed behind. They plodded through several hundred feet of scrub and briars that ended at a rusty, six-foot chain link fence surrounding the property. Vines covered the steel mesh, hiding the place from outside view. The fence ran out over the edge of the water, probably to keep out the animals, including the two-legged variety. Sam paced around the other corner to the front of the property and saw a dirt road leading through the woods to the place. The fence gate had a padlock with a heavy coat of rust, and he knew it wouldn't open with his pick. He went back to where the others stood.

"Give me and Simone a boost," Sam said to J.T. "We'll go check out the place."

"I don't think you should go," Harpo said.

Sam turned to the homeless man. "What?"

"Dr. Worth said to steer clear of the valley of evil. Old man Sherman was a mean man."

"Who's Dr. Worth?"

"My advisor." Harpo closed his eyes and cocked his head to one side, as if listening for instructions from the stranger inside his head. Obviously Dr. Worth. The machete hung from his hand by his side.

Sam said to J.T., "Keep an eye on him."

J.T. told him he would and gave Sam the boost. He peered over the vines on the top of the fence and didn't see anyone on the grounds. Boards covered the windows of the cabin, probably nailed there before the last big hurricane and never taken down. An old gravel path ran from the back door down to the water. While he knew the boat lay in the water down below the dock, he could see only the handlebars of the speed bike mounted on its rear deck.

When he dropped to the ground on the other side, Simone followed. Though the sun would be gone in a few minutes, glints of it still shone through the trees and illuminated the yard. If they tried to go down to the boat or into the cabin through the backdoor, they would be easy targets. They eased alongside the building toward the front, passing what appeared to be a toolshed built against the house. When they reached the corner, Sam peered around it and saw only an overgrown yard and the vine-covered fence. He wondered if this might be a trick.

They found a front door that stood ajar. Sam nudged it open with the tip of his shoe, his gun out front. Barely enough sunlight shone through to illuminate a kitchen inside. Old beer bottles and cans and empty food containers littered the floor, among a thin coating of dust.

A black spider raced across the top of the doorway and fell onto Sam's arm. His pulse spiked as he shook it off. It scampered into the weeds. Glancing at Simone, he shook his head. He recalled what Harpo had said: *Valley of evil.*

TWENTY-NINE

A VEHICLE APPROACHED on the road outside the fence, and Sam and Simone retreated around the front corner of the cabin. Sam heard two doors open and close, and a few moments later, a clanking noise, as if someone had fired a silenced weapon at the rusted lock on the gate. He peered around the edge and saw the front of a black SUV, like the one driven by the men who had tried to waylay him and Lora the night before. Two men stepped through the gate, one of them the man who had waved the gun at them to pull over. Only thirty or so, he had thinning black hair on top. He walked with a pronounced limp and a constant grimace on his face. Sam remembered the other man calling him Larson, assuming the other man had driven the SUV the night before. The second man wore a sling on his arm. Both had taken bullets, but here they were for another try at the computer card.

"They're the guys who work for the senator," Sam whispered to Simone.

"That means Knox told them we would be here, so he knows we were following him."

"Yep. So much for a surprise attack."

The sun had disappeared, and they would have only a few more minutes of light. Sam chanced another glimpse, and the men had disappeared inside. He called J.T. and told him about them. "No need in falling into their trap. We'll wait for Knox to make a break for it out the back door. The gate around front is open, so watch it in case he heads out that way."

After they hung up, Sam and Simone made their way to the back corner of the structure. They waited there a while, and sometime after darkness fell upon them, Sam heard the Cigarette start up, its engine revving. If Knox had come out of the cabin, they had missed him. They ran toward the dock and stopped a few feet from the sea wall. Sam could see the running lights of the boat down below, but couldn't make out anything else in the dark.

Just as they were about to hop down to the dock, someone turned on a flashlight in their faces. The man with the arm sling stepped out from behind one of the timbers and said, "Stop right there." He held the light in his sling hand, and a silenced semiautomatic, maybe a .45, in the other.

Sam fired and the man fell to the dock. A figure scrambled out of the boat cabin and opened the engine throttle. It sounded like a jet flying over. The bow rose into the air a foot or so and bounced back to the surface as the boat's pilot cut an arc in the canal, turning back the way he had come. Simone fired and must have hit her target. The boat sped toward the opposite shore about fifty feet away. It hit the edge of the bank, went skyward for a few seconds, its engine blasting, the prop singing. It crashed down into the earth with a *crack* and skidded back into the water.

As the noise ebbed, another replaced it. Footfalls behind Sam. He swung the gun around, just as Larson slammed the butt of his own gun into Sam's head. Simone yelled something he didn't understand, and then the dusky world went into a spin. The ground came up to slap the side of his face, but he felt no pain. Someone threw a light onto his face. He stared at the shine on the man's shoes in the dim light. Nice shoes. The guy had spent some money on those shoes.

SAM'S HEAD BOUNCED on the threshold, and he awoke as Larson dragged him through the doorway. His head throbbed, and he wondered about Simone. She'd said something right before he'd passed out, but thinking back, it seemed as if it might have been directed at Larson instead of him. Did he shoot her, too?

"I see you're awake," Larson said, throwing the bolt on the door. "Get up." He had a sizable paunch, and was breathing hard from the effort.

Though still a little dizzy, Sam struggled to his knees and stood. Larson held the gun on him with one hand and shoved him with the other toward a wooden table and chairs in the center of a large rectangular room. Simone sat in one of the chairs, her hands bound behind her chair back, her head slumped forward. The man with the arm sling stepped through a door on the other side of the room. In addition to the sling, he wore only a Kevlar vest on his upper body, and Sam saw a pucker in the chest area where he'd popped out the round Sam had fired at him. Probably had a cracked rib or two.

"You lock the door?" Larson asked.

"Course I did," Sling said.

Larson told Sam to sit down in the chair across the table from Simone. He pulled a large nylon tie from a plastic bag on the table and bound Sam's wrists behind him.

"Okay," Larson said, standing over him. "If you got

buddies anywhere out there, they won't be getting in here to help you, and we've called reinforcements to sweep the area. In the meantime, you're going to tell us where to find that computer flash card."

That didn't sound good. His head pounded. Beads of perspiration rolled down his cheeks.

"We don't have it," Sam said. He wondered how much time they had before the reinforcements came, or if that might be just a bluff.

Larson kicked Sam's chair leg. "We know you don't have it on you, but you know where it is."

"You'd better hope she isn't hurt," Sam said, nodding toward Simone, "or you won't ever get your hands on it."

"You talk big for a man with his hands tied."

Simone seemed to be coming around, her eyes blinking. The only thing they'd get by stonewalling might be some torture. These guys seemed more like the types who would use cutting tools, rather than water boards. If he could just get his hands freed, they might have a chance.

"I can take you to it," Sam said. "Just cut me loose."

"Not so fast. Give me some details and I might consider it."

After staring for a few moments, as if trying to make up his mind, Sam sighed and said, "We left it for safe-keeping with a guy in Iguana Key."

Simone took a deep breath, seemingly disoriented, and glanced at Sam and then Larson. She jerked at her bindings. "Hey, untie me!" she snapped, her eyes narrow slits.

Larson eyes cut her way and then refocused on Sam. "Give me a name."

"The acting police chief, Lonnie Cates," Sam said.

"I don't believe you."

"Don't worry, he doesn't know what it is. And for that matter, neither do we. I asked him to mail it somewhere if we don't show up to collect it."

The big man nodded. "Okay, we'll see." He stepped through the door the sling man had used earlier, which probably led to the kitchen.

Sling man came over and sat down. He laid his gun on the table and grinned at Sam. "Too bad you didn't know we were Federal officers when you shot us last night. We'll make sure you serve some time when this is all over."

"You're not Federal officers," Sam said. "Maybe contractors."

Sling man shrugged, but the grin leaked away. "Same thing."

Larson came back into the room. "You better be right. Somebody with authority is going to see the police chief. That flash card is government property, and if he's got it, he'll turn it over."

Uh oh, Sam thought. Figuring these guys for lowlifes, he hadn't expected them to send someone to see Cates.

A door slammed against the wall to Sam's left, and J.T. came out of a closet, his gun out front. Harpo followed. Larson swung his handgun toward the newcomers. J.T. fired three times before Larson could squeeze off a shot. The slugs knocked him off his feet. Sling reached for the gun with his good hand, but Sam kicked his knees from underneath the table and Sling's chair tipped over.

J.T. stepped around Sam and pointed the gun at

Sling's head. "Give me a reason to pop you, man. That vest won't do you a bit of good."

Sling put his good hand out in front of him as if that might protect him from a bullet. "Don't shoot! I'm not a threat!"

Harpo cut Simone's bindings first, and then Sam's. Larson sat up, groaning, and tore his shirt open. He wore a vest, also. The three slugs looked like shiny new nickels stuck to it.

"They called somebody," Sam said. "We need to get out of here."

J.T. bound both men's wrists and ankles. Larson's phone sounded off, and a moment later Sam heard the sound of vehicles out front.

"That's the guys I called," Larson said. "They're government agents, and it'll go easier on you if you just give yourself up."

"Yeah, right," Sam said.

They gagged the men with their shirts while someone rapped on the door. When they finished, Harpo said, "This way."

He led them into the closet, which was actually some kind of pantry.

Gallon jugs sat on shelves, covered with dust. The wall boards had been removed from a place in the corner about four feet high and two feet wide. Sam heard muffled pounding, probably men at the front door trying to break in.

"We used to sneak in here and steal old man Sherman's wine," Harpo said as he grabbed one of the gallon jugs and ducked through the hole in the wall. The others followed and found themselves in the toolshed Sam had seen from the outside. Yard tools hung from the wall, all brown with rust and rot because of a leaky tin roof.

They hurried out the door of the shed to a dark yard. Harpo led them a few feet to the fence. He lifted the wire from the bottom and made an opening large enough for a person to squeeze past. They crawled through, one by one. When they were on the other side, Harpo stuffed a snarl of vines through the hole and hooked the wire back into place. Sam heard loud voices as they ran through the brush toward the plane. The darkness made for rough going. Harpo tripped and dropped his jug of wine. Sam helped him up, and Harpo chuckled when he picked up the jug and found it still in one piece.

Lights went on behind them from inside the fenced property. Sam's pulse picked up a few beats. It would be a matter of minutes before the men found the hole in the fence. After that, chances of escaping would decline exponentially. He glanced back and saw more lights.

"Faster," Sam said. "They're not far behind us."

They made their way to the point where they had landed. Sam breathed a sigh of relief when the cockpit lit up and the engines began their whining windup. Two shots rang out, and Sam thought he heard the whistle of a round passing overhead. One smacked into a tree trunk a few yards away.

"Stop where you are or you'll die!" It sounded like Larson, maybe fifty feet back. Sam could hear their feet thrashing through the underbrush.

Harpo chopped the rope free from the tree trunk with one swing of the machete, and they scrambled aboard.

"Get us out of here," Sam said.

The pilot yanked back on the throttle and the turboprop engines reached maximum rpm as the plane lurched away from shore. The Gulf had smoothed out, and as they lifted off its surface, the powerful engines pinned them comfortably to the backs of their seats. They were airborne in less than thirty seconds.

"Anybody get hurt?" Randy asked.

"Sam and I have a headache," Simone said, "but I think they got the worst end of it."

"Why didn't you tell me about the hole in the fence before I climbed over?" Sam asked Harpo, who had taken the seat behind Simone.

"I guess I just forgot about it. I haven't been here since I was about twelve."

He closed his eyes and had a smile on his face, maybe reliving the memories of sneaking into the place and taking his first drink of stolen wine. The jug sat at his feet, and he opened his eyes and reached down to pull out the cork that had been there for no telling how many years. The pungent aroma of alcohol and some kind of berries wafted through the cabin.

"I'll have a drink of whatever it is you have back there," Randy said.

"You got any cups?" Harpo asked.

The pilot half turned and said, "In the overhead compartment."

Simone eyed Sam, a questioning expression on her face.

"Don't worry," he said. "It'll be okay." He reached and tapped Randy on the shoulder. "Did you see the Cigarette come out of the canal?"

"Yeah, he headed northeast, toward Miami."

"Did the boat look seaworthy?" He recalled the sickening sound it had made when it smacked to the ground on the far bank of the canal.

Harpo poured cups of wine and passed them around. Even Simone took one. Sam took a sip. It tasted like blackberries, with a hint of vinegar.

Randy took a big gulp of the wine before answering. "Come to think if it, it looked a little different, the bow riding too high. He was moving pretty fast coming out of the canal, and that boat should've ridden on an even plane."

"Could have a cracked hull," Sam said, "taking on water. If that's the case, he'll be getting another boat pretty soon." He tapped J.T. on the arm. "Is he still on the scope?"

"Yeah, he is. He made it to Biscayne Bay, and he's stopped there on shore. Might be at a marina. If he gets another boat, our signal is worthless."

Randy passed his cup back to Sam and said, "Pour me another."

THIRTY

SAM TOOK OUT his phone and saw a text message waiting from Lora. He realized that it had been sent about an hour before, probably while he was unconscious. Maybe Lora hadn't been abducted after all. Or, more likely, Knox had her phone.

He opened the message. *If I see the airplane again, I will kill her.*

Apparently, Knox hadn't discovered the tracking device J.T. had left on the boat, or he would have removed it. But he must have seen the plane more than once and put it together.

No one had said anything about why they continued to search for the man. Sam and Simone were on the hook for getting the lab's half-million back, and J.T. stayed on in hopes of getting his hands on some loose cash. Sam told himself that he wanted to get Lora back safely, but he couldn't deny the lure of that long-forgotten drug money. Split three ways, it would dwarf the fee their employer would pay. Besides, they didn't have Benetti anymore, and there was also that chance that their employer would turn on them once they handed over the flash card. Lots of things to consider. They might need that money to disappear.

Sam wondered about the message. Knox wouldn't hesitate to kill Lora, and Sam didn't want the guilt of that following him around for the rest of his life. On the other hand, the guy might kill her anyway, just to eliminate loose ends.

"I got a text from Knox," Sam said. "He knows we're following him. That's the reason he set the trap back there."

"What did he say?" Simone asked.

He showed her the message and she read it aloud so J.T. could hear.

After a couple of beats, she said, "We could land somewhere close to his location and get a boat."

"That sounds good," Sam said. "If we're a mile away, he won't see or hear the plane."

A few minutes later, Randy said, "Uh oh."

"What's wrong?" J.T. asked.

"The instrument panel is going haywire again. It's doing the same thing it did before."

"So, what does that mean?" Sam asked.

"It's really dark out here, and I can't see anything on radar. It's just like this thing to break after sundown. A couple of hours ago, I would've been fine."

"Can you land us?"

"I'll have to land at the airport, where I'll have lights and a visual of the runway."

"That's okay, we can get a taxi from there."

J.T. guided him in using the GPS on his computer, and twenty minutes later Randy landed and taxied to his boss's hangar. Sam dug into his bag for a couple of stacks of the cash they had taken from Chopin's wall and handed them to Randy. He grinned and told Sam he would be in touch about his situation.

They got into a taxi and headed to Sam's marina. There, they borrowed Jack Craft's car and rode to the location of the GPS signal. It turned out to be a marina in South Miami.

There had been no signal change for the last couple of hours, so Knox either thought he was safe, or had left the Cigarette. When they reached the marina, the four of them split up to search the docks.

A few minutes later, J.T. called Sam. "I found the boat, but he's moved on."

THE STERN LAY low in the slip. It was an amazing craft to make it that far with several hundred pounds of water in the hull. Knox had abandoned it, so he now had another boat or had commandeered a vehicle.

"I'll check with the office," Simone said. "Maybe somebody saw him."

"Worth a try," Sam said, "but it's dark, and there're a lot of unoccupied boats. It would be easy for him to limp in here in the Cigarette and hotwire another rig."

Sam and J.T. searched the broken boat. Knox had taken anything that might tie him to it. The racing motorcycle was gone, too. The police probably wouldn't find any prints, either, if they ever discovered the boat and put it together with Boozler's disappearance. Knox had probably wiped it clean.

When they neared the dock office, Simone stepped out.

"The night guy said the Cigarette came in a couple of hours ago, and the man running it paid for the night. He said another boat, a forty-five-foot cruiser, had the slip next to the Cigarette, and it left a little while later. The owners of the boat were out of town, and he thought they had come back early without telling him, so he tried calling them, but nobody answered."

"You get the boat number?" Sam asked.

"Yeah, I got it."

To J.T., he said. "You think we can track them on GPS?"

"Probably."

She handed him the note and they went to the car. Upon reaching the marina, Sam returned Jack's car keys and headed to his boat.

Simone and J.T. had gone ahead, and when Sam got there, J.T. said, "I found the GPS for the boat. It isn't far from here, going up the coast."

"Okay," Sam said. "I'll start the engines if one of you will get the tie lines."

J.T. said he would untie them.

"Hey, what happened to Harpo?" Simone asked.

Sam shrugged. "I don't know. Guess we left him at that marina."

HARPO HAD WATCHED the big boat for a while. Finally, the killer stepped out on deck, undid the tie lines, and went to the wheelhouse. The engines started a minute or so later, and Harpo wondered where Simone and the two men had gone. He'd walked around looking for them, and that's when he spotted the killer.

If the man got away, he would kill more people, and Harpo couldn't let that happen. Before the boat could pull out, he slinked down the dock and eased aboard, the machete hanging comfortably in his shirtsleeve. He could move quietly and hide like a cat. He'd had plenty of experience.

Dr. Worth had just signed off with a prayer and parting words: "Be on the lookout for the Devil and banish him." Harpo would be doing some banishing, all right, but first he had to rest. All this effort had taken its toll on him. The wine had just made it worse, and he regretted taking the first drink, which led to another and another. Now, he felt as if he might pass out. He found the perfect place for a nap on the back of the boat, inside a big horizontal locker. Several life jackets lay inside, but he squeezed under the locker lid and sank into cushiony softness. There were a couple of inches to spare between his face and the lid. It reminded him of the times he'd sacked out in the display coffins when no one was around. Best sleep he'd ever had, but getting situated in the darkness of the box, he thought this might be even better, except for the heat and the banishing chore he had ahead of him.

SLIPSTREAM CLEARED THE MacArthur Causeway a few minutes before midnight. The beacon on J.T.'s computer indicated that the new boat had passed Miami Beach, going north. It had at least an hour's head start. While *Slipstream* could cruise at about twenty knots, it appeared that the other boat had gone faster than that. If they kept going, the chances of catching up would be slim. Sam did have an inflatable with an outboard, and it could reach about thirty knots with two riders. That might catch up with Knox, but he didn't want to use it unless absolutely necessary, because it would mean one of them had to stay back with the boat. More speed, less firepower. Still, it was an option that he might be forced to take if Knox kept traveling at high speed.

They got lucky. The boat stopped, and they caught up with it in about an hour. As they neared, Sam slowed *Slipstream* to a crawl and asked J.T. to take over. He and Simone went out to the bow, where he used the field glasses and spotted the craft tied up at a private dock along the Intracoastal. He couldn't see anybody on the boat, and swept the glasses to the left. Party lanterns glowed around the back yard of what appeared to be a residence. Several people lounged on a patio next to a pool with lights underneath the water.

"Is he there?" Simone asked.

He handed her the glasses and she put them to her eyes.

"I couldn't make out the faces of anyone," Sam said. "Can you?"

"Just barely. A little closer and I might be able to." After another minute or so, she said, "I don't see anybody who might be Knox. All those guys are middle-age, or older."

Sam took the glasses back and scanned the crowd. Sure enough, all of them were too old to be their guy. "Maybe this is the senator's place and Knox is still on the boat with Lora."

"Let's go by slowly," Simone said, "and check it out."

As *Slipstream* idled past the boat, a man and a woman, both with gray hair, came out of the salon with glasses of wine in their hands and stepped onto the dock. They glanced at Sam and Simone and waved, headed for the party.

"Looks like a wild goose chase to me," Simone said.

"Yeah, I wonder if Knox paid that dock master to tell us about this boat."

"Could be. We could go back and give him some incentive to come clean."

"Might as well. We don't have any other leads."

HARPO AWOKE TO a man in his head selling cars. "How much do you think this baby is worth, Bubba?"

"I'd pay, oh, about twenty-two thousand for that car."

"Would you believe I'm selling it for five thousand off the sticker? Just nineteen-thousand-five-hundred? I must be insane for selling cars at these prices."

The homeless man tuned them out. He couldn't imagine ever having that much money, and if somehow he ever did have it, he surely wouldn't spend it on a car. Maybe buy Twyla and her boy a mobile home with air conditioning.

He heard the whine of a big diesel somewhere in the belly of the craft, and wondered how long he had been asleep. His stomach growled, and he tried to remember when he last ate. Probably the burger Simone bought him before they put him out at the hearse. At least eight hours ago. Surely they had food on this tub, but that would have to wait until his business got finished.

No light shone around the edge of the locker lid. Easing it open a few inches, he chanced a glimpse outside, but it was too dark to see anything. He climbed out and let the lid down. It slipped from his fingers and made a popping sound, so he stood there in the dark, listening to the engine and waiting to see if anyone had heard him. Nobody came running, so he slipped off his shoes and cat-walked down the side of the craft toward the wheelhouse, where he heard a man's voice talking on the phone.

"You need to get that flash card and kill them all, especially Mackenzie. Otherwise, it's going to blow up in your face. The end of your big career. Yeah, well, you should have thought of that before you hired that psychiatrist."

It sounded like he hung up. The guy had been talking about a flash card and killing people. He wondered what kind of card that might be, and why the person on the other end had hired a psychiatrist. Somebody must have been crazy.

He continued his soft shuffle to a porthole close by and peered inside. All lit up in there. The guy they'd called Knox, who had shot him and Alton, sat at the helm, drinking a bottle of beer. He had a towel wrapped around his arm, probably where he'd been shot. Knox picked up the phone and punched in a number.

"Something else. You need to take care of that lawyer in the hospital in Miami I told you about. He's trouble for sure. No, that's all I have." He hung up again and gazed out of the windshield.

This might be as good a time as any, Harpo thought, *while the man is having his beer.*

THIRTY-ONE

INSTEAD OF HEADING back to Sam's boat slip, they set course for the marina where Knox had left the Cigarette, which was only a few miles farther south. When they neared the place, Sam's phone chirped. He didn't recognize the number.

"Hello?"

"This is acting chief of police Lonnie Cates in Iguana Key."

Simone gave him a questioning look.

"What can I do for you, Chief Cates?"

"I'm trying to locate Lora Diamond. Her boss at the newspaper is in a panic. She called him earlier this evening and told him she was meeting a man in Marathon concerning this murder case we've been investigating. Then, before she hung up, she screamed and the connection died. He thinks she might have been abducted by the killer. Would you know anything about that?"

Sam didn't want to say too much, but he didn't want to jeopardize Lora's life, either. Maybe the police could help. "She called me, too, and said the same thing. She had to go, and I couldn't reach her after that. I wondered if something might have happened to her."

After a long silence, Sam said, "You still there?"

"Yes, I'm here. I knew you and Lora had been talking a lot with each other." He sounded like a jealous boyfriend, but seemed to catch himself and continued.

"One of our officers did some research on you and said you were with Special Forces in the Navy."

When Sam didn't say anything, Cates sighed. "I hate to say it, but with the way Chief Boozler skipped out, we're assuming he might be our killer. This job got dropped in my lap, and now I'm down a key police officer, too. I guess I'm in a little over my head and just wondered if there's anything you can do to help us get Lora back."

Lora had seemed to be in a big hurry when she'd called, but it sounded like she also phoned her boss after that. Sam supposed she wanted to touch base and let him know her status, since she'd been gone for an entire day checking on Charles Ford.

"What do you mean about being down an officer?" Sam asked.

"We tacked up some pictures around town of the type of boat Chief Boozler supposedly bought. This morning, a man called and said he thought he'd seen it in Cudjoe Bay, about twenty miles north of Iguana Key. Dudley Crew took the call and went to check it out. When he didn't return, and we couldn't reach him by phone, I sent another officer up there. He reported back that he'd found Dudley's cruiser parked at a marina, but no Dudley. I can't imagine any reason why he would've been kidnapped, so I presume something worse has happened to him."

Crew was the one who'd tried to arrest Sam before the FBI guy came to the rescue. He looked like a guy who could handle himself.

"I think it was a bogus phone tip," he said, "because we got another call about the boat being on Big Pine. I went up there myself and didn't find anything."

"Have you notified the FBI?" Sam couldn't believe he had asked that question.

"No, but I suppose I should."

Cates probably hadn't been any more impressed with Special Agent Crease and his sidekick than Sam had been.

"Well, since you aren't completely sure you have a kidnapping on your hands," Sam said, "you might want to give it a day before calling them. They tend to take over when they come in."

"Yeah, I know. That's kinda what I thought, too," Cates said.

If a forensics team combed over the Cigarette boat, they might find something that would help them capture Knox, and rescue Lora, if she was still alive.

"We went searching for her," Sam said, "and tracked the Cigarette boat to a marina close to Miami. When we found it, it was damaged and empty." He gave Cates the name of the place.

"Really? That's great news. I'll call the Miami PD and get them to look into it." He thanked Sam, a couple of times.

"I'll keep trying to contact her, and let you know if I get through."

They hung up as J.T. came into the wheelhouse. Sam relayed the conversation to him and Simone.

"Wonder how many people he'll kill before this is over," she said.

"It won't be over until somebody kills him," J.T. said. "We need to get whatever information we can out of this marina guy and get out of there if the Miami PD is coming." He frowned at Sam, never one to tell the police anything.

"Hey, it'll probably take them an hour to arrive, and we're about to turn in now."

Slipstream idled into the marina, and Sam parked it in an empty slip. J.T. stepped onto the dock and secured the lines. The three of them strode to the office and found a different manager at the desk. This guy resembled a TV wrestler; long hair, tattoos, and muscle bound. The nametag on his pullover shirt identified him as Stan. A bank of security monitors hung from the wall, covering each section of the marina.

"What happened to the guy who was here a couple of hours ago?" Simone asked Stan.

"He called and asked if somebody could relieve him early. His shift doesn't normally end until 5:00 a.m. You looking for a slip for the night?"

It sounded like the last manager might have come into some money and wanted to go spend it.

"You have any boats missing?" she asked.

Stan stood up from the desk. "Not that I know of. What's this about?"

"I'll tell you what it's about," Sam said. "A drug dealer came into this place a couple of hours ago, and your co-worker let him steal a boat."

Stan's eyes narrowed as he clenched his fists. Veins stood out on his forearms. "You don't look like cops."

Sam's patience was fraying by the minute. After going without any significant sleep for more than twenty-four hours, he didn't have time for this. He pulled his 9mm and pointed it at the guy.

"We don't have time for chitchat, Stan. Take a look at those security monitors and tell us which boat got stolen."

The dock man's eyes widened. He frowned at the gun for a few moments, and then turned to the monitors.

"Two of the yachts are missing." He picked up a log on the desk. "The Carsons signed out a little after 10:00 p.m., but the McCabes are in Canada for the whole summer."

The Carsons must have been the couple they'd followed up to Lauderdale.

"What's the McCabes' boat number?" Sam asked.

Stan sat down at his computer and clicked some keys. A picture of the yacht popped up. It was a sixty-footer, with the boat number clearly visible on the bow. The number also appeared in the corner of the screen, along with a GPS transponder code.

"Print that screen," J.T. said.

Stan complied and handed it to him.

Sam put the gun in his holster and peered over J.T.'s shoulder at the printout. To Stan he said, "We're with the DEA. Sorry about the gun, but we're pushed for time. A drug dealer paid your co-worker to let him steal that yacht, and now we have to find it or an innocent woman will die. We appreciate your cooperation."

"Is Roger in a lot of trouble over this?"

"I'm afraid so."

Stan smiled as they went out the door.

HARPO TWISTED THE lever on the door, eased it open, and stepped inside the semi-dark salon. It was like a plush living room, furniture and all. The helm was to his left at the far end of the room, raised about a foot above the salon level. Knox sat there, facing the instrument panel, his reflection in the windshield. That meant he might also see reflections from the salon, so Harpo got down on his hands and knees. The homeless man crawled along the bulkhead toward the step leading up to the wheelhouse. When he neared the corner of the room, Knox turned around, as if he'd seen or heard something, so Harpo ducked down behind a chair for a few seconds. When he peeked again, Knox had turned back around.

Loosening the slipknot on his wrist, he slid the machete out of his sleeve. The boat's engine suddenly slowed to an idle, and Harpo felt the propellers reverse. *Must be slowing down to moor the boat*, he thought. A minute or two passed as the boat's propellers went forward and then reverse, until the hull bumped against a dock. Expecting Knox to come out, Harpo made himself as small as he could behind the chair.

Knox descended the steps, just a few feet from Harpo, and strode through the salon to the door leading to the deck outside. Probably going out to tie up. The homeless man knew he couldn't stay there, because Knox would surely be looking his way when he came back inside. He saw a door on the far side of the room, maybe a closet, so he stood, tiptoed over and opened it. Inside, he found a tiny room containing some type of equipment. The mechanism hummed like an air conditioner. Though the free space was limited, he sat down in the corner, pulled his legs in, and closed the door.

"I COULDN'T FIND the GPS for the yacht," J.T. said as Sam got *Slipstream* underway again.

"What do you mean? I thought we had the code for it?"

Shrugging, J.T. said, "We do, but it doesn't show up on the tracker. Knox must've ripped it out."

Simone got beers from the fridge and brought them

into the wheelhouse. "Why don't we chill for a few minutes and think about this? There has to be a way for us to find this guy. We have a picture of the boat he has, and he probably won't paint over the numbers tonight."

Sam took a long pull on the beer and set it down. "Can you check on Benetti's location?" he asked J.T.

"Sure, I've been watching him off and on. The last time I looked, he'd made his way to South Miami." He brought up the monitor program. "He's still there, probably in for the night at a hotel or motel."

"Well, we might as well get some sleep and try to pick him up tomorrow."

They docked back at Sam's marina about 1:30 a.m. Sam gave Simone the use of the master stateroom, and he took the forward compartment. J.T. sacked out on the floor of the lounge.

SIMONE WOKE SAM at 6:00 a.m. "We'd better get going if we want to catch up with our guy. I found your coffee supply and made a potful."

Sam wiped sleep from his eyes, got up, and took ten minutes to shower and shave. He pulled on clean clothes and went in for the coffee. Simone sat at the dinette in the corner of the lounge, and J.T. clicked away on the keys of his laptop from one of the easy chairs.

"You have him on the monitor?" Sam asked as he walked through to the galley.

"Yeah, he's still in the same place. I've zeroed in on the location. It's a motel on Dixie Highway, south of Coconut Grove. We just going to take him, or see if he can lead us to Knox?"

He knew the answer J.T. wanted to hear, and this time he was in agreement with him. "I thought we'd follow him first. Maybe he knows something about Knox that we don't."

Sam called a taxi and they took it to a car rental agency nearby. Within the hour, they were headed inland on the MacArthur Causeway. They took I-95 South for a few miles and peeled off to South Dixie Highway. At 7:30 a.m. they turned into Benetti's motel. It had rooms opening only on the south side.

"This place doesn't have a restaurant, so he'll be coming out, sooner or later," Simone said.

They had stopped on the way at a fast food drive-thru for breakfast sandwiches, so they ate while waiting in the cool shade of a live oak in the back corner of the place. About an hour later, the sun had moved over the treetop, and Sam started the engine and turned on the air conditioner.

At 9:30 a.m., Benetti exited his room on the second floor, went down the stairs to a small blue Toyota, and got in. He started the engine, fiddled with the air conditioning vents, and unfolded a map. After studying it for a few minutes, he backed out and drove onto Dixie Highway, headed north.

THIRTY-TWO

HARPO AWOKE AND tried to push himself up, but his legs wouldn't cooperate. Dr. Worth and all the others had gone quiet the minute he'd climbed into the little fan room. Maybe the machine had caused some kind of interference, and without the voices inside his head, the whirring of the blades had lulled him into a deep sleep. Sleep he hadn't enjoyed since the explosion.

All quiet outside. Daylight spilled through louvers in the door. He turned the knob and chanced a glimpse into the big room. No one seemed to be out there, so he swung the door open, pulled his legs out of the cramped space, and stretched them out. They tingled for a few minutes as they came back to life. Full light outside, so it had to be at least 7:00 a.m. or 8:00 a.m.

The machete! What had he done with it? Then he remembered: he'd taken it out of his sleeve and stood it behind the machine. He retrieved it and got to his feet.

Maybe Knox was still asleep. Harpo crept down the length of the room to a passageway where several doors stood open. The first was a small bathroom, and two others were bedrooms that were nicer than any he had ever seen in any house. All empty. He kept going to the far end where he found a closed door.

SAM WATCHED THE car stop at a doughnut shop, where Benetti got an order from the drive-thru. He ate as he pulled back into traffic. Sam waited until a few cars had passed before following. Traffic got heavier several miles up the road as they merged onto I-95, and Sam lost him for a minute or so.

"Don't worry," J.T. said, "I still have him on the monitor. He's exiting onto Federal Highway."

Sam moved into the exit lane and spotted him again. He stayed within sight as they both turned right onto Rickenbacker Causeway.

"Going to Key Biscayne," Sam said. "He must think Knox is out there."

"That's pretty steep real estate," Simone said. "Maybe our Senator Blaine has a place on the Key."

J.T. said, "I checked all his residences yesterday, and didn't find one listed on Key Biscayne. He could own one, though, and have it listed in another name."

Across the bridge, Benetti took a right onto Harbor Drive, which wound around one side of the island. At one point, he slowed and turned into a driveway. Sam didn't think he had spotted them, but turned off on a small side street and pulled into the driveway of a home. A couple of cars were parked in front of a closed garage, but no one was stirring about.

"Let's go," Simone said. "He just went back the other way."

This time, Benetti slowed at an unpaved lane that led through a jungle of palms, pines and live oaks out toward the Bay. He turned in, and his car disappeared around a curve. A large red sign stood a few feet from the road that read: Danger. High Voltage Lines. No Trespassing Sam pulled onto the shoulder of the road and left the engine running. "Can you get an aerial view of this place on the computer?" he asked J.T.

"Yeah, I think so."

He brought it up and studied the screen. "There's a building back there. It's on the bay and has a big boat dock, but there's no boat there in this photo."

"Is it big enough for the yacht Knox stole?" Simone asked.

"Oh, yeah."

Sam wondered if this might belong to Knox, or somebody close to him. "Try to find out who owns it."

J.T. worked at the keyboard for a few minutes and came up with an answer. "It's a company named Geo-Watt. I couldn't find any websites, though, so it could be bogus."

"If Knox is in there," Simone said, "he might have cameras, and we'd be sitting ducks if we went down that road."

"Hey, wait a minute," J.T. said, eyeing the computer screen. "I just noticed something on the Palmetto monitor. A second person is showing up in there with Benetti."

That didn't sound good. Sam turned in his seat. "He must have enlisted another of his cohorts, and told him about the two million Knox has. Do you have a name?"

"Hold on," J.T. said. "Should be on Whitehall's list." A few seconds passed before he said, "Here it is. His name is Morgan Lockman."

Simone huffed a laugh, but didn't sound amused. "That's just great. I had a funny feeling about following Benetti. Now, if we decide to take him down, we'll have to deal with two goons instead of one."

"Don't get excited," Sam said. "This just means we need to back off and think the situation over before we make any moves."

J.T. set the computer aside. "You know, this other

guy could be somebody Benetti brought in. The two of them might have captured Knox."

"You're right," Sam said. "Let's find a place where we can get a good view of that dock and see if the stolen yacht is there."

They drove along the road until they found a house that appeared vacant. The place had a For Sale sign planted in the front yard. It included the name and number of a bank that was likely the beneficiary of a foreclosed mortgage. A two-story palace with a tiled roof, it would probably run several million in a good market. The lot across the street had a bulldozer and a back loader sitting idle, but no workers seemed to be present on the site. Sam turned into the circular driveway of the home and stopped the car near the front door.

Simone picked up the field glasses and said to J.T., "Bring up the picture of the boat."

Once out of the car, they walked around the house to the back yard that led down a gentle slope to an empty dock. It ran about sixty feet along the property. They hurried to the point that jutted out the farthest, and Simone used the glasses to gaze along the coast.

"A boat is docked there," she said. "Hard to say if it's the one we've been searching for, though. Trees are in the way, and I can't see a name or number on it."

Sam studied the picture the dock master had printed for them and handed it back to J.T. "Let me take a look."

She gave him the glasses and he put them to his eyes. The property curved inward, and a stand of palms partially obscured the dock area. He could see the rear end, though, and it appeared that a name on the transom had been painted over, the color slightly different. The hull sides were not visible from their vantage point, but he suspected any identifying information would have a fresh coat of paint. The parts of the craft that he could see, though, were similar to the boat in the picture. "I think this is it."

Back in the car, Sam drove toward the entrance to the property, but pulled to the shoulder before reaching it. "Okay, let's assume Knox is here and we want to go in. What are the scenarios?"

J.T. spoke up. "Like I said before, they could have already captured him. If we can sneak in, we could take all of them, no problem."

"Could be," Simone said. "But all three could have reached some kind of agreement to split the money, too. In that case, we'd have three guns to deal with, instead of two."

"There's another possibility," Sam said. "This Lockman guy could have hooked up with Knox. In that case, they might battle it out with Benetti before we get there." He said to J.T., "Is he still moving?"

J.T. looked down at the computer. "Nah, he stopped, and there's maybe a hundred feet between him and Lockman."

"If he stays put, maybe that means he's working alone," Simone said.

Sam shook his head. A feeling of dread swept over him, and he didn't know why. "We have to consider the hostage, too. Lora might still be alive, so we can't go in there spraying bullets."

Easy to say, but every way he examined the situation, it turned out to be a bloodbath.

HARPO PUT HIS ear to the door and listened for a few minutes, but heard nothing on the other side. He readied his machete, twisted the knob, and pushed the door open with his toe. Peeking around the jamb, he saw no one. The room seemed as large as the living room, and had a big bed, a dressing table, and two closets. A bathroom lay to the left, and he stepped over to it. No one there, either. Everything looked as if nobody had been in the place.

Making his way back through the passageway, he had the feeling the entire boat might be empty. He went out the main hatch and gazed ashore. A metal structure stood about a hundred yards away through the trees. That had to be where Knox had gone with his hostage. The smell of fresh paint wafted by his nose, and he wondered where that had come from.

He strode off the dock and into the trees, and worked his way toward the building. A green car sat next to it. As he got closer, going from tree to tree, he saw a sign that read danger, and something about high voltage lines. Maybe this was the site of a transformer or something, and he wondered why Knox would be here. *Could've just found it vacant and moved in.* Harpo had done that many times. Perfectly fine places that nobody seemed to need at the time. Just going to waste.

Dr. Worth started a sermon, saying, "Who's ready to go to heaven?" He repeated it several times, and the congregation answered each time, shouting, "We are!" Harpo thought about that for a minute. Though he did want to go to heaven, he had some things to finish first. The task of banishing this devil from the face of the earth still had to be done.

"Drop that blade and turn around." *Uh oh. Doesn't sound like the good doctor's voice.*

THIRTY-THREE

HARPO DIDN'T DROP the machete, but he did turn to see who gave him the command. A man stood there with a handgun pointed at Harpo's head. Someone he'd never seen before. "Who're you?"

"I said drop it!" The man thumbed the hammer on the gun.

"Okay, I'm putting it down." He bent over, as if to lay the machete on the ground, but instead swung it upward and hit the guy on the wrist with the sharp edge.

The gun flipped into the weeds. The man's eyes shot wide with disbelief, and he grabbed his wrist. Blood spurted between his fingers. His eyes found his weapon on the ground and he dived for it. As he grasped it in his bloody fingers, Harpo stepped on his hand and he jerked it back, letting go of the gun.

Now prone, the gunman rolled over on his back and watched blood cover his arm and hand. A moment later his eyes rolled up and he passed out.

Harpo took the gun and stuffed it into the pocket of his baggy pants. Remembering bits and pieces of his medical training in the military, he cut a wide strip of cloth from the wounded man's shirt and used it to fashion a tourniquet, twisting it tight with a piece of a dead limb. The blood flow stopped, and he was glad. Other than pulling a gun on him, Harpo had no quarrel with the man. He left him there, stood up, and peered around a tree toward the building to see if anyone had seen him. Nothing seemed to have changed from before.

Cameras were mounted high on each corner. Others were probably on the other side of the place. He hurried back to the water's edge and used the blade to scoop up a glob of black mud. Staying behind trees where he could, he worked his way back to the building, and ran under the eave at the nearest corner. While hugging the wall, he stuck a golf-ball-sized piece of the mud onto the tip of the machete and slapped it onto the lens of the camera. Within a few minutes, he had made his way around the building, blinding three more of the devices. Maybe the guy would come out in a few minutes. If not, he'd knock on the door and see what happened.

SAM PULLED THE rental into a dense stand of mimosa and scrub on the same side of the street as the property. He killed the engine. "We have to figure out a way to draw them out."

"I saw a bulldozer up the street," J.T. said. "We could roll in there with it and tear out a wall. That would bring them out."

"Yeah," Sam said. "That would probably work, but Lora might get hurt in the process. We have to be more subtle."

"I think we can get them to come out on their own," Simone said.

Sam turned to her. "How?"

"Call the reporter's phone. When Knox answers, tell him the police chief in Iguana Key told you that the FBI is closing in on a location on Key Biscayne."

"He'll wonder why I would alert him," Sam said.

"Tell him you don't want Lora to get killed in the

crossfire when the Feds come in with the heavy artil-
lery."

Sam thought about that for a few moments. "You
know, that might work." He took out his phone and
punched in Lora Diamond's number.

The phone rang several times before a man answered. "What do you want?" The voice sounded familiar. He couldn't quite place it, but it had to be Knox.

"Let me speak to Lora."

"Sorry, she can't talk right now."

"Is she still alive?"

"She might be. Why are you calling?"

Sam paused for a moment. "I have some information, but I'm not giving it to you unless I can talk to her
and know she's alive."

"What kind of information?" Tension edged into his
voice.

"The FBI knows where you are," Sam said.

Knox laughed. "They don't know anything about
me, much less where I am."

"That's where you're wrong. If she's still alive, let
me talk to her and I'll tell you the rest."

Several seconds passed before Lora's voice came on
the line. "Sam, is that you? He said he's going to kill me."
She sounded as if she had been crying.

"Don't worry," Sam said. "We're going to get you
out of there."

Knox got back on the phone. "Okay, she talked to
you. Now your turn."

"They think you're in a facility on Key Biscayne,
and they plan to storm the place within the next few
minutes."

He was silent for a moment. "Why would they think that?"

"The acting chief of police in Iguana Key said the FBI got the info from Senator Blaine's office."

After a moment, Knox cursed, then a clatter preceded a loud pop, and the line died.

"Did he buy it?" Simone asked.

"I think so. Sounded like he threw the phone down and stomped on it."

They conferenced their phones and decided to enter the woods from three different directions.

Sam pointed toward the driveway. "I'll head in this way. That's where they'll probably focus their attention." Likely the most dangerous path, too.

"Let's go," Simone said. "If we see cameras, we knock them out first." She took the middle of the woods.

J.T. took the far side, where the trees had been thinned for a utility easement. He said he would go straight to the shore and work his way over so he could cut them off if they ran for the yacht.

"I JUST SAW two guys heading for the dock," J.T. said on the speaker in Sam's pocket.

Sam put the phone to his ear. "You get a visual ID?"

"Not on the first one. He was too far away, but the one in the rear came a little later, and he looked like the homeless dude."

Harpo?

Sam passed the building about fifty yards to his left as he ran through the trees, briars snagging his pants legs. "Okay, I'm on my way. Simone, can you check on Lora in the building?" He almost tripped over a body on the ground and stopped. It was Benetti, his clothes covered with blood, a crude tourniquet affixed to one arm.

"Will do," Simone said. "I'm almost there."

"Benetti is out of commission. Somebody cut an artery and he's on the ground."

Sam thought about Harpo again and recalled the blade. He hurried on and saw J.T. ahead of him, stepping onto the yacht. The big diesel roared to life as he reached the dock, and he leaped onto the craft's deck.

J.T. stood outside the cabin, peering through a door that stood open. When he saw Sam, he said, "Harpo is unconscious on the floor in there, so Knox must be at the helm."

Sam edged forward for a peek through the side of the windscreen into the wheelhouse. Knox stood there working the controls, a handgun on the console just inches from his fingers, a frantic expression on his face. Sam recognized him and stepped back. *Dudley Crew*, the police officer who had tried to roust him.

It all fell into place. Crew had a prime position to observe Richard Boozler's every move, stay ahead of the murder investigation, and wait for the money to show itself. Sam told J.T.

They entered the cabin door, guns at the ready, as the yacht pulled away from the timbers. Harpo lay on the floor in the middle of the room. The wheelhouse was at the forward end, a step up from the rest of the room. It had sliding doors that were pushed wide open. Sam stepped to the far side of the room as J.T. eased forward along the closer bulkhead. It looked as if taking him would be easy, but then Harpo awoke and dropped his machete onto the hardwood floor.

Knox snapped his head around, grabbed the gun, and pointed it at the homeless man.

"Stop where you are," J.T. said.

The assassin turned to him. A surprised expression on his face morphed into a sneer. "Lay your weapon on the deck, or I'll shoot the bum."

He didn't appear to have seen Sam yet.

"No dice," J.T. said. "I'll splatter your blood all over that windshield."

"No, you won't. You're probably after the money, like everybody else, and I didn't bring it with me."

Sam leaped up the step and rammed Knox against the console. Knox sprang back and pointed his gun at him, but Sam knocked it away with his left hand and slammed his right fist into the side of his opponent's face. He felt bone give way under his knuckles. When the man staggered back, Sam twisted the weapon from his hand and tossed it to J.T.

Knox took a deep breath and sighed, as if outdone. Then, like lightning, he spun and threw a roundhouse kick at Sam's chin. Sam jumped back, feeling the wind from the man's foot as it whooshed past his face. He stepped in and kicked Knox in the stomach. The man doubled over, fell back against the console, and slid down to the floor.

"Watch him," Sam said to J.T.

J.T. moved in and dragged the killer to the corner.

Sam stepped to the controls, pulled back on the throttle, and reversed the propellers. After a few minutes of maneuvering, he had the craft back to the dock. *This might work out after all*, he thought. *Get off this boat and take Lora home*. He hadn't heard back from Simone and hoped she'd found Lora unharmed.

As he turned to go for the tie lines, Sam saw Harpo standing. In a blur, the homeless man flung the machete at Knox. The blade twirled end over end, like a boomerang. It struck the killer in the shoulder, and the tip of it sank a couple of inches into his flesh. He screamed and grasped the knife by the handle, pulling it free. Blood soaked his shirt from his neck to his sternum.

Knox stood up and swung the machete in J.T.'s direction, backing him up, and ran for the door. When he got within a few feet of Harpo, the homeless man fired a handgun at his head. It missed, and the killer slapped the pistol from his hand with the machete. He grabbed Harpo by the hair, pulled him close, and stuck the blade to his throat.

"Stay where you are," he said to Sam and J.T., "or I'll cut his head off. I mean it, no one move."

Knox forced Harpo to squat down with him as he picked up the gun. He dropped the blade to the deck and put the gun to the side of Harpo's head. Holding his hostage against him like a shield, he backed through the door. When he stepped onto the outside deck, Sam eased toward him.

Simone came into view behind Knox, eliminating any chance Sam would have for a clear shot.

"Hey, over here," Simone said.

Knox turned his eyes toward her and jerked the gun around.

She fired one shot. The killer's head snapped back, a crimson spot the size of a dime spattering on his forehead.

Harpo wriggled free as Knox fell back against the rail behind him and slid down. Sam strode to Simone's side. The dead man's eyes were frozen in a startled stare.

Peering down at the body, she drew a deep breath and exhaled. "Guess that's that."

J.T. came out a moment later, surveyed the situation, and made a clicking sound with his tongue. Sam knew he was thinking about what Knox had said about the money.

Sam put his hand on the back of Simone's neck. It felt warm and soft. "Good shot."

She turned to him, a thin smile on her lips. "He got what he deserved."

Maybe he did, and maybe he deserved a lot worse.

"Did you find Lora?" he asked, letting go of her neck and dropping his hand to his side.

"Yeah, she's okay. She was in a room in the back of the place. I left her waiting outside the building."

A muted *whump whump* of helicopter blades sounded off from the west. Sam stepped around the cabin to the stern and spotted the craft in the distance over Biscayne Bay.

"We'd better get going. I think those guys are coming here."

Simone joined him. "What about the body?"

"They'll take care of it. Let's go."

When they came back, J.T. said, "I got his wallet and phone. Might tell us something. He also had some keys."

"What about prints?" Simone asked.

Sam tried to remember what he had touched. The guys in the chopper would probably get rid of Knox's body and clean up the blood, but Sam didn't want to get hauled in on a boat theft charge because of his prints. He hurried into the wheelhouse and wiped down the helm with his shirttail. Back outside, he didn't see Harpo and asked about him.

"I don't know," Simone said. "I guess he ran off."

J.T. stepped toward the door. "I'm going back inside for a look around the boat."

The helicopter noise had gotten louder. "We don't have time for that," Sam said. He gazed skyward. "Those guys in the chopper will be landing in a couple of minutes. Anyway, Knox wouldn't have left that much money unguarded on the boat, and he didn't have time to hide it just now with Harpo on his tail."

J.T. stopped and shook his head. "Yeah, guess so. We were so close."

When they got back to the building, Sam didn't see Lora. "You think she went back inside?"

Simone frowned. "No, there was a car out here. She must've driven away."

While wondering if he should check for her in the building, a thought hit him. "Did you ask her about the other guy that was here?"

"Lockman? Yeah, I did, and she said he must have slipped out when Knox did."

"I didn't see anybody else," J.T. said.

Sam could feel his heart pounding in his chest. The sense of dread had remained with him from the moment J.T. mentioned the new assassin on the scene. Now, it was worse than ever, and he thought he knew why.

"Lora is Lockman."

THIRTY-FOUR

THOUGH HARPO HADN'T killed the man, he thought he
had helped with the job. Now he needed to get out of
there as fast as he could. If the police came, he would
be the first one they would blame. Running through
the woods, he came to a dirt driveway. As he stepped
into it, a green car came roaring toward him, its tires
throwing sand and gravel. He jumped back and fell to
the ground as it passed. The driver glanced his way,
but kept going. She looked like the woman from the
newspaper office.

He got up and dusted debris from his face and hair.
The vehicle disappeared around a corner and he followed, hoping for a path away from the death. As he
passed an area that seemed familiar, he remembered
the encounter with the gun-toting man. Wondering if
the guy might have died, he cut into the woods, but
didn't find him.

Angling back toward the drive, he spotted a car snug-
gled into the undergrowth and stepped over to it. The
driver's door stood open, and the man he had cut with
the machete sat slumped against the steering wheel.
Touching his fingers against the man's neck, he felt a
pulse.

What could he do? This went way beyond his medical
training. There wouldn't be any help from Dr. Worth,
either. The signal had died when the bad guy slugged

him on the boat. After a moment of deliberation, he went to the other side, opened the door, and dragged the wounded man over the console to the passenger seat. The guy landed upside down, his face jammed against the floor mat. Breathing hard from the effort, Harpo decided that was the best he could manage. He went back to the driver's side, got in, and started the car.

Though he had no idea as to his location, he thought he would try to find a hospital for the man. He backed out, drove about a hundred yards to the street, and took a left. A couple of minutes later he reached a highway and headed across a big bridge. The skyscrapers on the other side told him it had to be Miami.

The traffic going across moved swiftly, but when he hit the top of the off-ramp, everything ground to a halt. He could see several vehicles with flashing lights a quarter-mile ahead. Three police cars, a fire truck, and two ambulances.

A few minutes passed before anything moved. Then he saw the newspaper woman's green car cut out of the line about twenty cars ahead and roll down the shoulder around the emergency vehicles. He wondered why he hadn't thought of that himself, and did the same thing.

He idled by a five-car pile-up. Steam rose from broken hoods, fluids covered the pavement, groups of people stood talking. EMTs carried an injured man on a stretcher. Another EMT stepped out of an ambulance carrying a bag. Harpo jammed the brakes and jumped out of the car. "Hey, Doc, hold up."

The man turned around. "What is it?"

Harpo ran around to the passenger side, swung the door open. "This guy is in bad shape. I think he's dying."

The man frowned. "Was he in the accident?"

"He's lost a lot of blood."

Glancing back toward the wreckage, the EMT sighed and stepped over for a closer examination. He opened his bag and pulled out a stethoscope. "How did he get turned upside down?"

Harpo didn't answer, because he was already hurrying down the ramp on foot.

"Isn't that Harpo up ahead?" Simone asked.

Sam took a quick look, the traffic now moving at a stop-and-go pace. "I think so."

"Maybe he can tell us what happened to Benetti."

As they drew even with the homeless man, Sam lowered the window. "Hey, Harpo, get in the car."

The homeless man turned, gave them a frown. "No, thank you." He kept walking.

Sam drove alongside. "Come on. You're a long way from home."

He seemed to consider that for a moment then hurried over.

When they got underway again, J.T. said, "I can't find the woman on the monitor. Knox must've removed her transmitter before he left for the boat."

Sam sighed. "He probably knew exactly where to cut."

"Yeah," J.T. said, "thanks to your sharpshooting."

Sam tuned out the sarcasm. He'd felt bad about losing that connection to Knox, but he felt even worse about Lora Diamond. She had played him, zeroed in on him that first night, and he'd never had a clue. Too busy trying to play her. Though she hadn't done anything harmful to him, that he knew of, she had probably fed Knox information about what they were doing and maybe caused them to take some wrong turns. Thinking back, though, he didn't think he'd given her much, primarily so it wouldn't hit the news. He couldn't help but remember the morning on his boat when he had almost kissed her. How good she looked. The attraction.

"Hey, wake up," Simone said, "the cars are moving again."

Horns honked behind him. He pressed the accelerator and closed the distance to the next bumper.

It had been a surprise when Knox said he didn't have the money with him. They thought he was making his getaway. If he knew they were following, maybe he wanted to lead them away from the money, and double back later when the coast cleared.

Simone turned in her seat and said to Harpo, "Did you see another man back there, before you got on the boat?"

Harpo told her what had happened with the machete. "He was unconscious in his car when I came through there again, and I took him to one of the ambulances back there." He pointed over his shoulder with his thumb in the direction of the wreckage behind them.

She said to Sam, "We can probably find him in one of the hospitals."

J.T. spoke up from the back seat. "There's a note in Knox's wallet with two sets of numbers on it. One looks like a combination to a safe. The other might be a security system code. If only we knew where to go."

Same sarcastic tone. Sam had had about enough of the attitude. He turned and glanced at J.T. in the back seat. One more remark and he would be on the street. Sam's frown must have said it all. J.T.'s eyes got large for a split second then he averted his gaze to the computer and started clicking keys.

When they reached the I-95 interchange, Sam took the on-ramp leading to South Dixie Highway.

"Where are you headed?" Simone asked.

"Iguana Key. We can drop Harpo off and get the cars, but I also have an idea about where Knox might have stashed the money."

"What about Benetti?"

"He'll be there when we get back. ER always takes a while, and they might admit him if he's lost a lot of blood."

Two HOURS LATER they rolled onto Big Pine Key and headed toward the house owned by Knox's mother, Eva Crowne, the movie star. It had appeared vacant at the time, and Sam hoped Eva would still be away, maybe sunning herself in the south of France.

Sam turned into the driveway of the house with the For Sale sign in the yard, where they had parked before. J.T. got latex gloves from Sam's bag and they put them on. Leaving Harpo in the car, they got out, hurried past shrubs to the back yard, and crossed the next property to Eva's place.

When they reached the rear door, J.T. took out Knox's keys. There were four of them, and two fit the deadbolt and the knob.

J.T. turned to Sam. "Good guess, buddy. This is the place." His eyes took on a glow that Sam had seen before.

They pushed through to a small utility room and closed the door behind them. An alarm system hung from the wall. The digital display flashed the words "Enter Security Code."

"I'll try the code on the note," J.T. whispered. He pulled a piece of paper from his pocket and began punching numbers on the keypad. When he finished, the display stopped flashing and changed to "System Armed."

They split up. J.T. thought a safe might be in the den and headed toward the rear of the house. Simone said she'd check the bedrooms, and Sam took the living room.

Paintings hung from the walls. They looked like originals, primarily Gaugins and Van Goghs, but other classics, as well. Sam thought he would check behind the paintings for the safe, but he noticed an entryway to a library off the east side of the room. He decided to check in there first and eased over to the door, but heard a noise before entering and stopped. It sounded like rats scratching through newspaper, but he didn't think it was rats at all. In the back of his mind he knew what might be there.

Sam turned into the room, leading with his 9mm. The woman he knew as Lora Diamond crouched on one knee in front of a safe. She grabbed a handgun and jerked it around toward him. Dark circles framed her eyes, but she still looked beautiful. A large attaché case lay open next to her knee.

Something gnawed inside Sam's chest. "You planning to shoot me?" Sam asked.

"Of course not. I wouldn't shoot you." Her eyes widened.

Sure she wouldn't. "Then, drop the gun."

She hesitated for a moment. "Sorry, I can't do that.

I worked on this job for months. I can't just walk away from the money."

"Hard to picture you as an assassin with the Black Palmetto." He didn't know why he had said that. She had a gun pointed at him, and she probably knew how to use it.

"I wasn't. They recruited me because I killed a man. But I had a good reason, and I got out of the program as soon as I could. Check the records. Knox found me and asked me to help set up a con. I didn't know he was going on a killing spree. I had nothing to do with that. You have to believe me."

"What about Jake Bell? You had dinner with him right before he died."

"Knox gave Jake a hard time a few weeks ago when he got in a scrape over a girl. Then, the night before you arrived, he saw Knox beating up Benetti in Chopin's parking lot. When you showed up, he told me he was going to do something to get Knox in trouble. He didn't realize Knox saw him that night, too, and was following him. I didn't know he was going to kill him."

Sam wanted to believe her, but in the back of his mind he knew he couldn't. She had helped Knox and probably needed to die, too.

Something in his eyes must have told her what he was thinking.

"I tried to protect you," she blurted. "I made sure Ford kept you out of jail. Knox would've killed you in there."

"Maybe."

"Look, I only have half the money here. Let me leave and you take the rest."

"How much is there?"

She turned her case so he could see inside. "I counted five-hundred-and-ten thousand as I took it out. There's at least that much left in the safe."

The volume of the stacks in both places did appear to be about the same. "That would be only a million. It should be two."

"Yeah, that's what Knox thought. Boozler must have spent the rest."

"Knox give you the combination?"

A hint of a smile leaked into her eyes. "No. I got it from his wallet while he slept. He'd planned to give me a cut, but I saw what happened to him on the boat and figured I'd better get down here."

She closed the case, snapped the locks, and stood. "Maybe we can talk about this sometime, but right now I'm leaving, and I hope you won't try to stop me." Still pointing her handgun at Sam, she backed toward a door at the other end of the room.

Sam's heart raced as his finger tightened on the trigger. He said, "You're not going anywhere."

She just dropped the gun to her side, gave him a beautiful smile, and sidestepped through the door.

THIRTY-FIVE

J.T. PEERED INSIDE the safe, turned to Sam, and frowned. "You let her go?"

Sam nodded. "Yeah, I wasn't going to shoot her for the money."

Simone didn't say anything. She just stared at him, a wan smile on her face.

"She helped Knox, though," J.T. said, "and maybe killed some of those people."

"I don't think so."

Shaking his head, J.T. said, "She gave you a sob story, and you believed it. Man, you'll never learn."

The house phone rang. Sam stepped over to it and saw the name of a security company on the display. The security system had sent an alarm when Lora went out.

"We need to deactivate the security system." He turned to Simone. "Answer the phone and tell them you forgot about the system when you stepped outside. Say you're entering the code now."

J.T. thrust his hand in his pocket and pulled out the note with the code.

"She went out this way," Sam said, heading toward the door. It led to a small hallway that exited to a garden on the side. The alarm box hung next to the door.

J.T. punched in the code as he had done before.

Back in the library, Simone hung up the phone.

"They might've believed me, but I bet they'll come by here anyway. We have to get going."

"Get a bag," J.T. said as he turned to the safe.

Sam got two plastic trash bags from the kitchen and lined one with the other. When he returned, J.T. had put the cash on the floor in a neat pile and closed the safe.

"There's almost six-hundred thousand."

They stuffed the money into the bag and headed for the back door.

Outside, Sam peeked around the corner of the house to the street. A security car slowed and turned into the driveway. A lone officer got out, pulled a key from his pocket, and headed toward the front door. When he got past their view, the three ran across to the next yard and retraced their steps from before.

Back in the car, they didn't see Harpo. J.T. opened the back door and the homeless man awoke and sat up.

Sam started the engine and backed out. As they rode away, Sam glanced at his rear view mirror and saw the security man getting back in his vehicle. He might have been surprised that the woman who answered the phone had already left, but he wouldn't have found anything out of order inside.

About thirty minutes later, Sam turned onto Iguana Key and headed toward the place Harpo had left the hearse. He had been quiet since they'd questioned him about Benetti, but when they pulled in beside the maroon behemoth, he said, "Guess I'll have to turn the hearse in, now. Mr. Tim wouldn't want me to keep it, if he was alive. Have to respect the dead."

Before he got out, Simone said, "What are you going to do?"

"I don't know. I'll have to get another job. There's a

woman I want to go back to when I get some money to pay my way. She saved my life."

She gave Sam a pained expression, then reached over the seat into the bag next to J.T. and pulled out two stacks of the cash. "Here you go. This should last you for a while."

Harpo's eyes lit up even brighter than the night before when he'd retrieved the gallon of homemade wine from the cabin. "I don't know," he said, his voice breaking. "Is that real money?"

"Yes, it's real. Take it."

He hesitated, glanced down at his clothes. "I'll need to go to the funeral home and clean up, maybe borrow a burial suit from Mr. Tim's stock. If I try to spend hundred dollar bills looking like this, they'll haul me off for sure."

Harpo took the cash and thanked her profusely. He got out and hurried to the hearse, a skip in his step.

Sam drove on to Ford's cabin. When he finished loading the car and was about to get into the driver's seat, a man stepped out of the woods. He pointed a handgun at Sam's head. Simone stood on the passenger side. J.T. had just come out of the house with his bags, lagging behind. Everyone froze.

"Going somewhere?" the man asked.

He seemed familiar in his suit and tie. Then it came to Sam: the guy with the pet iguana. Edison.

J.T. started moving to the side, and the man in the suit turned the gun on him.

"Stop where you are. I won't hesitate to shoot."

J.T. stopped and dropped his bags on the ground. Sam's gun was stowed under the driver's seat. He wondered if J.T. had his with him. Simone usually had hers in a holster at the small of her back, but since they thought everything was smooth sailing, they had all relaxed.

"I didn't know prosecutors carried guns," Sam said.

"So you know who I am."

"How did you find us?"

Edison shrugged. "Wasn't too difficult. I figured your lawyer might be hiding you, and found this place in the court records. When I came out here, I saw the car. I knew it wasn't Ford's, so I expected you'd be back. You were here for the money. What did you do with the chief?"

"I don't know what happened to him. I heard he ran off when they found his fingerprints on that knife."

The prosecutor flicked his nose with his free hand and sniffed. A trace of white powder dotted his upper lip beneath his nostril. "Boozler's no killer. He's a dirty cop, but I don't think he ever murdered anybody. Did you plant that knife with his prints on it?"

"I've never even been to the place where they found it," Sam said.

Edison wagged the barrel of the gun back and forth. "No matter. Let's take a look inside your car. You two," he said to J.T. and Simone, "get over here so I can keep an eye on you." When they came around the car and stood close by, he said to Sam, "Open the doors and stand back."

Sam did as asked, and the prosecutor moved so he could see in the back seat first. They had put the bag of money in the back floorboard behind the passenger seat, and Simone had laid her overnighter on top of it. But the articles on the floor behind the driver's seat seemed to catch the man's eye first.

"That cap looks familiar. Morton Bell wore one just like it, and I'll bet that one has his DNA on it. And what's that beside it? Rubber gloves? *Tsk, tsk*. Doesn't look good, Mackenzie. You must have committed all these murders."

Simone touched his arm. He had told her he'd ditch the cap later, and had forgotten. His head throbbed, pulse pounding. The sun's rays felt like fire on the back of his neck. *There might not be a way out of this*, he thought. Could he get to his gun before Edison could fire? Killing a DA didn't fit in his bag of tricks, but death row didn't seem too appealing, either, especially for something he hadn't done.

"Let's see what's inside those bags. Get them out of there," Edison said.

Sam leaned in and pulled them out and onto the ground.

"Open the trash bag."

When Sam complied, Edison said, "Well, well, the evidence just keeps piling up."

The hum of an engine droned in the distance. Then it got louder, and Edison peered in the direction of the driveway. Sam smacked his gun hand to the side and tried to grab the weapon, but Edison moved surprisingly fast. He jerked the gun away and stepped back.

"Hey! You're a dead man if you try that again." He backed up farther and glanced at the driveway again. A police cruiser rolled into view through the trees.

Just great, Sam thought. His options were disappearing by the second.

The cruiser eased to a stop about a hundred feet away. Lieutenant Cates and a uniformed officer got out.

Cates's called out, "Mr. Edison, what's going on?"

The DA eyed the bag of cash and then glanced at Sam, a grimace on his face. He seemed to be agonizing over a decision. Seconds passed. Sam wondered if his brain might be fuzzy from the cocaine.

"I'm arresting this guy," Edison said. "He's the murderer."

"What? No, you've got it all wrong. Dudley Crew is the murderer. A detective on the Miami PD called me. He was at the hospital when Charles Ford woke up, and Ford fingered Crew as the guy who stabbed him. I spoke to Ford myself. We have an APB out all over the state, so we'll get him. Now, put the gun down."

Edison turned his eyes to the money again. "No, I think I'll keep the gun. You two get over here with them."

Silence. Cate's stared at him, seemingly in shock.

"I'm warning you," Cates said, his voice rising, his tone sharp, "drop that weapon on the ground."

"Better do what I say, Lieutenant."

The uniformed officer jerked out his handgun and pointed it at Edison. "No, you do what the lieutenant said. Drop that gun or I'm going to shoot."

Cates held up his hands. "Hold on, everybody. We don't want to—"

Edison fired, hitting the gun-wielding officer in the shoulder, but the policeman returned fire, two shots. Both rounds slammed the DA in the chest, dead center. He stumbled back a couple of feet and fell to the ground. His eyes gazed skyward, unmoving and unseeing.

Cates ran over to him and kicked the gun out of his hand.

"He's dead," Sam said.

The lieutenant stared for a moment, worry gripping

the features of his face, then went back to the officer, who had his hand pressed against his shoulder wound. Cates examined it. "The bullet just grazed you. You'll live." He got the radio from the cruiser and called for EMTs. When he finished, he stepped back over to Sam, who had cinched the moneybag and tossed it and the overnighter back in the car, covering up the cap.

"Okay, now, what was he really doing out here?" the lieutenant asked, his eyes narrowed. "I don't buy that business about him thinking you were the killer, and he wouldn't have come looking for you carrying a gun without a good reason."

"Did you notice his nostrils?" Sam asked. "He's full of cocaine. That might have something to do with it."

Cates stepped over to the body and squatted down. "Yes, I can see it, but he didn't seem impaired." He stood again and shook his head. "His death is going to be hard to explain. There's something else you're not telling me." He stared at Sam.

"Well…"

J.T. spoke up. "He came here to kill us."

"Why would he do that?"

Yeah, buddy, why would he do that?

"We knew his secret, one that would take him down. When we thought he might be the killer, we dug into his background. He worked for the DEA in Miami several years ago and got caught with his hands in the cookie jar. They fired him when a load of cocaine went missing from a major bust. You'll probably find what's left of it at his place."

Cates raised an eyebrow. "That doesn't sound right. The city would've checked out his background before appointing him as the prosecutor."

"Yeah," J.T. said, "they probably did. He somehow got his DEA records sealed. I'm sure you can get them, though, with a formal request to the DEA."

"Huh. Then how do you know about all this?"

"We found somebody at the agency who remembered him."

WHEN THE EMTs arrived a few minutes later, they dressed the officer's wound and hauled the dead body away.

"Ford told me you might be out here," Cates said. "He asked me let you know about Dudley. I tried calling, but you didn't answer."

"I must've left my phone in the car while we packed to leave. I appreciate you coming out, though." Cates would never have any idea how much Sam appreciated it.

"I'm just hoping Lora is okay when we find Crew. The detective didn't seem to know anything about her abduction."

Sam could see real concern in his eyes, and maybe something a little stronger, too. "Yes, I hope she's okay, too."

When he had gone, Sam asked J.T. about the DEA information. "Was all that true?"

"Yep, all true. My contact called while I was packing my bag. That's why I was late coming out of the house. I'm sure Edison knew about the missing cash and knew Boozler had it. He had to be pretty patient to wait a year for it to come into play."

"And he saw this as his last chance to get his hands on it," Simone said.

Before they left, Sam called Jackson Memorial, the

same place Charles Ford had been admitted, and found that the injured people from the Rickenbacker Causeway accident had been treated there. They caravanned back up the Overseas Highway. When they reached the hospital, Sam got out and Simone took the wheel. She said she would circle while he went into the ER.

Sick people and family packed the waiting room. He went to the information desk and asked for Spanner, assuming he probably still used an ID with that name on it. The receptionist studied the computer monitor in front of her and pressed some keys.

"We released him just a few minutes ago."

Sam hurried outside and scanned along the curb. He spotted him standing on the corner, probably waiting for a taxi, and called Simone.

"Yeah, I see him," she said. "I'm headed that way."

The former assassin turned and started to run, but Sam grabbed him and twisted his good arm up behind him. Simone pulled to the curb and Sam opened the back door with his free hand. Benetti screamed out, maybe in pain, maybe just to get attention. Sam shoved him into the back seat and went in behind him, pushing him over. He pulled his gun and pointed it at Benetti. The injured man gave him a hurt look.

Simone pressed the accelerator and the car sped away.

"Don't turn me in," Benetti said. "They'll kill me."

Sam tuned him out, but Simone peered at him in the rear view and said, "Who do you think will kill you?" She turned onto the highway and into traffic.

"The Palmetto bunch. I been doing some thinking, and I believe Mackenzie here had it right. He said organizations like that never go away. They just put on a different mask. Those guys say they're doing psychological research, but I've seen the people they're studying. They look spaced out, just like we did. I know a killer when I see one."

"You're wasting your breath," Sam said.

"You two probably won't make it out of there either," Benetti continued. "You know too much about that tracking system."

Simone glanced at Sam in the mirror, her face a question mark. "Maybe he has a point."

Her remark seemed to embolden the man's plea. "Why do you think they sent a couple of lightweights like you two after me?" He turned to Sam. "No disrespect, man, but they have people to do this kind of thing."

Sam stared for a moment. It was something he had pondered. What if Blaine really hadn't closed shop, and had just lain low until he could reestablish the group?

"Yeah, I think we've met a couple of them, already." To Simone, Sam said, "We need to have some kind of resolution to this. If we just avoid them, we'll spend all our time from now on looking for laser dots."

ABOUT TWO HOURS LATER, Sam and Simone entered a coffee shop in Coconut Grove. They got cappuccinos at the counter and took a table next to the far wall. A few minutes later, two men stepped inside the place and spotted them. They appeared to be in their thirties. Both wore loose shirts with the tails out, probably to cover handguns holstered at their backs. One carried a portable computer bag.

Sam took a sip of the coffee—too hot—and set it down. "You recognize either of them?"

"No. The assignment was all handled by phone, and they sent Benetti's photo in an e-mail. They look like contractors, though."

The men stepped over to the table and took a seat. One smiled at Simone. The other laid the bag on the table, took out a laptop and turned it on. He kept his eyes on Sam, a serious expression on his face.

"So, you have the thing?" Smiley asked.

Simone laid an envelope on the table in front of him. He slid it over to Serious, who removed the flash card and plugged it into the laptop.

"I don't think it's any good," Sam said.

Serious glanced up from the computer. "What do you mean?"

"We plugged it into a computer, but couldn't get it to do anything."

He went to work on the keyboard. A few moments later, he stopped keying, watched the screen, and then turned to Smiley, who nodded. They obviously knew the nature of the system and had the decryption key. Blaine had probably gotten the information from White-hall and given it to them. So the people in Homestead were still working for the senator, along with the guys who had twice tried to waylay them. If they were willing to kill them then, they probably would now, too, if they got the chance. That settled Sam's mind about what they planned to do.

"Okay," Smiley said to Simone, "what about Spanner? On the phone you mentioned a problem."

She sipped her coffee. "We tracked him to a motel in Iguana Key, but he got away."

Smiley raised an eyebrow. "Then how did you locate the computer card?"

"He left it with somebody who didn't know what it was, and we found it."

All true.

"What about the money he stole. Did you find that, too?"

Simone shook her head. "No. He must have escaped with that. We could spend another couple of weeks searching for him, but we don't have any leads at this point."

Serious, spoke up. "That's okay." He studied the screen for a moment. "We can take it from here. We'll send your fee to your bank account." He closed the computer and they stood to leave.

"That's fine," Simone said. "Something we should tell you, though. The FBI is after Spanner, too. We met an agent in Iguana Key who told us Spanner sent them a copy of a computer system, and the names of people involved with it. We assumed it was what's on that memory card. He wouldn't tell us any more about it, though."

All lies.

The smile leaked away from Smiley's face. "You're kidding, right?"

"No, I'm not." She took a drink from her cup. "You know, this is pretty good stuff. You should get one on the way out."

Smiley stared for a moment then turned to Sam, as if trying to divine the truth from their faces. He turned to his partner and said, "Let's get out of here."

Sam and Simone followed them to the door and watched them glance up and down the street before hurrying to a familiar black SUV parked on the street. The men got into the back seats, Serious on the curb side and Smiley on the street side. Before Smiley closed his door, Sam got a glimpse of the driver. Larson. They all worked for Blaine.

"I don't think we'll have to worry about them," Sam said.

Simone smiled. "No, we gave them something much bigger to worry about."

"YOU SEND THE e-mail to Agent Crease?" Sam asked J.T.

They had met up in the parking lot at Carling Research, a company that produced study aids from human cadavers for colleges and medical schools. The place supplemented its income by serving as an underground Emergency Room for the Miami crime industry. Sam and Carling, the pretty blonde owner, had dated off and on. At the present, they were off, but still friendly.

"Yep. I told them everything we know about the Black Palmetto. They'll be swarming the place in Homestead by nightfall."

Sam felt an impulse to ask if they would be able to trace the e-mail, but knew that would offend J.T.

Within a few minutes, Benetti exited the door of the facility and headed for J.T.'s car. He grinned and held up the tiny transmitter that Carling's people had removed.

Sam and Simone followed J.T. to a car rental agency where they dropped Benetti. Sam handed him a stack of the cash through the open window.

"Is that it? Come on, you can do better than that."

"Don't press your luck," Sam said.

Benetti grinned, then pointed his index finger at Sam, his thumb up like the hammer of a gun. He blew Simone a kiss and headed inside to get a car.

ON THE WAY back to Sam's marina, his phone chirped. He took it out and glanced at the display. Though he didn't recognize the number, he had a bad feeling about it.

"Hello."

"You won't get away with this, Mackenzie. That little trick with the FBI might shut down my operation, but they won't touch me, and I'll get you for killing my son. You'll die a slow death."

THE NEXT DAY, all the major networks carried news stories about the FBI arresting a dozen or more members of a murder-for-hire operation. They mentioned nothing about the government or Senator Blaine being involved. Sam wondered if Agent Crease had some tricks up his sleeve, or if Blaine had gotten to him. It wasn't the outcome he had hoped for, but it would keep Blaine busy for a few weeks. That might be the best he could expect. If Blaine or his hired help came for him, he would be ready.

THIRTY-SIX

RICHARD BOOZLER AND a pretty brunette sat in chairs beneath an umbrella, sipping tall drinks, their bare feet in the cool beach sand. They seemed happy, chatting and laughing, but J.T. couldn't hear their words through the window from inside their villa. It had taken him a week to track down the former police chief to the Chilean coastal community. Boozler had left no trail, but his girlfriend had been careless. She purchased airline tickets on a credit card. Few people left Iguana Key that week for another country, so J.T. played the hunch.

A note with the account number and PIN had been taped to the underside of the bottom drawer of the dresser. A rookie hiding place. Boozler probably didn't have much experience with that sort of thing. J.T. thought of his actions as teaching him a valuable lesson, among other things.

With one last glimpse through the window at the happy couple, J.T. silently wished them enjoyment for this moment, because when he finished, they would have only enough money for a few meals and a ticket home. Alas, such could be the life of a criminal on the run. With a smile, he went out the door of the villa and headed for his rented car.

THIRTY-SEVEN

SAM GOT A cold bottle of beer from the fridge and stepped out onto the deck of *Slipstream*. He took a seat in one of the chairs under the awning at the stern. Pete, the pelican with the lame foot, stared at him from a timber a few feet away. Sam wished he had something to feed him. A fish jumped nearby and Pete snapped his head around toward the noise. He dived into the water, came up with something in his beak, and floated there for a minute while he swallowed it.

Though Sam had been home for several days, he had slept with one eye open, until the night before. He'd had dinner at the marina bar and grill, and a news alert came on the TV behind the bar. Senator Blaine had been found dead on the sidewalk outside his Georgetown condo. The reporter said the authorities thought the senator might have been shot by a robber. Sam had gone back to his boat and slept for ten hours straight.

Footsteps rattled the dock boards and he turned to see Simone nearing the boat with an overnight bag in her hand. She looked stunning in shorts, blouse, and sunglasses. When she stepped aboard and saw him, she smiled behind the shades and headed over.

"Simone." He stood, took the bag and set it on the locker close by. "What's the occasion?"

She gave him a quick kiss on the lips. "I thought we might celebrate."

Sam smiled. "Yeah, I'm up for that. Gin and tonic?"

"That sounds good."

"Okay. Coming up." He headed toward the door and glanced at the bag on the way by. A paperback book protruded from the side pocket with an airline boarding pass stuck inside. Slowing for a better view, he saw that it was for a flight that morning, from Washington Dulles to Miami. He went on and came back with the drink.

"You see the news about Senator Blaine?" he asked, handing her the glass.

Simone took a sip of the drink. "Yeah, I saw that."

"You suppose they'll ever catch the killer?"

"Not a chance." She took off the sunglasses, lay her head back, and closed her eyes. "This is so nice. Why don't you take me on a romantic cruise, maybe over to the Bahamas? We can hit the beaches and relax for a few weeks, maybe spend some of that money."

Sam's pulse swished in his ears. He could think of nothing he would enjoy more than cruising the islands with Simone, remembering how terrific she looked in a bikini.

"I'll check my calendar, but I think I can swing that. You break it off with Karl?"

She gave him a smile, and something fluttered in his chest. "You were right, before. I just made him up."

* * * * *